DECEITFUL MOON

By
RICK MURCER

PUBLISHED BY:
Murcer Press, LLC

Edited by
Jan Green-thewordverve.com
Carrie Murgittroyd

Interior book design by
Bob Houston eBook Formatting

For my wife Carrie, who still believes in me.

For JC, who loves me and keeps me on the path; I'm grateful.

To Jessie, Sarah, Marie, and David for being the best editing team ever.

To Josh and Buzz . . . this is for you.

Deceitful Moon

A Novel

By

RICK MURCER

Chapter-1

"Hey Manny, hear the one about the pig, the priest, and the chicken?"

Detective Manny Williams rolled his eyes and turned toward Sophie Lee, his partner. She was slouched in her chair, looking at the screen of her laptop, wearing that smartass look she wore when she was bored. The diminutive, Chinese-American cop reminded him of his fifteen-year-old daughter when she moped around the house complaining there was nothing to do. Manny would point out that her room needed cleaning, but apparently that wasn't something "to do."

"No, Sophie, I haven't. And would it matter?"

"Nope. I'm going to tell you anyway."

"Am I going to laugh?"

"Don't know. I just need to tell it."

"How are you coming on that report?"

"Don't change the subject. You're not gettin' out of it that easy. Besides, I don't do B&E reports."

"You do now; at least until someone in our fair city decides murder is their God-given right."

"Whatever." Sophie sighed.

Manny knew how she felt. Once you worked homicide, nothing else came close. Some people thought homicide detectives were a little crazy; hell maybe that was true, but there was no substitute for putting a killer away, not to mention the thrill of the chase. It was like comparing Boone's Farm to Dom Pérignon . . . and this busywork of writing and filing reports was driving them both insane.

Maybe he should consider that other offer. The pay was way better and there was no shortage of work with the FBI's Behavioral Analysis Unit. He was pretty sure they didn't do B&E paperwork either. But would it take him away from his family even more?

"Okay. Tell me."

"Okay, tell you what?"

"Tell me about the pig, the priest, and the chicken."

"Nah."

"What? Why?"

"I don't think you'd get it. You're all blue-eyed and blond, not Chinese."

"Remind me to kick your ass later."

"Yeah, like I'm going to do that. I just live for having my butt kicked."

"No problem. I'll remember on my own."

"At your age? Pssfftt. I'm safe."

"Oh, I won't forget. Trust me."

"It's because men can't get me off their minds, isn't it? Admit it." Sophie winked and blew him a kiss.

Manny caught it, put it in his pocket, and winked back. It was amazingly good to see her bouncing back to her former self. The whole thing on the cruise ship three months ago had affected them all, maybe for a lifetime. Sophie had not only lost a good friend in the murdered Lansing DA, Liz Casnovsky, to a psychopath, but she had lost an ex-lover as well. Sophie's affair had just happened to be with Liz's husband Lynn. That kind of guilt and remorse would put anyone in a different place. Manny knew about those different places.

The first two months back had been tough, but Sophie was reverting back to her old persona, even though that meant she was going to be a pain in the ass from time to time. Some types of pain are just worth it.

Argyle. He was still out there, and that fact made Manny more than a little nervous. The psychotic doctor had left bodies strewn all over the Caribbean and then disappeared after they had tracked him from Aruba to New York. Manny's newfound friend, Special Agent Josh Corner, claimed the FBI had Argyle high on its radar and was monitoring the Good Doctor's every known contact and source. But Argyle was clever, wealthy, and worse, the most ruthless killer Manny had ever encountered. Not a good combination.

That wasn't all. Argyle had put them all on notice that the books weren't balanced, and there were more paybacks coming to the Lansing law enforcement family. It was a promise that triggered some sleepless nights for Manny and added more fuel to his workaholic streak. Manny wanted no more of the pain and loss he'd suffered on the *Ocean Duchess*.

The time was coming when they would meet again. Argyle seemingly controlled when that encounter would happen. Manny would try to be ready.

Meanwhile, there had been extra security put into place surrounding the families involved in the cruise ship incidents, and they were doing all they could. He hoped it was enough.

"All right, I'm done with this report. Where do I stick it?" panned Sophie.

"You can't figure that out? I'm going to have to–"

The phone on Manny's desk rang. He looked at the number and quickly snatched the headset from its cradle. "Williams here."

Manny listened, then hung up without speaking. He stood, ran his hand through his hair (an old nervous habit from his teen years), tightened his shoulder holster, and motioned to Sophie. "No more reports for you or me today. We've got a dead parolee, and it ain't pretty. Let's go."

Chapter-2

Eric Hayes knew he wasn't alone in the dark. The duct tape over his mouth and eyes proved to be efficient enough, but he *heard* his captor. Worse, his captor heard him. He knew the large man was staring at him from the other side of the small table situated in the middle of the suite on the ship's eleventh deck. Eric was sure his captor had taken great pleasure in his attempt to demand and even coerce his freedom with angry actions that had evolved to desperate, silent screams. Then, as harsh reality showed its aberrant face, terror-stricken sobs had forced him to hold hands with helplessness. Lastly came a hushed acceptance that was somehow more terrifying than the act of being bound in a chair at the whim of a maniacal stranger, all his pleas smothered by the gagging effects of the tape.

The strong man doubling as his jailer had planned this attack well.

Eric never could resist a story, or the thought of one, and the mysterious note had assured him that if he came to this stateroom at the proper time, he would be part of a blockbuster story that would make him famous—more than famous, a household name. He didn't know what that meant for sure, but the cruise ship was docked in St. Thomas for the day, so how could he ignore a guarantee like that? It was like promising dope to a junkie, and he had chased the promise like an addict.

One giant hand over his face, a rag immersed in chloroform, and voilà, instant prisoner.

My God, he was still so naïve.

Eric, for the hundredth time, speculated about the purpose, and maybe more importantly, the reason, for being bound in this room.

Did this glimpse into hell have anything to do with his career as a small-town reporter for the *Lansing Post*? He would be a liar—any reporter would— if he said he didn't worry about writing something, somewhere down the line, that would offend someone to the point of repercussion. The public was as fickle as any weather forecast, and even in the land of the free, you had to watch your ass.

He didn't have to wait long for the answer.

"Mr. Hayes. It is so good of you to join me for this happy fiesta. Well, happy for me."

The voice was powerful and confident. Eric also detected a hint of enthusiasm. The thought of his captor being excited at his prey's confinement sent a horrifying chill up his spine.

"I know you are wondering what you are doing here, and I assure you, I won't keep you waiting.

But first, I'm going to remove the tape from your eyes. That's the least I can do."

The feel of ripping tape against his skin caused him to let loose a muffled scream as the hair of his eyebrows left his face—with precious skin attached. Almost as pointed, however, was the sudden flood of light. Eric blinked and squinted his way to the realm of focus and, after a few moments, succeeded. Immediately, he wished he hadn't.

He recognized the man standing across from him. Anyone in Lansing would—and maybe half the nation. Dr. Fredrick Argyle had added a blond goatee, but it was him.

"Do you remember me, Mr. Hayes? I assure you that you have not been far from my thoughts for years. I couldn't be more pleased that we are finally together. I love reunions. Ask anyone at the Lansing Police Department."

Argyle's eyes rolled, and he laughed wildly, almost like a cartoon madman. Then he brought it under control so quickly that Eric jumped. He began a new round of struggles against the bindings.

"I assure you, Mr. Hayes, that your efforts to escape are futile. Duct tape is a wondrous invention to be sure. Besides, you don't have my permission to leave. But you'll have it soon."

The big man slammed his fist on the small table, and Eric felt his heart skip beats. "You must atone for the things you have written about me. About my research. You'd write anything to sell a piece-of-shit newspaper."

The doctor bent close to Eric and pointed to the table. Eric's smartphone sat so very close to the longest knife he had ever seen. "I'm going to offer you a chance to right wrongs, understand?"

Eric nodded with desperate enthusiasm.

"This phone will inform your rag of a paper that you were wrong. That the *Lansing Post* should never have printed the drivel you wrote. Do you have a problem with that?"

Eric shook his head and felt a little relieved. If that was all Argyle wanted, it would be the best damned retraction ever printed. He wanted to live. Swallowing some pride seemed a small price in exchange for that opportunity.

"Excellent, Mr. Hayes. A wise decision to be sure. Shall we begin?"

Before Eric could blink, Argyle snatched the knife from the table and plunged it deep into the left side of his neck. He felt the blade came out the other side, and he suffered the accompanying agony. His eyes grew wide watching the crimson spray that, somehow, didn't seem to be his.

Just before his world went dark, he heard Argyle laugh.

"Never mind, I've had a change of heart."

Chapter-3

Reaching to turn off his computer, Manny saw the e-mail notification pop up. He recognized the sender, a local reporter named Eric Hayes. The e-mail had an attachment. Manny would have to look at it later. His crew had a crime scene waiting for them.

Eric and he had worked some cases the way reporters and detectives do, but weren't exactly on each other's Christmas-card list. Manny knitted his brow, decided it could wait. Maybe this was another reason to get a smartphone instead of the one he'd had for years. But answering e-mail and downloading data to and from a phone appealed to him like snakes in the shower. People already had enough ways to mess up his day—and night. He flipped off the computer.

"What?" asked Sophie.

"Nothing, just an e-mail from Eric Hayes. I'll check it out when I get back. Kind of odd though. I don't really talk to him much. Come on, let's get to the car."

Sophie hurried to catch him as he hit the steps

to the parking garage. “Get a smartphone, Williams. They don’t bite. Then you could look at his e-mail while we are traveling. It’d take your mind off my driving.”

“Nothing could do that. And who says those phones don’t bite? Besides, it’s probably one of those ‘Don’t break this e-mail chain or you’ll have 8,000 years of bad luck and grow a third ear on your arm—with little pink flowers in the background.’ ”

“Maybe. The firewall would have caught it though. And that doesn’t change the fact you’re such a baby with this stuff. I’m going to talk to your wife. She’ll straighten you out . . . and don’t get kinky on me.”

Manny rolled his eyes as they reached the unmarked cruiser and climbed in. It was a Ford Taurus with a twenty-four valve turbo that kicked ass and took names when the pedal hit the metal.

They pulled out of the underground garage, Sophie driving, and screamed down Cedar Street, lights flashing.

“Where we headed, I forgot to ask?”

“Where else? Behind the White Kitty. Sex, rock and roll, and now murder.”

“Awesome.”

They reached the strip club in record time, and Manny reminded himself to take Sophie’s keys away. The woman was a great driver and fearless behind the wheel, but he’d had to liberate her cell phone when she tried to text her husband Randy while driving seventy-five miles-per hour.

He stepped out of the car and gave her the look, tossing her phone at her.

"What? I always drive like that."

"Consider your license revoked. You're going to kill us one of these times."

"Damn. You *are* getting old."

Manny and Sophie ducked under the yellow tape and moved to the back of the parking lot near the rusting trash bin that also served as roadblock to the narrow alley running away from the strip club/adult theater. The September sun was warm, even at four in the afternoon, and it did little to improve the mixture of scents emanating from the crime scene.

Day-old, decaying human flesh combined with the truly ripe odor of hot garbage didn't stir anticipation for Manny's next meal. He didn't know how the CSU guys did it, but it never seemed to bother them. That, or secretly they enjoyed it, harboring some kind of warped fetish. He chose not to dwell on that one.

Alex Downs, his good friend and head of the LPD's CSU, was bent over a small swatch of cloth near the corner of the trash heap, dark streaks of perspiration running down his pink shirt and khaki slacks. The pudgy CSI was already working hard.

"What do we have?" asked Manny.

Alex stood, cracked his back, and flicked away sweat with his latex-covered hand.

"Not nice. Thirty-five-year-old, white male, based on rigor, dead about fourteen hours. Lividity indicates he's been on his back. He was partially hidden by the trash dump so none of the patrons spotted him. The janitor noticed the smell and called it in."

"Dispatch said he was an ex-con out on parole," said Manny.

"That explains his choice of establishments," smirked Sophie.

Alex smiled. "Three years is a long time without getting laid. Anyway, his name is Mitchell Morse, and he got out two days ago."

"Cause of death?" asked Sophie. "I mean, other than this ungodly heat."

"Funny you should ask. Let me show you something. Oh. You may want to cover your noses. It gets worse."

Alex led them around the corner, and he was right, it did get worse, much worse. Manny eyeballed Sophie as she covered her nose with one hand, then the other, eyes watering like she had been cooking with the harshest onion known to man. He felt her pain.

After a few moments, Manny was able to control his gag reflex, and Sophie seemed to adjust as well. Alex stood next to the body, grinning.

"You think this is funny?" he said to Alex.

"I sure as hell do. But you two have come around, so let's get to it."

"Paybacks, just remember paybacks," threatened Sophie.

Alex waved his hand and bent close to the

body. "The body is bloated and I'll have to see the toxicology and autopsy reports to confirm, but I'll tell you what I think . . . and it's weird."

"Bloated? Good God. He looks like a blimp," said Manny.

"Not unusual in hot weather, of course," responded Alex. "You can see the bullet holes in his chest and the one in his forehead, four total, looks like a small caliber. He was also tied up with black leather straps. But that's not what I want you to pay attention to. See that area by his groin?" Alex was pointing to a raw patch of skin bulging through Morse's blue jeans near the left inner thigh. The jeans were perforated diagonally toward his crotch, displaying raw, disfigured muscle tissue—and a small lump of flesh where his penis should be.

Manny squeezed his legs together and cringed. "Oh man! What caused that?"

"It looks like an acid burn, and if I were a betting man, I would bet his testicles—if I could find them—got the same treatment. Those burns probably came from hydrochloric acid; he was one hurting puppy before he checked out."

"Whoa. Someone burned his pecker off and then shot him four times?" asked Manny.

"Yep. Definitely antemortem. Someone had to get real close and loving to do it, too. And that's not all." Alex asked one of the coroner's people to help him turn the body on its side.

Manny followed Alex's hand to the place where a small tip of jagged bone pressed just under the purplish-red skin of Morse's back.

"His neck was broken, postmortem, in several places. The ME will let me know for sure, but see these marks?"

Manny did see them. "Looks like boot or shoe prints."

"There's hope for you yet. Yeah, it is. I think the killer did the Watusi on this guy for more than a few steps. There are some other deep marks that I can't ID yet, but I will when I get back to the lab."

"So whoever killed this guy was pissed," said Sophie, "like a crime of passion?"

"Bingo. You win the Kewpie doll."

"Any shell casings?" Manny asked, already suspecting there wasn't.

"None, so far."

Alex scowled, made a small clucking sound in his throat, and removed his gloves. "There is one more thing. There was quite a bit of blood, but not as much as there should be."

"You mean it was almost a dump site, but maybe not," said Sophie.

"I don't know what I mean. It just doesn't add up, yet."

"Well, if he was inside, chasing the woman of his dreams, it stands to reason he was killed here," stated Manny.

"Makes sense," said Alex.

"All right, boss. Let's find out if he was here, and who he wanted to make friends with," said Sophie.

"Okay. But we have one small problem."

Sophie stared at him, and then began to laugh. "Never been inside one of these places, huh? Come on straight-laced boy. I'll hold your hand."

Chapter-4

Manny walked through the gray-tinted, glass door with Sophie at his heels. He noticed the metal detector, but went through it anyway. The siren was loud and immediate and got the attention of the two women behind the long display counter and the two security goons who were hanging out near the DVD section of the store. The larger of the two men, sporting a dirty blond mullet and black, fingerless gloves, rushed them like a bull chasing a red flag. Manny's police ID stopped him in his tracks. The bruiser gave him a dirty look, but said nothing.

"Good afternoon, folks. Now that we have your attention, we have a few questions. We'll ask politely, you answer with honesty overflowing from the goodness of your hearts, and we'll be fine? *Capisce*?"

The tall blond, wearing little more than a sheer negligee, five-inch stilettos, and Koi fish tats above each fleshy breast, stepped calmly to the counter. "Can I help you?"

"What's your name?"

"Charity. I'm the night manager."

"Charity? Is that your real name?"

"Real enough for the pervs that come in here. Evelyn Kroll is my legal name."

"Okay, Evelyn. Were you working last night?"

"Yes. I came in about 6:30 and closed up about 3:30 a.m."

Manny motioned to Sophie, and she handed him her phone with the freshly downloaded picture of Mitchell Morse on the screen. "Do you recognize this man?"

"Is that the dead guy?" she shivered. "That's so freaky. Yeah, he came in about 11:00 and went right into the theater."

"Was he alone?"

"Yeah, just him and his five friends, Rosy Thumb and the Four Finger Sisters."

Sophie snorted and glanced away. Manny ignored her.

"How long was he here?"

"I'm not sure. We were busy last night, full moon or something. We had a couple of fights and tossed a hooker out on her ass. I do remember seeing him about 1:30 or so."

"What was he doing?"

He heard Sophie throttle a cackle. He gave her the evil eye.

Evelyn smiled an anxious grin. "He was standing by the door, talking to one of the ladies, and trying to get a paid ride around the world. She told him that was illegal, and that she wasn't interested."

"I'll need that girl's information."

Evelyn looked to the ceiling, then back to Manny. "It was me. He was talking to me. Okay? I kicked him out and that's the last I saw of him . . . until now."

Sophie had regained her composure. "Scout's honor? Because we're going to go over the security tapes, and we don't want any surprises."

The tall blonde made eye contact with the other security guard and shifted her feet nervously. Manny didn't like what he saw.

"There. . . . ah . . . was a problem with the system's cameras last night, and we didn't get the whole night on video."

The club had committed one too many violations to suit the city and, as a condition of keeping the doors open, was required to keep sixty days of security tape, inside and out, in archive. Although the outside cameras didn't cover the area of the parking lot by the trash bin, Manny thought there could have been information that might help.

"That could be grounds to shut you down, you know that, right?" asked Manny.

"I know. I know. And they were working fine until just before he left. Then we got this snowy screen, like interference or something, and they just stopped recording, but they came back on like nothing ever happened right before we closed up. The camera company said they couldn't find anything wrong and that sometimes the system just gets bottled up." She looked at Manny, then

Sophie. "Scout's honor."

"We'll need the tape anyway, statements from all of the employees who worked last night, and a complete list of all employees."

She nodded and folded her arms over her ample breasts, causing the tats to change shape.

"Did you notice anyone unusual or out of the ordinary?"

Evelyn stared at Manny. "No, not in here. Our clientele is the salt of the earth. Cops, firemen, preachers, social workers, you know, all pillars of the community."

"Okay, smartass. You know what I mean. But maybe you could concentrate better down at the station."

"Sorry. Really. I get like this when I'm nervous. We've had some stuff go on in here, but nothing like that junk outside."

She looked at the counter, and then Manny watched her eyes grow big.

"Wait. There was this one chick. At least I think it was a chick. Tall, thin, wearing all black, face covered with a hoodie. The real weird part was the black gloves. I couldn't see the hands. People walk in here hoping no one will recognize them; she made sure."

"Good girl. What time?"

"Right after my dinner break, so just about 1:00 or so, I think. She might be on the video before it crashed."

"That could be helpful. One more question. Do you own a gun?"

Evelyn blinked her eyes, looked at the floor, then back to Manny and Sophie. "Yes. I have a permitted handgun, Smith and Wesson .38. But I keep it in the bedroom at my apartment."

"We may want to see it, but I think we're done, for now. We'll set up interview times for your people. Make sure they show up, okay?"

"Okay."

Manny watched a small smile form on Evelyn's face, and her blue eyes began to twinkle.

"Now I have a question for you, Detective Williams."

"Fire away."

"It takes a big gun to set off that metal detector. Just how big is your . . . weapon?"

Sophie released a belly laugh that caused Manny's face to turn an even deeper shade of red. But he grinned anyway.

"Cute. It's still not too late to shut this place down."

"Yes sir. I don't get good-looking cops in here very often and—"

"Just get us what we asked for and don't dink around." He grabbed Sophie's arm and ushered her out the door.

"Was that your doing?" he steamed.

"No, no. I think she likes you, and she's the kind of woman who doesn't beat around the bush. Sometimes, you slay me. You're the best detective I've ever seen, but when it comes to most women, you're clueless. Really."

"Not one word to any—"

Manny's cell rang. He pulled it out of his pocket and cocked his head. Eric Hayes. The call seemed to carry a sense of urgency that made Manny uncomfortable. He answered.

"Manny Williams here."

No response.

"Eric, is that you?"

There was another moment of silence, and then hell came calling.

"Detective Williams. How lovely to hear your voice."

He froze in mid-stride, unable to speak. Argyle was on Eric's cell phone.

Chapter-5

Mitchell Morse's killer sat, her legs crossed, at the oak table in the breakfast nook located at the south end of the house. The late afternoon sun was bright and cheerful, forcing the room to glow with a special comfort. The last of her summer roses gave the room an unmatchable aroma. The sun warmed the enigmatic area of her heart that turned cold when thoughts of murder evolved into the real thing.

Evolved or . . . snapped?

The term "snapped" was always just out of reach, at least for her, when it came to understanding what people do and why. It was simply a convenient phrase to explain the actions of someone who had truly decided, voluntarily or not, that living in the realm of psychoticism was preferable to any other reality. Fair enough.

"Snapped" also doubled as an excuse to disguise uncontrolled rage aimed at a cheating spouse, a crooked partner, or a BFF who had stabbed you in the back.

But what of her killing of Morse? Had she

snapped or made a rational decision? Perverts like him would never stop doing what they did. Morse's third trip to prison had only been three years. Is that all raping and sodomizing his "dates" was worth? Shouldn't someone do something? Didn't three strikes mean you were out? Way out? Enough was enough.

"Losing it" didn't apply here, not to Morse or the rest of the deviates who did what he did. Ridding society of men like these sick bastards was the right thing to do, and if the justice system couldn't, or wouldn't, do it, then well . . .

And if the system had worked, *she'd* still be here, laughing and joking, singing that stupid song, and causing everyone to laugh. Cheering up rooms and lives—like only she could.

It was more than awful to miss the little things, maybe worse than having her actually gone.

But paybacks were a bitch for some, and she was going to start with Siggie Ashcroft.

She ran a long finger over the black-and-white picture of Ashcroft she'd printed from his online sex offender file. He'd raped and terrorized four women and only served five years in prison.

What a deal for him.

Ashford was released yesterday and would need a day to get settled into his new state-sponsored domicile before the piece of shit began the hunt for his next good time. That was okay. One day wasn't a long time, and patience was a virtue. She was living proof.

Chapter-6

"What do you want, you sick prick?" asked Manny, in a low, controlled voice that hid his anger, his dread.

"Now, now, now. Is that any way to speak to a long-lost friend? I thought we cared for each other, Detective Williams. No?" Argyle laughed that familiar laugh that said he was still sleeping with insanity.

By now, Sophie had walked back to him with a curious look on her face.

He mouthed Argyle's name.

Her eyes grew hard, and she grabbed Manny's arm. "GPS trace?"

He shook his head. There was no reason to try to trace the call. Argyle would be done in a few moments, and it would be an afterthought. The real questions had to do with Eric and what Argyle had done to him. He was pretty sure Eric hadn't lent his phone to Argyle because his car was broken down and he needed a wrecker.

Manny remembered the earlier e-mail sent from Eric's address and felt his insides turn inside out.

What was in that attachment?

"We're not friends. We'll never be friends. You and I don't think the same way. For instance, I think you should be fried in the hottest electric chair ever created or eaten alive by hungry piranha. I bet you don't think that way. Right?"

The quiet was more than ominous, and Manny felt the man fighting for control. He had pissed off the Good Doctor. Too bad.

"You keep saying things you'll regret, detective, and you call *me* arrogant. I called to make sure you got my e-mail and see if you had any questions."

"About what?"

"About the message or the . . . pictures. I so love the pictures. I fancy myself as an artist, and they are very good."

"Where is Hayes?"

"Oh, he's very near, but I don't think he'll be writing any more disparaging columns of pure bullshit about me or anyone else. I think he's learned his lesson."

What has Argyle done?

Intimacies with the bizarre and cruel were not unusual for Argyle; in fact, it was his way of life. He had invented tortures to make medieval dungeons proud. Manny's angst for Eric escalated to a different level—the one that said his wife was a widow.

"Detective Williams? The cat got your tongue? Where is that smartass mouth now?"

"I'm here. I'm going to take you and your perverted logic down, you know that?"

"I don't think so. But we will meet again, when I decide the time is right. Meanwhile, know that you have inspired me. And I would appreciate your critique of my work when you see the pictures. Stunning, if I say so myself."

There was empty air as the connection went dead. Manny squeezed his phone, then smashed it on the parking lot's surface, pieces flying in every direction like black dirt in the wind.

"Sophie?"

"Yeah, I'm already on it. I called the paper. Apparently, there was a staff cruise set up for the *Post*'s employees. I have the itinerary right here. They're on the *Ocean Empress*, one of Carousel's ships, and they're docked in St. Thomas."

His eyes moved to hers, and she turned away. This was too familiar, too close to home, for both of them. To take this ride down memory lane and focus on what had happened on the *Ocean Duchess* wasn't where either one of them wanted to go. But psychopaths like Argyle got off on his previous "accomplishments" and had no intentions of letting them forget. Why would he? It made his world go round. Manny could feel the self-absorbed bastard laughing.

Manny flexed his shoulder and picked up what was left of his cell phone. "I think I'm going to need that new phone after all."

Sophie smiled. "I'll take care of it. Good arm, though."

Chapter-7

Gavin Crosby, Manny's boss and Lansing's police chief, stood behind Manny's desk, looking over his shoulder, along with Sophie and the LPD's computer forensic expert, Buzzy Dancer. Manny sat in front of the twenty-two-inch widescreen computer monitor, opened his e-mail account, then highlighted the message from Argyle. He wasn't sure if he was ready for what was inside the cyber message from hell, but there was only one way to find out.

Buzzy rolled up Sophie's chair and sat close to Manny, flashing him a quick smile. He smiled back and noticed how her red horn-rimmed glasses clashed with her bright-blue eyes and pink hair. She was pretty, about twenty-five, a few pounds underweight, loved wearing anything pink, and would probably win the title of office drama queen. She had also earned a reputation for being incredibly bright, which translated into *incredibly useful.*

"There's probably not anything you'll need me for, but if Argyle got clever, I might be able to see it," she said, snapping her gum.

"Okay. Are we ready?" asked Gavin.

Manny could still hear the sadness in his old partner's voice. Argyle had savagely murdered Gavin's new daughter-in-law, Lexy, on that ill-fated cruise three months ago, and the chief was still living it. His wife, Stella, seemed to be doing better than her spouse, but that wasn't saying much. Gavin said the pain of losing Lexy had invaded like a fever and simply wouldn't leave. Manny knew it would get better, but there was no timetable. Each death harbored a grieving life of its own, maybe even an agenda. He hoped it would come sooner rather than later for the Crosbys.

Their son Mike, Lexy's widower, hadn't come back to work at the police force yet, and Manny was glad because he wasn't sure if Mike would, or should. Who could blame him? Cop or not, getting over what he had gone through—especially with losing your wife of four days—wasn't going to happen overnight, if ever. Seeing her like that, ravaged beyond recognition, had sent Mike nearly insane and into intense therapy with the department's shrink: a path all of the passengers on that cruise followed, to varying degrees. It was mandatory protocol for LPD staff, but that didn't mean the healing was mandatory. He knew that game, too.

"Ready. Wait," begged Buzzy. "You're sure this isn't just a joke or porn or something?"

"How did you guess?" smiled Manny.

"Well . . . I've never really . . . okay, I get it.

Sorry."

"Let's see what's what." Manny clicked the e-mail and the JPEG attachment exploded into life.

The first picture set Manny back in his chair and Buzzy rolling away, covering her mouth, stifling the yell that came as an involuntary reflex.

The close-up of Eric's face showed his bulging, brown eyes, stained duct tape sealing his mouth, and a jet of blood flashing to the right of his chin. The Power Point show switched to the next shot that came from farther back. Gray duct tape had Eric bound to a chair, but Manny's eye was quickly drawn to the gleam dancing off the tip of the knife protruding through the side of Eric's neck. The angle of the sun reflecting off the gleaming blade made it impossible not to focus there. Clever work. Manny was helpless not to dwell on Argyle's claim of artistry.

"Shit," swore Sophie.

But that wasn't the worst. The slide show displayed four more pictures and ended with something conceived only in Hollywood, designed to totally shock its audience.

Eric's severed head rested on the small table of the cruise ship suite. His body was still taped to the chair, sitting a few feet behind the head in a strategic position. The horrible look on his face told a tale that Eric took to his grave. On the bottom of the picture, in front of his chin, was a two-word epitaph: "I'm sorry." It was written in blood.

Gavin hadn't moved, but Manny heard him

clear his throat and felt him finally turn away. Buzzy was losing her lunch a couple cubicles down. Sophie swore again.

He clicked off the screen and bowed his head, his hands clenching a thousand thoughts.

The murders on the *Ocean Duchess* and on the islands had been bad, but Argyle had clearly taken his game up a notch. He wanted everyone to know that he was in control and that to even out the score, as he had put it, was still his number one agenda. This meant no one was safe. No one.

"Are you going to call him? Agent Corner, I mean?" asked Gavin.

"Yes. I don't see a choice. You know Argyle's no longer on the ship, but they'll want to see if they can pick up his trail," answered Manny. "They'll need to get lucky for that to happen."

"He'll want you to go with him," said Sophie.

"Maybe. But we do have a case here."

"Don't worry about that. I'll reassign it to Wymer and Ross. We need to find that murdering son of a bitch." More of that awful sadness crept into Gavin's voice.

Buzzy walked slowly back to Manny's office, her skin as white as a Goth junkie. "That was real, wasn't it? I . . . I've never . . ."

"As real as it gets, Buzzy, as real as it gets," said Manny, reaching for the phone.

Chapter-8

Special Agent Josh Corner looked at the clock and decided it was time to go home. He'd been in the office for over twelve hours and had earned the day's wage. Besides, he had promised his boys he would read their bedtime story tonight, *My New Friends at the Zoo*, by Pops Burkett. The very best reason to get out of the office.

The phone rang as he turned to pluck his navy, pinstriped jacket from the coat rack, deciding to let it go to voicemail. He'd call back tomorrow because tomorrow was soon enough. It would have to be.

"Josh. This is Manny. Pick up. I know you're there; you never freaking leave."

Williams. He smiled. Maybe he'd changed his mind about the job offer. Fine with him. Any day the FBI could land a cop like Manny was a great day for the good guys. He rolled his eyes. He might as well answer. Williams would just call him on the cell if he didn't. It's what friends, and relentless cops, do.

He snatched the phone from the cradle. "Hey,

big boy. What's up, but make it snappy. I got a bedtime story to read." Josh turned on the speaker phone so he could wiggle into his suit coat.

"Hi, Josh. What the hell do you mean you're going home? Getting soft? Real cops are just getting warmed up about now."

Josh shook his head. Next to most cops, he was the workaholic, but compared to Manny—well, there was no comparison.

"Yeah, okay. I'm slacking off after twelve hours. I want to see the boys again before they start shaving and dating."

"Well, that's weak, but almost understandable."

"Thanks for your undying compassion."

He waited for Manny to speak again and felt his own uneasiness grow. "This isn't about the job offer, is it?" Manny didn't speak. Not good.

"No, it's not. Argyle's back. He called me about an hour ago, just after he sent an e-mail showing what he did to a local reporter. I'm forwarding the e-mail as we speak. Josh, he's escalated things, his MO. He's gone deep."

Josh rubbed his face with his hands. "Great. Do you know where he is . . . or was?"

"Yeah. He was on a cruise ship, the *Ocean Empress*, docked in St. Thomas. But you're right; he's long gone. He's too organized not to have his escape route in place. Wherever he is, he's not on that ship. But I don't think he's had time to leave the island."

Just then, Josh's computer told him he had a new message. "Hang on."

He pointed the mouse and opened the communication Manny had forwarded.

This job was always full of surprises—demanding, at its best. But having Argyle show up now, like this, took Josh's breath away. He turned away and laid his family picture face down on his desk, hoping it might insulate them from what was screaming through his monitor.

He let out a long breath. "Who was he?"

"His name was Eric Hayes, a local reporter. About six years ago, he wrote a series of articles about the complexity of the human mind and got some facts wrong involving Argyle's research. There were threats, even a lawsuit, but nothing too desperate . . . until this."

"I'm sending a plane. I'd like to have Sophie come too. Alex, if he can make—"

Before he could say another word, Sophie was talking.

"Josh? Sophie here. I'd be more than willing to help. Really. Thanks for asking. Maybe we can discuss some of the details over dinner, my room?"

Josh heard Manny tell her to go pack. She was in the background, talking fast, but he could make out her fading comments.

"Woo hoo. Road trip to St. Thomas. Best one ever . . ."

Josh laughed. "I guess she wants to go."

"That's an understatement. I'll check with

Alex. I know he'd like to be involved, if he can."

"Good. Meanwhile, I'm going to call the folks at Cyril E. King Airport in St. Thomas and have them delay all outbound flights until we can determine if he's trying to leave that way. I'll meet you there. Okay?"

"Sure, Josh. We'll be there. What about the ship? It's due to sail in about ten hours."

"I'll see if they'll delay until we get there. Carousel owes us that much."

"Good enough. One more thing. I'm sorry about the story-reading time with the boys. I missed a few of those with Jen."

"Thanks. But I'm going to go home and do it anyway. I've got an hour or so before they'll have the plane ready. Besides, they ain't leaving without the man in charge."

"I'd do the same. Oh, I'm bringing my own gun this time."

"Me too. And lots of ammo. Maybe we'll get a chance to save the taxpayers some money."

"Okay. Is that it? Because I can't think of—ah shit," Manny blurted.

His tense tone surprised Josh. Maybe scared him too. "What is it?"

"I just got another e-mail."

That caused Josh to stand to his full six-feet. "From the reporter's account?" His stomach somersaulted when he heard Manny's reply.

"It's from Eric's wife."

Chapter-9

Gavin Crosby did everything he knew to comfort the newest member of the Argyle Widow Club, Katie Hayes, before hanging up, knowing she was sitting on the bed of her stateroom aboard the *Ocean Empress*, taking comfort from her sisters and the ship's security staff—but it could never be enough. He had said all the right things. But he knew that it hadn't really mattered—that it wasn't enough. How could it be? There weren't words in any language that could perform the instant healing Katie's soul longed for. He knew she felt like the loneliest woman God had ever created and nothing would fix that, at least not now. Her children would help when she got back to Lansing, but until then, she would simply zombie through the process of getting home, alone, and wonder a billion times over what had just happened. He snorted. Argyle had just happened again, that's what. Gavin's hatred for the deranged doctor smoldered.

The large picture window in the southern corner of his fifth-story office looked over the

Capitol building. Gavin stood in front of it, his wrinkled hands held behind his back, looking at everything and seeing nothing. But that's how things had been the last few months.

He had always enjoyed watching the sunset, reflecting off the Capitol's pearly dome, but he barely saw it tonight. In fact, he'd hardly seen it at all since they got back from the cruise from hell. His mind kept drifting back to the horrible scene in Mike's cabin and the carnage Argyle had left as a reminder that he hadn't cared for Gavin's opinion of his research. He shook his head. That was it, nothing more sinister or complex than that. If there had been something unforgivable, some heinous wrong that the Crosbys had perpetrated to ruin the doctor's life, at least Gavin could understand that. Lexy was ravaged over a professional disagreement, a damned argument.

The pack of smokes in his shirt pocket called his name, and he listened, lighting up. He had quit for over twenty years, but started again when they returned from the Caribbean. Who knew exactly why? Did it matter? He supposed it did, but he didn't care. It calmed his nerves.

It was against the rules to smoke in the building, but he was the police chief; what were they going to do, fire him?

He exhaled a gray, wispy haze, and again tried to focus on positive things: what was good for his wife Stella, for his son Mike, and even for him. There were moments that it worked, but usually it didn't. Today was one of the days that positive things were as far away as Shangri-La.

Stella. His wife of thirty-seven years was holding them all together, like usual. She spent time reading about healing. She went to Tae-Bo classes with women like Manny's wife, Louise, and Alex's wife, Barb. Her friends wouldn't let her drown in a funk, but instead helped to pull her out. They were there for her. But he choose the opposite . . . alone was better.

He bowed his head. Stella was working hard at moving on. Mike and he needed to follow suit. They would, eventually, but nobody had said how difficult it would be.

And lately, being home with her was . . . harder. She would never blame him, but he felt guilty, almost dirty around her. It was why he'd spent a few nights in the office over the last month. People married as long as they've been didn't have to talk to communicate, and he'd felt *something* was off. But things would come around. They always did—he hoped. He wasn't sure how much more he could take.

Gavin moved away from the window, sat at his desk, and began to leaf through the personnel file of newly appointed district attorney, Jessie Grace. The circuit court judges in Ingham County had named her to replace Liz Casnovsky.

Jessie had a reputation for being fair-minded, but unbending in her approach to serious criminal offenses while an assistant district attorney. She was incredibly prepared and bright. Maybe a little raw with the people skills, but that would come. It would have to. Serving the public was as much about image as getting the job done.

"Welcome to the world of sleepless nights and the realm of 'they don't pay me enough for this shit,'" he said to himself.

Gavin finished his report on the e-mails Manny had received and then went over the preliminary findings of the murder at the White Kitty. Morse had been no Citizen of the Year candidate, but dying like that wasn't how anyone should go. "Brutal" only touched the surface of this one. He frowned. Somewhere, way back in one of those secret places of the mind, he called himself a liar. Maybe dying like that *was* justice.

"Hey, honey."

Gavin looked up from the oak desk, stared, and then broke into a tired grin. Stella was standing at the door, her expression more relaxed than he could remember seeing in months. She looked good too. Real good. Her long legs were in great shape, and she had changed the color of her hair.

"Hey baby, good to see you. Sit down."

Stella walked around the desk and kissed her husband. "No, thanks. I can't stay that long. Things to do. Just wanted to say hi and give you this."

Gavin watched as she pulled the .22 from her purse and promptly shot him in the chest.

Chapter-10

Siggie Ashcroft threw his black duffel bag on the worn couch of the dilapidated bedroom and stood silently, taking in his surroundings. Even the musty smell seemed liberating. He'd been confined to a six-by-eight cement-block cell, with color-coordinated steel bars, at the Jackson Correction Facility for the last five years, and that made this seem like the White House. But then again, what wouldn't? There weren't any rats waltzing around the stained windowsills and no turds sprinkled around the floor or in the bed, at least that he could see. That made this halfway house apartment just that much better. Score one for him and the bleeding-heart liberals who thought he deserved another chance.

Still, nothing could compare to what he had six years ago, before those sleazy bitches took it away: decadent salary, big house on Lansing's Southside, SUVs . . . and a family, a family he would never see again. His ex-wife had made that abundantly clear. His young son and daughter would grow up not knowing who he was, what he had sacrificed to give them a leg up in life. Worse, the old lady didn't *want* them to know. Stupid heifer.

So what if he liked getting it on in a different way? Those women knew what they were getting into. They had to. The way they'd all looked at him, showing their tits and all of that leg, begging him to take them down a road they'd never been. And let's not forget those shoes. The ones that said do me, do me now. He'd just done what they had asked. Where was the crime in that?

His jerk-off attorney said he would be smart to plead guilty and get a reduced sentence. If not, he could go away for a very long time. Rape on multiple counts wasn't funny. So he had pleaded guilty. But he and that faggot lawyer would talk again. Real close up.

"Rape, my ass," he whispered. The word caused his searing anger to burn even hotter. "Paybacks, bitches, paybacks."

He kicked off his shoes and stretched his thin, wiry frame, then headed to the kitchen. There was supposed to be some food in the fridge and a few things in the cupboard to tide him over until he could go shopping. Minutes later, he realized he was going to have to go out. There wasn't anything in this shithole that he had a hankering for. He grinned. Nothing the pantry or refrigerator could give him.

He needed something else, and he wasn't going to wait.

Having playmates in prison wasn't the same as

having them on the outside, and he more than missed the ones out here. They were softer, more compliant. He loved compliant.

Ashcroft waited another two hours until the fall sun had almost vanished over the red Michigan horizon, slid into his brown loafers, flipped the hood over his head, and went out the door. He stood on his stoop, looked up and down the street, and realized how much freedom he had. There was no one around telling him what to do, what to say, or even watching him take a piss. No more.

Ashcroft could no longer suppress what his appetite said he had to have, what he needed. This was going to be some lady's lucky night. What a country. He could hardly contain himself.

Chapter-11

The woman in black watched Ashcroft shudder like he was gripping a downed power line, then grow still. It was fascinating and eerie at the same time. She almost felt him leave this world and enter the next. But it wasn't heaven, or any other promised land filled with God's mercy and presence. He went straight to hell, to the kingdom of eternal suffering. It's what he deserved.

Her breathing began to settle as she rose from her knees and, once again, glanced down both sides of the dusk-shrouded street. They were off the beaten path, but it never hurt to be cautious. She had more work to do and getting caught wasn't on the agenda.

It had been easier this time. Ashcroft hadn't needed much coaxing to get his pants off, not after she had promised him whatever he wanted. She had worked the hooker angle, and he drew to her like iron to a magnet. Thinking with his little head had cost him his miserable life. What a surprise.

After putting the bottle of acid back in her bag, she began wiping blood and strands of tissue from her face and legs with the moist towels she had brought. She peeled off the black hoodie, short skirt, and the four-inch stilettos, putting them in the thick garbage bag. Then she put on jeans and a sweatshirt. She found the shell casings and put them in her pocket. Next, she removed the bloodied rag from his mouth. That had shut up the perverted whiner, but she supposed most people were cooperative with their wrists adorned with black leather straps and a .22 handgun massaging their face.

At that moment, the mercury-filled streetlight flickered on, changing shadows to reality, and she jumped, grabbing her chest. In that brief millisecond, her mind ran the full gamut of what she had done, was doing—from the shock and disdain of her family, to spending the rest of her life in prison.

She quickly envisioned herself as a shriveled old woman sentenced to a dirty, diseased-infested prison cell, where her best friend was another decrepit, forgotten woman who hadn't done anything wrong. They were just victims of the system.

"We're all victims of the system," she whispered in a voice that didn't sound like her. That was okay. Her voice wasn't the only part of her struggling with who she was.

The streetlight bled Picasso patterns into the area behind the tall, silver maple—just turning colors, anticipating the cycle of life the four seasons dictated—where Ashcroft lay. She tilted her head, curiosity outweighing revulsion. His crotch no longer carried the hard woody he so desperately wanted to relieve just a few moments earlier. He had thought he was going to get the blow job of his life, and in a real sense, he had. She grinned at that.

Her eyes moved to the three crimson holes ripped into his chest and the third eye staring up between the other two. The black powder residue bordered the wound like eye shadow, and the escaped gases from the gun's barrel gave it a more pronounced, jagged appearance. There also seemed to be more blood this time. A lot more. But she really hadn't taken time to notice the last time. It had been darker, and she had been much more concerned (first-time jitters) with dragging Mitchell Morse away from her car and planting him at the dumpster. It had been farther than she thought. Maybe thirty yards, but adrenaline was an amazing ally.

Things you learn.

The air was cooling, the way Michigan fall evenings do, and she could smell the faint crispness of autumn riding the breeze as she raised her face to the sky. But there was another scent, unpleasant, out of place—a stench really. One that threatened to spoil the jealous euphoria she had created. It was him. She felt her blood pressure rise. He had to ruin the moment, didn't he? The narcissistic degenerate couldn't even die gracefully. But what did she expect? Zebras never changed their stripes.

The woman in black slid the stilettos silently back over her feet and fastened the large silver buckles. She promptly kicked Ashcroft's right ribs so viciously that she heard bones crack. She kicked again and felt the pointed tip go deeper. It was on. There were no thoughts of anything else, no other picture. Just red rage that spoke in a straight-line language she understood, no need for an interpreter.

When she finally stopped, she was breathing hard, sweat trickled down her temples, and her ankles hurt. She looked at him and noticed he was lying on his face, several bones pressing against graying skin at weird angles, not breaking through his beaten hide, but close. She had no real recollection of turning him over; but using him as a trampoline remained vivid. One last point to make.

Somewhere, a siren wailed, reverberating through the clear evening. Maybe someone saw or heard. Maybe not. Had she screamed? Perhaps. At any rate, it was time to go. She picked up her bag and moved in the direction of the grocery store parking lot two blocks over. She pulled out of the lot just as a red sports car sped by, chased by an LPD cruiser. They were both driving like bats out of hell with each driver's destiny at different ends of the justice spectrum.

She smiled.

Chapter-12

"So, geniuses, what's a six-letter word for guardian or protector?"

Manny looked up from his book, *Devil's Moon,* by Rebecca Stroud. Alex Downs was passing time on the flight to St. Thomas working crosswords with his usual intensity. He sat across the aisle of the FBI's swanky, corporate-like, Gulfstream G-V, Sophie sitting to the left. Alex's glasses rested on the bridge of his pointed nose. He looked like a serious, no-nonsense judge from the 1770s.

Sophie cocked her head to the right, pulled out one earphone, and turned the volume down on her pink MP3 player. "What did you say?"

"I said, what's a six-letter word for guardian or protector?" repeated Alex.

She scrunched up her nose and looked up to the ceiling before suddenly clutching Alex's chubby arm. Manny placed the bookmark in his book, closed it, and waited.

"Oh my gosh, I've got it. Condom, the word is condom."

"What? Is that all you think about, woman?

The word is not condom."

"No? Are there any letters?"

"Yes, an N."

"Where?"

Alex rolled his eyes. "It's the . . . ah . . . third letter."

"Do you have any other letters?"

Manny saw the exasperation forming on Alex's face.

"No! I don't have any more damn letters, yet."

Sophie leaned back in the plush leather seat, putting her earphones back in. "Then how do you know I'm not right?"

The CSI got out of his chair. "I've got to take a leak . . . and it's not condom."

"Whatever you say. But if you're going to act like that, I'm not going to help anymore."

She winked at Manny and dialed up her music as Alex marched to the rest room, mumbling something about wise-ass detectives.

Never a dull moment.

Manny put his book on the floor, beside the other one, a Tim Ellis thriller, and turned on his laptop, waiting for it to fire up.

So this is how the FBI worked, at least the BAU. Nothing seemed out of their reach, if it was needed. Like this jet, for starters. It wasn't just your everyday, run-of-the-mill, executive plane. This one had all of the state-of-the-art communications equipment, including satellite links. It was comfortable, quiet, fast, and even the food was good. Not to mention all of the amazing criminal databases and latest forensic research provided by the bureau's ERT units and NCIS case data dancing at their fingertips. These types of resources would be an amazing upgrade to what Lansing had to offer, and he could be part of it. Josh had made him an incredible job offer with more leeway than he'd ever had or dreamed of. Extremely appealing. But leaving Lansing, home . . . well that was the conundrum, wasn't it?

Which way is the right way?

He gazed out the curved window and flirted with the star-filled night. The stars winked back a million times over as his thoughts turned to the rush of the last four hours—and what kind of hell Katie Hayes was now living.

The e-mail she had sent was in response to one that came from Eric's account, telling her to contact Manny right away, that it was a matter of life and death, giving her Manny's e-mail address. The message to Katie also had one of the pictures of Eric attached, up close and personal. He could almost hear her screams.

Gavin had volunteered to call her and do the best he could to explain the situation, as well as they knew it anyway, and shooed Manny out the door. As he was leaving, he heard Gavin tell Katie as soon as the cruise ship's security staff could locate which suite Eric was in, or at least had been in, they would contact her. He asked if Katie had anyone close by. Gavin was still talking in that quiet, comforting voice, contradicting the gruff exterior that Manny had heard so many times before. All the while, Gavin tried not to show his own tears already adding twenty years to his face.

As he left the office and climbed into his Ford Explorer, it occurred to him that in this day and age of *Me First*, he was grateful to work for a man who didn't operate that way. Gavin Crosby truly cared about others.

When Manny had arrived home to get his travel case and tell Louise he was on the way out, he could smell her famous spaghetti and meatballs. The smell of garlic and tangy tomato sauce swirling through the modest ranch home was amazing, but he wouldn't be eating any of it tonight.

Louise had been a cop's wife too long. When Manny put his hands on her shapely waist and found her eyes, her look turned from "glad to see you" to "what's going on?" He explained as much as he could, grabbed the already-packed travel bag from the closet, and walked to the front foyer. She hugged him ferociously, told him to be careful, and pushed him out the door.

She knew there would be no peace for the Williams family as long as Argyle was out there and wanted him put away, or in the ground, as badly as anyone.

The laptop blinked brightly into existence, bringing Manny out of his deep thoughts just as Alex plopped back in his chair. Manny had a message from Agent Corner saying that he and his people would meet them in Miami, and they would fly to St. Thomas together.

The ship's security people had found the suite where Eric Hayes had been murdered, and the reporter was still there, just like the last grisly picture had depicted. No Argyle to be found, of course.

The cruise line was going to wait for them, but at least security and some of the local detectives would do the leg work of interviewing passengers and staff. Manny knew there wouldn't be much to act on. That's how Argyle operated. But maybe this time . . .

After shutting the top on his computer, he rubbed his eyes with a thumb and forefinger and reclined the seat. They had a couple hours to sleep, and sleep was a precious commodity.

He took one last look at Alex and remembered his question. "Minder," he said.

"What?" asked Alex.

"The word is 'minder.'"

The CSI squinted and then nodded. "Good one, Williams. It fits and beats the hell out of your partner's guess."

Manny thought Alex was right: it *was* a much better word. But he wondered how to convert the concept of guardian and protector into action with animals like Argyle roaming the world.

Chapter-13

The FBI's jet skidded along the runway at Miami International and rattled to a manageable speed. Manny threw a quick glance Sophie's way, grinning. "How you doin' there, partner? How was that landing? I personally liked that bouncing part."

"Not funny, Williams. You know I hate the landings," answered Sophie, obviously relieved that the plane was taxiing up the runway. "We could have died really. Twenty-five percent of all airplane accidents happen during the landing, you know."

"Yeah, and fifty-seven percent happen while the plane is in the air, so I'll take the landings."

"Are you lying? If you are, I'm going to shoot your ass, right here." Sophie released her grip on the seat as the jet settled at the private gate, and she patted her holster. Manny could see her finger impressions imbedded in the tan leather.

"When was the last time I lied to you? And I've seen your targets at the firing range. No worries for my ass."

"You're not kidding? Are you? Just great. I'm walking to St. Thomas."

"Long walk," stated Alex.

"Sharks too," added Manny.

"You guys suck."

"Just trying to help," smiled Manny.

"Okay. I'm renting a car. How deep can the ocean be?"

The passenger door swung up and open. Josh walked through the door followed by two agents. One Manny recognized as the very talented forensic expert, Max Tucker, who had teamed up with them on the *Ocean Duchess*. The third agent was a woman in her early thirties: long, red hair; demanding, green eyes; curvy build; wearing a dark pants suit; and a serious look clouding her pleasant features. Very pleasant features. She walked with a barely discernable limp.

Agent Corner zeroed in on the Lansing crew and broke into a huge smile, accented by those startling, pilot-blue eyes. He stuck his hand out, moving to greet them.

"Manny. How the hell are you?"

"All right, under the circumstances. You're looking well."

"Thanks. Been working out," he laughed.

Corner turned to the other two. "Alex. Good to see you. Sophie, glad you could make it."

Alex shook his hand and nodded. "Always good to see you guys."

Sophie took his hand. "I can tell."

"Tell what?"

"You've been working out, big boy."

Manny watched as Josh's face shaded red, and he tried to release Sophie's hand quickly, except she wouldn't let him. His partner held on for a second or two longer, then reluctantly let go. Manny nudged her. She ignored him.

Josh cleared his throat. "You remember Max Tucker, and this is Chloe Franson. Chloe recently transferred into my department from Domestic Terrorism. Lots of experience in the field, and we're happy to have her."

Chloe greeted everyone with a tight, professional smile and a slight grimace, which she almost succeeded in hiding, but not from Manny. She caught his eyes and allowed a slow grin to come to life.

"Gunshot," Chloe said, a trace of Irish lilt filtering through her voice.

"Western Ireland?"

"Galway Bay." Her quick smile, the real one, was brilliant.

Sophie and Alex looked at him and shook their heads in unison.

"You're doing it already," said Alex.

"Doing what?"

"Profiling the new help."

"I'm not either. I just noticed the accent and the limp, and she was in a little pain."

"I didn't," said Sophie.

"Me either," said Alex.

"That makes three," said Max.

Manny rolled his eyes. "You call yourself

cops?"

Chloe turned to Josh. "He's better than you said." Then she turned back to Manny. "It happened about two months ago. A raid in New York City. My calf is still sore, but getting better. I'll be back to normal in no time." She glanced to the floor and then back to Manny. "Don't worry, I won't be a liability. I'm able to do everything I could before, physically, but it hurts a wee bit."

"Mentally?"

"You *are* on top of things. The Bureau shrinks cleared me. Seems being shot didn't bother me that much."

He smiled. "Not bad yourself." He gazed another second or two, then turned away. She was better than not bad in all the right ways.

Josh motioned for everyone to sit. "Okay. We'll take off in a few minutes. Before we do, I want to go over the file on Eric Hayes, at least what we have. The locals have done a great job of getting pictures and reports to us, but they are holding the room, and the cruise ship is not going anywhere until we get there."

Corner nodded to Max. The CSI sat up straight and handed out the plain brown folders marked with the official Bureau logo. Max still had that same asthmatic wheeze and the tiny tremors in his small ebony hand. But the smallish, bespectacled agent never allowed his breathing problems, or his internal angst, to get in the way of his tenacity operating in the forensic world. Nice trait.

Max reached into his pocket, took a hit from his inhaler, snared a deep breath, and sat down.

Josh glanced at Manny, then around the table, and began. “You all know about Argyle, seen his work up close, with the exception of Agent Franson, and she has been well versed on his psychotic tendencies and traits. Which had been pretty consistent, up until a few hours ago.”

“You mean because of the way he killed Hayes?” asked Chloe.

“Yes, there’s that. But there is something else.”

Manny nodded his head. “He was bold before, but in a controlled, almost careful way. Like he wasn’t totally 100% confident in what he was doing, that maybe he could be caught. He’s arrogant, but the fact that he didn’t want to risk close contact with us, instead choosing to leave a video message, meant that he was not totally self-assured, no matter what he tried to portray in the DVD on the *Ocean Duchess* a few months ago.”

“Do you think that was because he was in the restricted cruise ship environment?” asked Sophie.

“Maybe. Or even that acting out his fantasies was all pretty new to him. Whatever the reason, his methods never involved leaving forensic evidence of any kind. The bleach, the gloves, his shaved body, and the biting were remarkably consistent with victims DA Casnovsky and Lexy Crosby. Controlled mayhem, if you will,” said Agent Tucker.

“He was good at covering his tracks, no debate

there," agreed Alex.

Max took a drink from his bottled water. "These new pictures indicate that he didn't care about covering his tracks. The blood on his hands, no gloves, his goatee, the knife, and fibers from his clothes could all lead to where he's been, what he's been doing."

"So this attack was almost careless, disorganized. Like his anger was getting the better of him. Even losing control to the point of total rage," added Manny.

The images of how they had found the two women—his friends—came screaming back like a haunting, recurring nightmare. He dismissed them from his mind. He was getting better at it, but he wondered if they would ever go away completely. Besides, dwelling on Liz and Lexy wouldn't help find Argyle; it would just feed the emotion that could cause him to miss something. Maybe something critical. "It doesn't really fit for him though. He could be playing mind games again, trying to lead us astray when he has a completely different agenda in mind."

"You mean like leaving the message on the mirror of Detective Castro's stateroom on the last cruise?" asked Sophie.

Chloe stopped tapping her pencil on the table. "I'm not totally sure. Who could be? But he did it once and I don't think he'll go down that road again, at least not that way. I think he's evolving, or devolving, if you will. He's had to lay low. His narcissistic propensities won't allow him to do that forever. He loves his 'watch me' moments." She looked around the table and settled on Manny. "And he doesn't strike me as a patient man."

Manny returned the look and caught himself staring again. "You're right about that."

"So maybe he's escalating things?" said Josh.

Manny shrugged. "That's a good guess. All psychopaths obsess on some segment of society that represents a means to an end. Sexually or otherwise. The thing about Argyle that's been different is his versatility. He'll do anything to exact revenge, and that makes him dangerous and mostly unpredictable. Combine that with his intellect, and nothing is out of the question. We do have one advantage, however. We know he's focusing on anyone who caused him grief within the Lansing law enforcement family, and Argyle is compelled to scratch that itch."

"Some advantage," said Sophie.

Chapter-14

Argyle leaned against the faded yellow stones of Blackbeard's Castle and stared down the hills to the bright lights of Charlotte-Amalie. The sultry Caribbean breeze touched his face and brought a scent of ocean and flora that even a man like himself could appreciate. He was such a complex dichotomy, was he not?

To his left, a mile away from the city, the glowing, colorful outlines of two cruise ships shined in the St. Thomas port. Each mammoth vessel originated from a different cruise line, and each with a different story to tell. He smiled at that. There would be no tale like the one saturating the staff of the *Ocean Empress*. He was sure they hadn't seen anything like the calling card he'd left. Ever. They should be honored. He didn't show his genius to just anyone. And it *was* genius. Maybe Eric Hayes and his lovely wife wouldn't think so. Perhaps Detective Manny Williams, his slut partner, and the worthless morons from the FBI would disagree. Everyone's a critic these days.

The doctor wiped at the perspiration that was as natural to the Caribbean as teal waters and swaying palm trees. Leveling the score with Eric had been all that he'd expected. Not to mention, it had been a hell of a way to announce his return from his self-imposed sabbatical. Hiding was for cowards, for the weak. He was many things, but weak was not on the menu. Men like him were prudent. He'd had to hole up because people knew him, maybe even saw him through the different colored hair and beard merry-go-round. It was difficult to mask his height and his strong build, but there were ways to make one's self invisible, even for gods. But no longer.

As ironic as it sounded, his patient, Eli Jenkins, had helped to show him the Way, the truth about himself, and how special he was going to be. He had learned his lessons well and had become the Master. He grinned. He wondered what the deceased Eli Jenkins would think about the passing of that torch.

He focused on the Carousel Cruise Line ship and wondered when Williams would show with his cronies. He guessed they would be there in another three hours or so and, predictably, run right to the suite to see his handiwork. They were thinking that he had become sloppy, careless, and was out of control. Fools. Besides, if you wanted to find someone, why look where they *weren't*? No problem, however. They would all enjoy a "family" reunion soon enough. He could hardly wait.

"Beautiful view. It really captures the

imagination, doesn't it?"

Argyle glanced in the direction of the young, dark-haired woman standing a few feet to his left.

"I believe you're correct. Well said."

They were alone. She wasn't exactly what he liked, what made his whistle blow, but not bad. She would do, and he did have a little time before the real party started. Not to mention, it had been awhile.

What a night this will be for her.

"Listen, at the risk of sounding bold, I have a few hours to kill and wonder if I could buy you a drink?"

Argyle felt her size him up through the shadowy lights careening from the castle walls, and then the quick smile. "Sure. Why not? It's not like you're a serial killer or anything, right?"

He held out his arm, and she looped hers though.

He feigned a horrible look. "What a totally awful thought."

Chapter-15

"He's watching us."

Alex Downs and Agent Tucker had already progressed through the ship's security station, hurrying to get to the suite where Eric was murdered before any more evidence could be compromised. Manny stopped at the foot of the gangplank and laid his shoulder bag on the tepid concrete of the pier.

Josh backed down the steps, and Manny felt him touch his shoulder.

"Argyle?"

He nodded.

"How do you know? It's dark, it's late, and you can't see him."

Manny turned his head to the left, looking through the ten-foot, chain-link security fence and catching the colorful lights of the St. Thomas Cable Car Sky Ride as it stepped up the island's hillside toward Paradise Point.

"I can feel him, Josh. This is too good for him to pass up."

By then, Sophie and Chloe had joined them.

Sophie touched his arm. "Are you going into spooky mode again?"

Agent Corner grinned. "It's not like we haven't seen it before."

"Yeah, true enough. At least he's not in one of those trance things," said Sophie.

"He does trances?" questioned Chloe. "Can I watch?"

"Funny. If you guys would pay attention, you'd get it too," explained Sophie. "It's all about his profile, what he gets off on, and how he *has* to be involved. He has no choice, even though he thinks he does."

Chloe shifted her feet and looked Manny squarely in the eyes.

He felt her intensity, maybe perhaps anger, even through the oblique illumination of the pier's mercury lights. Was this personal with her? They'd have to talk later. He found himself looking forward to talking to her alone.

"What's too good? The crime scene?" Chloe questioned.

She was direct, no doubt about that. Another first-class trait. "Me. Maybe us. Maybe anyone who wants him stopped. He thinks he's won again. But he has to take part in the victory, or it would be like it never happened. The deranged animal has to control everything. But I think this could be about me, my family. When we got home from the cruise in June, he had somehow put a note with three black rose petals in my wife's purse. The note said 'one never knows.'"

Chloe nodded. "It's consistent with him. He's obviously trying to scare and manipulate you, but how could he be watching us? There's police everywhere, and he wouldn't risk getting caught."

"He could be using a long distance camera or an easily concealed one closer to us. Maybe on one of the mall buildings," offered Josh, pointing to the group of red-roofed buildings to the right of the fence.

"It's possible. It'd have to be pretty sophisticated equipment to let him see what he has to see. Besides, I think he needs it to be more personal," said Manny.

He shifted his gaze to the ship, and eventually upward along her balconied flank, focusing as far as the lights would allow, and then back to four Virgin Island officers patrolling the fence. "Security said he left his suite and then the ship about three minutes before I got the pictures. That was about an hour before he called."

"So we know he didn't stay on board, and it's impossible to book the same cruise, even under another name, so he has to be off the *Ocean Empress*," said Chloe.

Manny tapped his foot and ran his hand through his hair. "What would I do if I were him? How would I get up close and personal?"

Then it came to him like those enlightenments do. He turned to Sophie. "What was the alias he used to book the cruise?"

She took out her notepad. "Ahhmm. Well, he was found in a suite booked by a—Steve Decker.

Yeah, Steven Decker."

"Josh, stay casual, relaxed, and call your contact at the local police department. Ask for the names on the duty roster of all the Virgin Island Police assigned to St. Thomas. We need to compare it, particularly to the ones assigned to Customs and pier security."

"Why do we need to do that? I don't get . . ."

Manny watched his face light up like a new sunrise.

"Are you saying he's one of the patrol officers?"

"I don't know, but it's what I would do if I wanted to get close to the action. The rest of you, don't look at the patrols. Keep talking and nodding until we cross-check the reference list."

Agent Corner pulled out his cell and made the call.

"Say that's true, how would he know who was assigned to this gig on such short notice?" asked Chloe.

"If I'm right, he knew that Steven Decker would be working this shift. He always does his research. It's part of his game, his taunting. It's an irony he doesn't think we'll get because we're not as bright as him."

"So the real Steven Decker . . ." wondered Chloe.

He bowed his head. "My guess is the real Steven Decker's family isn't going to see him again, alive at least . . ."

"You're paranoid, or Argyle's even scarier than I thought," shivered Sophie.

Josh moved closer to the steel fence and slapped his phone shut, walking back in Manny's direction. One look from the Fed was all Manny needed to see to know he wasn't paranoid, and that Argyle was enjoying the view. Maybe his favorite view.

Chapter-16

Josh put his phone in his pocket and smiled at Manny. “So how do you want to play this? We could have the place crawling with cops in five minutes.”

Manny clapped Josh on the shoulder, looking relaxed and unconcerned. Argyle had balls; he had to hand it to him. “He knows it and has that contingency covered. I would.”

“So what would be the most unexpected thing we could do?” asked Chloe as she moved closer, switching her leather bag to the other shoulder, stretching and yawning in the process.

“Distraction?” asked Sophie. “Maybe I could go over to the fence—with Josh—and scream for help, that I was being raped or robbed. Or just drunk and having fun. I take off my clothes—with Josh—and make it totally realistic. Then we can see which guard doesn’t come running.” Sophie’s eyes opened wide. “You know I’d take one for the team—with Josh.”

Josh stared at Sophie and shifted his feet.

Manny had never seen Josh that nervous

before. The funny thing was that Sophie was just crazy enough to do it—with Josh.

"Thanks, partner. I'll remember that for future reference."

Manny ran his hand through his hair. Argyle was scary bright and always a step ahead. His plans, his plays, were faultless. Mistakes were not in his makeup. So what was the answer to Chloe's question? "We need to talk to the officer in charge. I'll see if I can get to the security shack and talk to the guards. We need to know how many patrolmen are out there and where Decker should be stationed. But if we all start walking that way, he'll know something's up, so I want you three to check in with security. Once we find out where Decker is supposed to be, I'll radio his location, then we can call for backup."

"Isn't that a little dangerous for you?" asked Chloe.

"No, I don't think so. If he wanted to make a move on me, he would have tried by now. He wants a bigger stage when he goes after that prize."

"There's another exit on the other end of the ship for passengers. After you radio the ship, the three of us will exit there and rendezvous with you," said Josh.

"Sounds good." Manny picked up his bag and turned to Chloe. "I don't know, agent. I don't know what he would least expect us to do." He grinned. "Hell, maybe Sophie's right. Maybe we should all rush the fence naked and see what happens."

"My brilliance is so underappreciated," moaned Sophie.

Chloe shook her head. "I don't know about the naked thing, since I just met you all. I guess it could be fun—with Josh. But I think you're right about not letting him know we think he's out there. Good luck."

The others moved up the silver-railed gangplank as Manny faced the security shack, about sixty yards to the south and began to walk. As he sauntered along the pier, he tried to see without looking. The long shadows away from the well-lit pier weren't cooperating. Argyle was out there, lurking in the shadows. No doubt about that now.

Manny brushed at the sweat beading like small pools of salt water on his face. Could this be it? Could they actually have a step-up on the crazy doctor?

His insides roiled with anticipation, with bold possibilities. How good would it be to see the man in cuffs? Better yet, in a meat wagon?

The door of the small, green building was cracked, and Manny pushed it open. According to the sign on the door, Officer S. Treadwell was in charge. "Hello? Officer Treadwell? Anyone?" There hadn't been anyone standing outside and no one sat behind either of the small, worn, wooden desks. Not good. The hair straightened on the back of his neck, and he reached for the Glock .40 holstered under his arm. He quickly cleared the area around the front of the shack and saw no one heading toward the checkpoint from outside the fence. There was no sound, except the party music floating softly from the Lido Deck of the *Ocean Empress*.

What the hell? Argyle?

On full alert, he moved back inside the shed, searching for the two-way to call the ship, when he heard the rustle from behind the narrow door to his left. Just as he leveled his gun, the warped door burst open. Samantha Treadwell's plump body did a twirling dance step, dreadlocks flying, while listening to a tune through her earphones. The sergeant's last spin, hands flailing in the humid air, brought her dark, oval face inches from the barrel of Manny's gun.

Her eyes grew wide and she stopped moving, staring at the gun like it was the last thing she would ever see. "Jus take it easy. My dancin' wasn't dat bad, my brudder. No reason to shoot a woman for dat."

Manny holstered his gun and smiled, despite the 100 miles per hour his heart raced. "I'm sorry, officer. When I didn't find anyone around, I thought the worst."

She took the hand from her chest and let out a strangled breath. "You need to relax, mon. It's late, so my partner went to get dinner and I had to . . . well, you know." She grinned. "I tink I might have to go again."

"I'm sorry again. Really." He leaned against the door and watched the local cop recover. "I need your help. I'm Detective Williams, and I'm with the

FBI crew that was brought in to investigate the murder on the *Ocean Empress*."

"I know who ya are, mon. I saw you when ya came tru da checkpoint, and I never forget a pretty face." She sat down in her padded leather chair. "Whew. Now dat my chest is done poundin, I might be able ta help. What do ya need?"

"What area is Steven Decker patrolling?"

"Decker? He be on the very south end, jus on dat side." She pointed over Manny's shoulder. "Why?"

Before he could answer, the square, glass window to Treadwell's right exploded as a large rock blurred past her face, bounced off the desk, and settled on the sweating wooden floor. He jumped away and dove for cover. Treadwell followed suit, yelling in surprise.

The smell of the floor was sharp, like sweat and dirt, as Manny stayed low, gun raised facing the door, waiting for Argyle to show. His concentration was on the door when it dawned on him that Treadwell was still screaming. But not a shriek of fear or being startled, but one of horror, outright panic. Rolling to his left, he rose, slammed the door, and turned in Treadwell's direction. She lay face-to-face with the rock, except it wasn't a rock at all, but a woman's severed head wrapped in a clear plastic bag. Manny could see the head's wide, dark eyes staring at everything and nothing, the expression of terror still etched on her bloodied face.

Manny pulled the sergeant to her feet and told

her to call the ship's security. He sprinted out the door and stopped cold after three frenzied strides. There, lying on the ground, the heartless floodlights exposed another mutilated body, a St. Thomas cop with his head staged on his chest. Manny closed his eyes and felt his stomach twist like a pretzel. It didn't take an expert to figure out that Steven Decker wouldn't be going home to his family tonight.

"Where are you, you gutless son of a bitch?" he yelled. "You're a damned coward! Come get me."

Silence ruled the night until he heard the footsteps racing from the ship along the path of the security fence. Manny turned back to the body. A note was pinned to the blue lapel of the dead cop's shirt. He pulled it off and read the perfectly printed block letters:

EXCELLENT TO SEE YOU, DETECTIVE. GLAD YOU MADE IT. AS YOU CAN SEE, I'M STILL AHEAD IN THE GAME, BUT WE'LL GET TOGETHER SOON.
P.S. EVER NOTICE HOW PEOPLE DIE AROUND YOU?

Chapter-17

"We're searching everywhere, but we haven't located Argyle," said Josh, rubbing his eyes with the heel of his hand.

Manny looked up from his seat in the ship's swank conference room. "Yeah. They won't find him. He's had this planned for weeks. The question is, what's he going to do next?" He gazed at the note Argyle had written. It continued to burn in his hand. The all-too-familiar guilt ran roughshod through the empty hole where his heart should be. These latest murders, these invitations to the party, were mostly for show, for Manny.

The inner voices argued. One whispered it wasn't his fault, that Argyle killed without warrant and nothing could prevent that. The other voice blamed him for every hurt, every death. His dad used to say, "Knowing and believing are two entirely different matters." Manny let out a slow breath and fought to ignore the persecution the inner accuser wanted to keep vividly alive. His dad was right, but it wouldn't do any good to throw a full-blown pity party. Maybe later, most assuredly later. But for now, he needed to focus on the living—that meant Argyle.

Alex, Sophie, Chloe, and Max sat with him at the dark mahogany table. Each appeared tired and defeated. Manny was sure he mirrored their collective conditions.

"Well, one thing's for sure. The locals are going to need more help. Alex and I can't process three, maybe four, different crime scenes. Not that it's going to do much good," said Max. "We found nothing in the room where the reporter was killed that Argyle didn't want us to find. We bagged what we could, but by the time we ID any particulates or fibers that could help us know where he might have been, he'll be long gone."

"He might already be," added Alex.

"Count on it," answered Manny. "He's like the freaking invisible man."

"They can only lock down the island for a few hours, or maybe a day, before they have to get back to normal," said Sophie, drumming her fingers on the table. "People need to make a living and tourism is their main thing."

"He knows it too," said Chloe. She leaned against the table, frowning. "So why the change?"

"In his MO?" responded Manny.

Chloe nodded, not taking her eyes from his face.

"I'm not sure. I think he's changed, but he may think it's intentional. He is always looking to confuse us and wants to hide the real purpose for doing what he does." He sipped from his coffee cup. "His profile is odd because serial killers aren't typically motivated by revenge."

"Except for women serial killers," corrected Chloe.

"Right. The thing is we know he wants to settle the score, as he sees it, with anyone from Lansing who he believes crossed him. But these murders, the decapitations, indicate more anger, more frustration. Like he can't control it anymore, and victimology doesn't matter." Manny shrugged. "But he is forever bright and seems too organized to make a mistake that will get him caught."

"So it's about the game. About winning," said Chloe.

"I think it has been all along. But like I said, I don't think he realizes totally that he is devolving and driven more by rage than ever. And that could be good for us."

"Ppfftt.Yeah. If we live through it," snorted Sophie.

Josh's cell phone rang, and he moved away from the table, finger in his ear. Manny watched the FBI agent slump just a little more as he flipped his phone shut and moved back to the table.

"They've located the rest of the young woman's remains behind a clump of palms and bougainvillea bushes near the old Butterfly Farm. She was a passenger on the other ship in port. Argyle must have recently met her. Maybe up at Blackbeard's Castle. There was a brochure in her pocket from there." He plopped down.

"What, Josh?" asked Manny.

He shook his head in disgust. "She was raped and bitten. She was so ravaged that it was almost hard to believe she was human."

"Even worse than what he did to the women on the cruise?" asked Alex.

"Sounds like it."

"My God. How could it be worse?" whispered Manny. A question he knew no one could answer, not even Argyle.

Josh stood and clapped his hands. "All right. Here's the deal. It's 2 a.m. and we're all beat. The ship has a few rooms left, so we'll sack out here." He smiled a tired smile. "Apparently hurricane season is less than peak vacation time for cruise lines."

"The ship leaves later this morning at 9 o'clock. We'll meet on the dock at 8:30 and see what the locals came up with."

"Sounds good to me," said Alex.

"I'm willing to sacrifice my room and bunk with Josh, for the good of the team," said Sophie.

"You're such a team player," smiled Manny.

"Just trying to do my part."

"Thanks for the offer, but I think I'll be fine."

As they began to trudge out of the room, Manny grabbed the condemning letter and stuffed it in his pocket.

"It's not your fault. You know that, right?"

Without looking up, he answered Sophie. "I know, at least my head does. The soul is still coming around. I'll get there."

She put her hand on his shoulder. "There's nothing you, or any of us, could've done."

"I know you're right . . . it still stings. We have to get ahead of him soon. He looks like he's heading for a spree. Hell, maybe he's already riding that train. Three murders in ten hours qualify, I guess." He patted her hand. "I should have sent you to the fence, naked—with Josh. Could've worked."

Sophie rolled her eyes and laughed. "Or scared the passengers and cops away. Maybe even sent them streaking for the other ship for safety. Get that? Streaking?"

"Yeah, it's late, but I got—" His thoughts suddenly focused on something Chloe had said that Sophie's joking brought into focus. He called to the others before they moved too far down the aisle.

"What?" asked Josh.

"Remember what Chloe said about not being able to book the same cruise ship at the same time?"

"Yes. It would be impossible to check in more than once because of the imagery software," agreed Josh.

"But it's not impossible to book two different cruises with different cruise lines at the same time. Some ships pick up passengers at different ports along their itinerary and then eventually return them to their original embarkation port. This ship will sail from St.Thomas to Dominica, where it will pick up more passengers."

"So he could be on the *Sea Fantasy*, the other ship in this port, because the itineraries cross?" Sophie asked, doubt tracking through her voice.

"Think about it. How is he going to get off this island without being caught? Everyone's looking for him. He can't leave by air. The Harbor Patrol is on every boat or yacht like white on rice. He sure as hell isn't going to walk away. And he's not going to hide under a damn rock."

"Because he's started this spree, this 'look at me thing?'" asked Chloe.

Manny spoke. "I keep coming back to what I would do. I'd try to get out where I wasn't noticed obviously, but still throw it in law enforcement's face. Who would suspect that he was leaving on the other ship with 5,200 others? It's a perfect hiding place."

The room grew quiet.

Josh pinned his eyes on Manny. "You were right with the police patrol scenario, and if you're right here, we have him."

Chloe frowned. "If your theory is true, how do we find him? If we do a door-to-door, especially this late, he might catch wind of what's happening and disappear."

"You're right. We'll just have to take—" Manny felt his heart jump, and he rose from the table. "He'll want to out-clever us, to mock us with that unhinged sense of humor." He turned to Josh. "How fast can we get a passenger/crew list from the other ship?"

"I don't know. Let's find out."

Fifteen minutes later, the first officer, Anthony Amalia, hurried into the room lugging a large laptop, put it on the table, and fired it up.

"We cross-referenced our database with theirs and came up with no matches for Decker or any other alias you gave us. But I think there is something you should see."

He quickly opened a PDF file and, running the curser down the list, stopped and pointed his shaking finger at a name and cabin assignment.

The collective surprise was almost palpable as they gathered around the twenty-two-inch screen.

"Well kiss my skinny ass and whistle Dixie," whispered Max Tucker.

It appeared that Detective Manfred R. Williams was leaving St. Thomas in room 7880 of the *Sea Fantasy*.

Chapter-18

"It's done. It wasn't as hard as I thought it would be. You know, after all those years together?" Stella Crosby shifted the cell phone to her other hand, its small, square screen the only light emanating from the darkened study in the Crosby home, the one she and Gavin had shared for thirty-four years.

"Did you do everything else we talked about?" asked the voice on the other end.

"Yes. I didn't have to go through security, so explaining the gun was no issue. Besides, the cop on duty has seen it before."

"Good. You made sure no one else was on the floor and left down the stairwell?"

Stella reached for the cigarette smoldering in the ashtray on the glass coffee table, her hand remarkably steady for a woman who'd just shot her husband. "I did. By the way, thanks for taking care of the security cameras on that level and the lights around the ground floor exit. It was just like you said: unguarded.

"I also locked his office door when I left, like we

discussed, so maybe no one will find the sniveling worm until early morning. Although once in a while, the night cleaning crew comes in ahead of schedule. Actually, they could be there about now. Either way, I'm ready."

Static rolled softly to her ear as her new confidant, one of them, grew silent. She heard soft breathing filter through the handset. It reminded her of rhythmic waves echoing against the ship's hull while Gavin and she had held each other in their cabin on the *Ocean Duchess*. Gavin had insisted on leaving their balcony door open as they sailed the Caribbean, and he had been correct; the effect was almost magical. At least he'd been right about one thing.

But that's where he lost it, wasn't it? That's when he stopped being the cop, the man, the protector she had fallen in love with. He'd changed. He was no longer Mike's hero or her knight in shining armor, her lover and her rock, but instead a pathetic, depressed old man scared of his own shadow. She felt the anger rise like heat in a sauna, her disgust evolving from a crevice to a canyon.

He had failed to protect Lexy, like a good cop would have, and let her die like a slaughtered lamb. Now their son's life was in shambles. The boy was so far down the well of despondency that he might never crawl out. It made her heart ache like only a mother's can. But she couldn't really blame Mike; it wasn't his fault. Seeing what Argyle had done to his new bride, her precious daughter-in-law, would widen anyone's path toward insanity.

Stella crossed her long legs and exhaled. She sensed the smoke twirl and waltz, responding to a sonata it alone could hear.

Gavin had failed at his most basic assignment: *protect thy family*. The FBI, Manny Williams, and all of them were responsible, but Gavin was the patriarch of the Crosby clan. It all fell on him. But not anymore. His reign was over. If he couldn't *handle* things, she—they—would. The law had let her down and ruined everyone close to her. It was time to balance that scale.

"You did the right thing, Stella. You know that, don't you?"

Emotion surprised her with unexpected resolve. It rushed the steel wall of disdain and hatred she had constructed against her husband. For a brief moment, it threatened her newly-discovered religion. She massaged away the lone tear. It *had* been the right thing to do. Weakness could no longer be tolerated, and Gavin Crosby had come to personify frailty. That made him expendable, husband or not.

She sat up straight and steadied herself. "I know."

"Remember what we've set out to do," encouraged the voice.

"It's all I think about. I knew it wouldn't be easy, but we have a chance to make a difference."

"I'm sure men like Mitchell Morse and Siggie Ashcroft wouldn't agree, maybe even Manny and the rest, but they don't get a vote. Not anymore."

Stella heard the tiny laugh at the other end and found herself smiling, too. "And the last two nights are only the beginning."

The land line rang and the caller ID said it was from the Department. "It's them. We'll talk later." Stella hung up.

She let it ring three more times and finally answered in her best "you just woke me up" voice. "Gavin?"

There was a small, pregnant pause, and she heard someone catch their breath. "Mrs. Crosby, this is Officer Swift down at the station. Ma'am, I've sent a car to pick you up—"

"Why? What's going on?" she interrupted, false panic searing through her voice.

"I'm not sure how to say this, but the Chief has been shot."

Chapter-19

"You're not as bright as I thought, are you, my fine Detective?" said Dr. Fredrick Argyle, wiping away the last of the temporary blond dye that had covered his now wavy, brown hair. He dabbed at a few last streaks watching the slow, confident smile spread over his chiseled face. They would never put it together. He was going to sail out of St. Thomas, free as a bird, and move forward with the end game he'd so meticulously put together over the last three months. Too bad. He would have preferred the other contingency. Plan A would've been ideal.

So this is the best law enforcement available? No wonder the country was going to hell in a handbasket. But then again, who was like him?

He stretched to his full six-foot-four frame, ogled the mirror, and marveled at his physique. Gods had to look the part, too, and he certainly had accomplished that. There was no match mentally, and he could hold his own with anyone physically. God was a good word.

After one last look, Argyle moved back to the

bed, finished unpacking, and then moved to the balcony facing the harbor and Charlotte-Amalie. The waxing moon appeared to be almost full, sending glittering moonbeams off the ocean. It was beautiful by any standard. Yet, dichotomies like the deceitful moon existed everywhere. Shining beauty hid the dark, cold, unseen, and even deadly persona that everyone possessed. He was just more honest than most. More real. More god-like.

But he *did* recognize beauty when he saw it. The misconception that men like him were incapable of such appreciations was not entirely true. Most of the social interaction was an act, a lesson in mimicry. But appreciation wears many faces, and he did enjoy the island qualities; it seemed to enhance his fairly new journey from prison drudgery to absolute liberty.

He felt the blood rush through his body. He could do anything he wanted. The lack of inhibition, of any dictated moral compass, allowed it. Freedom. The very word resonated truth. So what if there was collateral damage? A small price to pay to see his genius manifested.

Shifting his feet, he frowned. Men like Manny Williams failed to understand, but he would do his best to help with the detective's education, and soon. After that, when he was through with Williams, his family, and the rest of the Lansing idiots, he'd make an unexpected visit to an FBI agent or two. The attractive Chloe Franson could be an endeavor worthy of his attention.

Worthy indeed.

Then he would dedicate himself to a more far-reaching purpose, one worthy of his vast abilities. His disdain for politicians in general could be cultivated to include some serious accountability for the corrupt, the crooked. Maybe a face-to-face with the President could be arranged. What about getting an audience with Billy Graham or even the Pope? The things they could "discuss." But who knew for sure? The world was his oyster, and there was no one to stop him. Life was good, *his* life.

Argyle strolled in from the balcony and removed his shirt, turned out the lights, and spread out on the bed.

His overloaded mind began to unwind just as the knock came to his door. Ah. It was time.

He sat up, realizing instantly that someone had figured out his location . . . and that Manny Williams couldn't be in two places at the same time. He smiled.

Let's see how good they really are.

He slipped on his shirt, grabbed his bag, took one last look around the room, and went to the verandah door. He would simply swing down or over to another balcony and make his escape that way. They really were dense to think he didn't have this part of the game planned. He'd give Williams kudos the next time they met. No one else would have gotten this far.

He slid the glass door open, and stepped directly into the barrel of a Glock .40. Two more weapons pressed against the side of his head and chest.

"Good evening Dr. Argyle, you have no idea how nice it is to see *you* again," taunted Manny.

Chapter-20

Three thirty a.m. never felt so good. Manny watched as Argyle, surrounded by armed and ready local officers, was folded into the backseat of a small police cruiser. As the taillights of the miniature convoy disappeared en route for the island's police headquarters, he simply couldn't stop grinning. His body was fully alive, awake, like he had drunk a little too much coffee right after a chocolate rush. Adrenaline will do that to you, but he thought it the best feeling he'd had in years.

They had done it. Dr. Fredrick Argyle would never hurt anyone outside of a prison again. The FBI's field agents from San Juan would pick Argyle up in a few hours, process the paperwork, (there was always paperwork), ship him to Miami, and then in a few days or a week, to Lansing where he would stand trial for the murders of Sylvia Martin, Liz Casnovsky, Lexy Crosby, and Eric Hayes. No case was ever open and shut, but this would be as close as it came.

"So, you going with me to interrogate this creep?" asked Josh.

More grinning. He looked to the others standing in a loose huddle, talking in excited, low tones. Then back to Agent Corner.

"I wouldn't miss it, but I doubt he'll say much. He'll talk when he chooses to. It's part of the whole control thing."

"I know, but it'll be fun to watch the son of a bitch squirm. Maybe we can even piss him off."

Manny grinned. "That would be worth the effort."

Chloe left the others and stepped close to Manny, maybe too close. "That was some of the best profile work I've ever seen. How did you know?"

"Don't encourage him; it'll go to his head," said Josh.

"Let me guess; it was a 'feeling?'" grinned Chloe.

"Something like that. You know how this stuff goes; you just try to put yourself in the guy's head, that's all. He did what I might have done, or at least one of the things I would have done. Alex and Max believe it's a subconscious gathering of facts . . . but they're science geeks. They don't believe in the Way."

"Well, I have to admit, I'm more of a believer than before. Okay. What was the other thing?" asked Chloe.

"Run like hell."

"What?"

Manny winked. "It's just me, but I would've run like hell."

Chloe gave him the best smile he'd seen from her, and it was dazzling. When she relaxed like that, laughed, she was more than beautiful, and he wasn't sure she realized it. But that *something* remained underneath it all, that reason for guarding herself. On the outside, she appeared to be a hard-charging professional ready to climb the ladder at the Bureau. Except she was driven by a need, perhaps a pain, a hurt hidden deeper than any psychological exam the Feds had administered. He was sure about that. But she was handling it by burying herself in her work. He knew that one. Not always healthy, but a defense mechanism that would keep her out of the nuthouse. He knew that one too.

Manny found himself fantasizing about finding out what that pain was and helping, even getting to know her better. He shook it aside. This feeling would pass. He'd experienced infatuations before. That's all this was. Right?

"That would have been my choice, for sure," said Josh, giving Manny a curious look.

Just then, Sophie left the two CSIs, shaking her head. "Those guys need to get a room."

"Why?" questioned Manny.

"All that science talk. Damn. I think they're getting horny talking about particulates, DNA, bodily fluids, poly-something evidence bags, and new kinds of latex gloves."

"Yeah, well it's not like Alex has a lot of people like Agent Tucker to talk with," said Manny, happy that Sophie had interrupted Josh's attention.

Manny had stared at Chloe a little too long.

"Whatever. They seem entirely too excited about that stuff," Sophie moved a little closer to Josh. "What do you think about latex?"

Josh frowned. "Gloves?"

"Gloves could be part of it, boots for sure, but I mean in general. You know. Like black or red . . . camisoles . . ."

"Sophie!" warned Manny.

"What? I only wanted to know what he thought." She blinked at Josh. "Still do."

Josh stepped closer to Manny, away from Sophie. "Ah. I think it's time to go. Let's get down to the station, talk with our special guest, and then see about getting some rest."

Manny watched relief landscape Josh's face as he changed the subject. But there was little doubt Sophie would pick up the matter again at the first opportunity.

That's twice she had flustered Josh, and she seemed to be enjoying the hell out of it. Still, they would have to talk about professional conduct. But not today. For the moment, life was too good to go the downer route.

Just then, Sophie's cell began playing a tune from *Phantom*. She scowled, looked at the number, then up to Manny.

Thinking back, he had no inkling how quickly the good mood would change. How one call could disrupt not only the moment, but turn part of his world upside down?

"It's the office. Hello—whoa. Wait. Slow down,

Buzzy."

Manny watched the color drain from Sophie's face as she handed the phone to him, tears already glistening in her big, brown eyes.

"Buzzy. What happened?"

He heard her sob and then make a heroic effort to get control of the hitch blocking her throat. "I tried your cell a hundred times . . . so much blood . . ."

Panic punched Manny's chest. "Whose blood? Tell me what's going on, Buzzy."

There was a brief silence as Buzzy caught some air. "Just get back here. Gavin's been shot."

Chapter-21

The FBI's jet lifted from the runway, banking gracefully over the thick, shadowy green of St. Thomas and straightening over the glassy ocean just as the sun began to climb over the eastern horizon. Manny looked away from the window and down to his watch. They had lifted off before the pilots had gotten their FAA-required eight hours of continuous rest. But with the FBI, everyone did what they were told. This time, he was okay with it. Getting back to Lansing was the only thing on his mind.

"Just get back here. Gavin's been shot."

Putting the cuffs on Argyle had been special, and there was no telling how many lives would be saved because of it. If the profilers could get him to eventually talk to them, which was something Argyle was helpless to resist, he might reveal an insight or two into how these psychopaths thought, how they worked. Even if Argyle talked just to hear himself speak, they would learn something. Manny wouldn't be there for the first run. Josh, Max, and Chloe stayed behind to brief a crack team of the FBI's Behavior Analysis Unit, which could lead to an opportunity to learn more about Argyle. Josh wanted Manny to leave the Lansing PD to work for that unit. He ran his hand through his hair. Changing jobs, even for one with the BAU, was the last thing on his mind. He had to get home. Nothing was more important.

Buzzy had been near hysteria. He had finally talked her into handing the phone to one of the EMTs.

Gavin had been found in his office with one shot to the chest. He was hanging in there, but barely. "He's lost more blood than anyone still breathing has a right to lose," said the tech. "Just keep praying we weren't too late."

Praying was something he could do, and did. He believed that God listened and even intervened from time-to-time to show the world He was God and the rest of mankind wasn't. This was one of those times, he hoped, that God would listen.

And what of Stella and Mike? How much more could they take? What Argyle had done to Lexy was hard to digest, maybe even impossible to reconcile fully. A quick vision of how she had looked when she'd been found in her stateroom gouged his thoughts. He flinched. Only animals did that to people, especially to someone as beautiful, inside and out, as Lexy.

Now Gavin. If he died, and it was past touch-and-go for him, Mike and Stella would lose two of the most important people in their lives just months apart. Talk about a recipe for the loony bin.

And why did this happen? Who had the balls to do it? A cop makes enemies over the years (he had a few of his own), but shooting the police chief in his office? It was spitting in the face of all law enforcement. Maybe that was the idea.

He glanced around the cabin. Alex was dead asleep on the sofa. Not a bad idea. They had all been up for over twenty-two hours, and Manny would have to follow suit soon. Sophie caught his eyes, left her seat, and plopped down next to him, looping her arm through his.

Sometimes, in spite of the smart-ass remarks and the almost fearless bravado that was genuinely her, his partner seemed like a lost little girl looking for a place to hide, a safe haven. But hey, didn't everyone feel like that, at least once in a while? Maybe more than once in a while.

"What is rattling around in that slick brain of yours?" she asked.

"How tired I am . . . and visions of Josh Corner in a red latex tutu."

She snorted. "You ain't the only one." She squeezed tighter. "What's *really* going on in there?"

"Besides what would happen with Stella and Mike—and the rest of us—if Gavin doesn't make it?"

"Yeah, besides that." She hesitated, swallowing hard. "We had our moments, the Chief and I, but I love the guy like a father. This doesn't happen to your dad, you know?"

"I do know." He patted her arm. "As for your

question: Who? Why? How did they get in? The usual."

"Me too. What about the unusual? That's *your* thing."

"I don't know, girl. I'm tired and not exactly concentrating. You first."

"Oooo. All right. Me first. Why only one shot? And how did someone get close enough to him for that?"

"So you think he may have known the shooter?"

She nodded. "Also, don't most shooters click off more than one round, just to make sure?"

"True. They do."

"So maybe this is someone who has never done this before and didn't know any better. Or maybe doesn't quite have the stomach for blowing someone away."

"You may be on to something. If that's true, then it makes it tougher for us. If the shooter left any trace DNA or fingerprints, they won't be in any database, and ballistics won't get a match." Manny frowned.

"I felt that. What are you frowning about?"

"We need to see more evidence, but this almost feels like—"

"Like what?"

"Maybe a woman perp. There doesn't seem to be any rage, no overkill, and he was shot in the chest, not the head. More than half of male shooters go for the face or head. It could be a woman."

"Say you're right. He wasn't fooling around or anything, correct?"

"I don't think so. I think the whole family was still struggling with what happened to Lexy. No inclination for extramarital affairs. Besides, he's not exactly Don Juan."

"Yeah, that's true, but it takes all kinds. Trust me, I know."

"Things I don't need to know." He shifted to look at Sophie. "But maybe the wife, the sister, or maybe a daughter of someone he put away thought it was time to even the score." Manny rubbed the stubble on his cheek. "But I'm just spitting into the wind until we get there and look at everything."

Sophie let go of his arm and reached into her pocket, where her phone was vibrating.

"I'm starting to hate this universal communication stuff. Maybe being a Luddite like you is a good thing."

She opened up her phone, read the text message, and handed it to Manny. "When the dam breaks, it really breaks."

The text was from one of the detectives, Frank Wymer, who had taken over the Mitchell Morse case at the White Kitty: **GLAD YOU'RE ON YOUR WAY BACK. EVERYTHING THE SAME WITH THE CHIEF, BUT WE HAVE ANOTHER PROBLEM. WE HAVE TWO MORE VICS LIKE MORRIS. THE SAME MO. MORE WHEN YOU GET HERE.**

Manny leaned his head back against the seat.

Three makes it official; they definitely had a serial killer on their hands. Just what they needed. "Shit. Does it ever stop raining?"

"And why don't we have a damned umbrella?" sighed Sophie.

Chapter-22

"I'm going to go freshen up. A girl has to look good, even when interviewing a deranged serial killer," said Chloe.

The three FBI agents had just entered the St. Thomas police facility, such as it was. The pastel-blue building had been annexed with new construction, combining the old with the new, and making it at least interesting. It was hardly what she was used to seeing. But this was the Caribbean and the place was buzzing, especially for 4 a.m. Argyle was surely the most high-profile killer arrested in St. Thomas since the pirate Anne Bonny.

"You look fine," said Max.

"Ah, thanks, but I gotta pee too."

"Pee? You can't go to the head while on duty—that's FBI regulation 601, section b-u-l-l-s-h-i-t, I think," answered Josh.

Max looked at Josh. "Man, you need some sleep or more coffee. That was lame, even for you."

"Really? Lame? I take pride in my sense of humor."

"You know what they say about pride before a fall?" pointed out Max.

"So, what are you saying?" smiled Josh.

"Do I have to explain everything to you?"

Chloe shook her head. "I'll see you two in a few."

She walked through the heavy, steel door adorned with a sea-shell lettered sign telling her it was the Big Girls' Room and put her leather purse on the black granite counter. She splashed water in her face, dabbed away the excess, and stared into the mirror to make sure she got it all. The stare lingered. It had been a strange fourteen hours, and it hadn't ended the way she'd anticipated, with Argyle in chains. Courtesy, mostly, of Detective Manny Williams, or maybe she should say future FBI Special Agent Manny Williams.

She leaned closer to the mirror. He was another reason the day hadn't ended as she had expected. In fact, he was the biggest reason today was a total enigma.

No doubt about that.

Josh had talked about Williams, what had transpired on the cruise. It had sounded a little concocted, but she should have known better. Agent Corner didn't work that way. What he didn't bother to mention was how good-looking the Lansing detective was. How wide his shoulders were, and how his eyes looked like they were torn from the bluest sky on record.

"I guess he wouldn't have, would he?" she

grinned to herself.

Chloe had known good-looking men before, dated several, a couple she had even liked. But it wasn't just his looks, those eyes, those shoulders, but it was how he carried himself, who he was. It was how honesty seemed to exude from his pores—a certain vulnerability and strength from the emotions he wore so well on his sleeve. She felt herself growing a little warmer.

After they'd shaken hands, she felt the electricity shoot directly to her heart, causing her pulse rate to jump. That had never happened to her. She read about it, even fantasized about it, but those things didn't happen to women like her. The thought of jumping him right there, in front of everyone, had run briefly though her mind.

Not a great way to broaden my career path. But . . .

Reaching into her bag, she took her cinnamon-shaded lip liner and went to work. She had done her best to hide it. She'd been trying not to stare too long or move too close, but it hadn't worked entirely. Even Josh had seemed to detect—something. More importantly, Manny had noticed. She knew that much was true. One too many glances her way, his smile was a little too friendly, even the brief glance at her mouth. He wasn't the only profiler in the group.

Part of her was embarrassed; the other part, however, didn't give a rat's ass. There had never been, for her, a fascination, an attraction—or whatever the hell you wanted to call it— like this in only six hours' time. She released a small sigh. It was disconcerting to know her luck with men hadn't changed over the course of her thirty-one-year life; he was happily married.

Married men weren't off limits for some women. In fact, a few of her friends preferred the no-attachment thing. They said it made the sex better and the gifts amazing. But her mum had raised her with good, old-fashioned, Irish values. She'd rather live alone than be the reason a family was destroyed. She brushed her long hair back behind her ears.

Detective Manny Williams had momentarily shaken that value with just a touch of his hand. That excited, breathless feeling fluttered from somewhere deep in her core. But she'd do the right thing, be the right kind of woman, just as soon as she got him off her mind—and as long as he never touched her again.

She straightened her jacket, picked up her purse, took one last glance in the mirror, and walked to the door.

The wild yelling coming from the smallish, dimly lit hallway startled her as she instinctively reached for her gun, clutching the door handle at the same time.

That's when she heard the first gunshot, quickly followed by another.

Chapter-23

Stella Crosby rose slowly from the sagging, red-vinyl chair positioned mere feet from her husband's bed in the ICU of Eagle Memorial Hospital. Her hazel eyes burned a hole into her husband's face. The rhythmic sound of the breathing pump and three beeping monitors featured quiet, soughing echoes. The newest technologies were designed for only one purpose—the desperate attempt to keep Gavin Crosby from meeting his Maker, to advance to the proverbial "better place," whatever that saying truly meant. She was sure the syncopated noises would drive her crazy. That and the smell of arbitrary hospital odors she'd never been able to quite identify. She bent closer, staring harder, as if she could will him into the afterlife.

None of this would be an issue if he would have cooperated. Why couldn't he just die like he was supposed to? The pansy-ass couldn't even do that right. Who lives with a shot to the chest, at point blank range no less? But she was no expert, at least not yet, and shooting him twice would have been wise.

Learn something every day.

And why was she agitated? Because he wasn't dead? Guilt? Because she had just shot her husband and people who did that went away for life? Stella shrugged. None of those scenarios seemed to fit exactly. Maybe it was a combination of everything.

Getting caught wasn't a major concern, which would take some time, and if the cops did put things together correctly, dotted those damnable "i's" and crossed the "t's," it would still be too late. They had planned too well to get boxed in. She supposed that's what everyone who intentionally danced on the wild side of the law thought, but they weren't just anyone, were they? Their purpose was . . . noble, just, and right. Maybe that was it. The law wouldn't recognize that what they were doing possessed any of those attributes. They would be branded as people who couldn't play by the rules.

To hell with the rules. Rules didn't help Lexy.

In all of her years as a cop's wife, she had heard Gavin slam the vigilante mentality that was growing in America's fractured, frightened society.

"The law, the cops, will find them, get it done. People have to be patient," he would say.

She rolled her eyes. Law enforcement bellied up to the challenge so much that only *half* the murders in America remained unsolved. Yeah, that's getting it done.

Why did more than sixty percent of rape

victims fail to go the police? Not just from the embarrassment, but the knowledge that nothing would be done, or that the victims must have somehow brought it on themselves. What bullshit. She felt the rage rise again. She took deep breaths, like the Yoga instructor told her to do when her anger threatened to blow her out of the calm into the fire. It helped.

Stella moved to the third floor window and watched the sun's earliest rays begin to usher away the predawn darkness. It reminded her that all things were new in the light of another day, and that a fresh radiance could put a new slant on her problems. And she had a big one: Gavin was still breathing.

The hand on her shoulder made her jump. She whirled, grabbing her chest.

"Whoa. Easy," said the ICU nurse.

"You startled me."

"I see that, and I'm sorry. But you have two visitors, and they seem anxious to see you."

"Who are they?

"They said they're friends of yours and just want to see how you're doing."

Stella's pulse rose higher. This wasn't good. They weren't supposed to meet like this. She gathered herself. "Okay. Thank you. I'll be right out."

Straightening her blouse, she stood taller and left the room. Her friends, partners, were standing in a secluded corner of the waiting room. She moved toward them, butterflies doing the fandango in her stomach.

The two women hugged her. “You hanging in there?” asked the tall woman.

She nodded. “But what are you doing here? This isn’t supposed to happen.”

“Relax. We’re here as friends only trying to console our hurting compadre. And if you hadn’t screwed up, we wouldn’t be here, at least together.”

“I know. I thought he was—”

She was interrupted by the shorter visitor. “You’ve got to fix this, you know that, right?”

Stella stared at the floor. “Yes. Just trying to figure out how.”

“Don’t figure too long. We’ve worked too hard to get here.”

“I know. It’s not that easy in here.”

The tall woman leaned closer. “We don’t care how you do it. Smother him, pull the plugs, shoot him again, screw him to death for all we care. Just do it. Besides, tonight’s your night to keep things rolling.”

The shorter woman touched her arm. “And try to look like a grieving wife. There are no tear streaks on your face. You’re not wringing your hands or acting like you’ll break down any minute. You’re not doing any of the stuff we discussed; a cop like Williams will notice that.”

Stella started to answer, but the loud siren exploding from Gavin’s room interrupted her, causing all three women to jerk their heads in sync. Several nurses and doctors sprinted into her husband's room. She looked to the others, moving away. "Maybe I won't have to worry about it. His damned heart has just stopped."

Chapter-24

Chloe opened the heavy door and swiveled to her right, then left, gun poised and ready for anything. Her first thoughts had been that Argyle had tried to break free and was lying in a pool of his own blood. She was half right.

Argyle was spread flat on the stained, tiled floor in front of the Big Boys' Room. Josh Corner, Max Tucker, and a huge, maybe 300-pound, USVI cop sat on various sections of Argyle's body. They were surrounded by seven other officers, all with guns pointed directly at the killer's head.

She lowered her gun. Talk about a Kodak moment. She quickly pulled her phone from her purse and shot the picture that she was sure would mysteriously circulate through the bureau's intranet.

"So, you boys having fun, are you?"

"He tried to take . . . my gun . . . even with full . . . lockdown chains and cuffs," heaved Max. "Had to . . . smack him . . . and in the excitement . . . my weapon . . . discharged." Max glanced up where two holes, side-by-side, had torn small rifts in the white hanging ceiling.

A small hissing sound, accompanied by subtle rivulets of steam, escaped through the freshly bored openings.

She had a feeling the FBI was going to get a repair bill, a big one.

Josh glowered at Argyle. “What the hell’s wrong with you? Where in the universe did you think you were going to go?”

Argyle didn’t respond. He simply raised his head, searching Chloe’s face, and suddenly flashed that beyond creepy trademark grin of his. His eyes seemed to go right through her and settle on her soul. She knew what he was thinking, what he sought. He was telling her, in his own special way, that he wanted her to be his next good time. The sooner the better.

Chloe shivered. She had seen a few things, monsters even. They came in all sorts of packages, with all sorts of agendas. The terrorism gig had shown her that. But nothing like Argyle. Pure, unadulterated evil. She shivered again.

“Get his ugly ass up and strap him into the interrogation room. We’re going to talk,” said Agent Corner.

The big cop was the last one to rise, and Argyle took a deep breath. He should have been gulping like a fish out of water with a man that size on his back. It was like he’d been prepared for how his little drama would play out. Was he that smart, that organized? Chloe fought the uneasy feeling building in her stomach. They had him. He wasn’t a threat. Right?

The crowd of blue ushered Argyle through a small wooden door, and he disappeared down the hall.

"I'm not cut out for this shit. I'm a scientist, a forensic guy. I don't think I should even have a gun," moaned Max.

"Hey, you did good. Except for the part where you let him get his hands on your weapon—and shooting a poor, innocent, defenseless ceiling." Josh clapped him on the back. "That was a nice punch, though."

"My hand hurts, and he never flinched. It felt like I hit steel."

"I go to the restroom and, *wham*, I miss all the fun. That ain't right," Chloe chuckled.

"They have medicine for tiny, leaking bladders. I saw it on TV. Didn't you, Max?"

"Yep. Diapers too. I think I can get her a sample of each."

"You two are amazingly kind. Remember, things have a way of coming full circle." Chloe thought about the picture on her camera. "Karma is a wonderful thing."

"Just trying to help," smiled Josh.

She watched him put his gun away and saw his demeanor change. "Let's go see what Argyle has to say for himself."

Five minutes later, Chloe and Josh sat across from the well-restrained Argyle. He was docile, almost unconcerned. She found that disconcerting, like he knew something they didn't.

Josh had instructed her to not speak, that neither one of them would, until Argyle broke the tense silence. It was a way to begin to assert control over him. But he was a psychiatrist, and he had to know what they were doing. They didn't have to wait long to find out.

"We are such a cozy trio, don't you think? It's a shame that Detective Williams isn't here. I was looking forward to getting reacquainted."

"Why does that matter?" asked Josh.

"Because he's the only one I'm going to talk to." Argyle became even more serene.

What the hell is going on here?

"You still don't get it, do you? You're not in control here," said Chloe.

"Perhaps you're right, Agent Franson." He drew out the enunciation of her name.

Chloe flinched. It sounded so dirty coming from his lips. She wanted to rush to the nearest shower.

"But I suspect that you're not entirely correct on that point."

"So tell me the error of my way," said Josh.

Argyle sat motionless. Chloe thought he was savoring the moment, like the last morsel of a gourmet meal cooked to utter perfection. Then his eyes turned as black as any darkness.

"Detective Williams is the only one that I wish to tell about the others."

Chapter-25

Manny jammed his Ford SUV into park, jumped out, and headed for the hospital's elevator, Alex and Sophie on his heels. There was a crowd of reporters, a few from Detroit, approaching him and Sophie, moving in for the kill like hyenas circling an injured impala.

"I'm sorry. We don't know anything yet, and we'll let you know." Questions rained like hail in a storm, but fell on deaf ears. He, Sophie, and Alex pushed through the group and into the hospital's foyer.

"Damn. That's always fun," complained Sophie.

"Yeah. I just wished they'd act like they at least cared."

The elevator ride to the third floor was a silent, excruciating one. The damn things never moved quickly when it was necessary. Finally, the door parted at the third floor, and Manny burst through it like a running back headed for the goal line.

Stella stood at the window of the waiting room

and turned to face him, like she felt he was there. Maybe she did. Her emotional state had to be at hyper level.

He hesitated when he saw her face. Stella looked every bit her age, and then some. It was a tough few hours for a family that had endured their fair share of horrendous days and sleepless nights the last few months.

He quickly noticed the woman standing close to her. Manny's heart leapt a little. He didn't remember being so glad to see someone. Louise was holding Stella's hand, and speaking softly, the way women do and men can't seem to fathom.

He'd called her on Sophie's cell, and she had gotten there quickly. That was just like her; always on the spot. Ready to help. Manny reached for Stella's other hand.

"Hey, girl. How you doing?"

Stella blinked at him and tried to smile through quivering lips. Her eyes were red; streaks ran down her angular cheeks. Her hair was a little less than Stella perfect. She was the absolute picture of grief, and his heart instantaneously ached for her, even more than it hurt for himself.

She hugged him fiercely. "Oh, about as good as you could expect," she whispered. "Thanks for coming so quickly. You must be exhausted."

"We caught a few Zs on the plane. We're fine."

Stella stepped back and held him at arm's length. "Gavin used to say he was getting too old for this shit. I think I know what he meant."

Sophie and Alex came close and hugged her.

Manny watched fresh moisture cover her eyes with each embrace. He wondered how many tears she had left. How many *anyone* would have left.

Louise reached for his hand and squeezed. He hugged her. His wife's perfume shook his senses, and he couldn't ignore the merciless pang of guilt that stabbed him with an almost physical force. Chloe Franson. She lingered in his thoughts just a little too long, longer than any infatuation had the right to do. But those eyes could take him to cloud nine if he let them.

More guilt. How could he be thinking of Chloe when Gavin was in such rough shape and while he held the most wonderful woman in the world? He pushed thoughts of Chloe away. He wanted them to stay gone. Sometimes wanting and getting were great enemies.

"So, Argyle's in jail?" asked Louise.

"Yeah. We got lucky. I'll tell you about it later."

She nodded.

The ICU doctor came from Gavin's room and walked straight to Stella. "He seems to have stabilized after that last incident."

"Incident?" quizzed Manny.

The doctor looked at Stella.

"It's okay. There are no secrets here."

"All right. His heart has stopped twice in the last three hours. Not long, but enough to make me consider, if he makes it, well . . ." She shifted her feet and continued. "Combined with the huge blood loss, those two episodes may have caused oxygen deprivation to his brain. I'm sorry. Only time will tell."

Manny felt his body grow numb.

"That's not all. Once the bullet stopped rattling off his ribs, it ended up lodged close to his aorta. Way too close. Surgery would be risky; although I've seen worse situations turn out just fine. The key is to get in early. It could conceivably move closer and make the surgery more risky."

The doctor smiled her best reassuring smile. Bedside manner wasn't completely dead.

"I know. Lots of ifs and maybes. But it's all we have for now. Let me suggest you keep churning out those prayers. They never hurt." She touched Stella's arm and left.

"I'm going to go see him," said Manny.

"He'd like that," whispered Stella.

Gavin looked frail, pale, and vulnerable, like a newborn in an incubator. The machines hooked to the police chief did little to enhance Manny's state of mind. Tears welled up, then crawled down his face. The last thing his friend would ever want was to be helpless. It didn't fit.

Manny smiled one of those half smiles born from memories that grief couldn't eliminate entirely.

Gavin loved westerns and was a big John Wayne fan. Going out in a blaze of glory, amid a hail of bullets, like the Duke in one of his movies, would suit him more. Not wired up in the damned ICU of a hospital. He laid a hand on Gavin's arm and prayed that his boss would get to see another ending.

Chapter-26

"I'll stay with her. You three can't help Gavin, or anyone else, sitting around here," reasoned Louise.

"I don't know," Manny hesitated, rubbing his face with both hands, "if I can concentrate on anything right now."

"I think she's right," agreed Stella. "We'll let you know if anything changes. Besides, you know he'd take a hunk out of your collective asses if he thought you were sitting around feeling sorry for each other and him. He'd want you to be out looking for the bastard who did this."

Sophie rubbed her backside. "Yep. Been on the end of that one."

A tiny smile tugged at the corner of Stella's mouth. She put her hands on Manny's shoulders. Her firm grip was warm, reassuring. "Manny. You've always been amazingly good at separating the job from your emotions. What do they call that? Compartmentalizing? It's what makes you who you are, the best." She looked away from him. "That's why Argyle's behind bars. I need you to go to work, okay?"

Damn. How could anyone say no to that?

"All right. We'll do it for both of you. But you have to keep me posted."

"I will," said Stella.

He kissed Louise and said he'd see her for dinner, hugged Stella again, and let Sophie and Alex escort him to the elevator.

Once in the car, Alex moved into CSI-mode quickly. "Where do you want to start?"

"Gavin's office. We need to see what we can find." He ran his hand through his hair. "If there's anything *to* find."

"Buzzy said Alex's folks gave it the once over and found nothing. No shell casing. No unusual prints. Just hits from people that had reasons to be in Gavin's office," said Sophie.

"Were you on that list?" asked Manny.

"Yes. I . . . Oh, I get it. You mean because I was in there getting my butt reamed?"

"Just asking."

Her eyes narrowed, and she zoned in on Manny. "I think I remember you taking a trip in there a time or two."

"Me?" Mock surprise billowed across his face.

"Whatever. Hey, maybe they dusted for prints on his Nat King Cole CD collection. If they did, we'll finally know who's been taking them."

He shrugged. "They're always returned, right?"

"Yeah, but he always got pissy when one went missing."

Alex cleared his throat. "Anyway. My people

also didn't think the hair and fibers would help either. But we won't know until it's all processed. I'm betting the particulate forensics will probably be a dead-end. There was so much traffic in his office that it's just not going to be a good source of evidence."

"Manny. Did you see how the man tried to change the subject?" Sophie gave Alex the evil eye. "It's you, isn't it? You're a closet Nat King Cole groupie. Admit it."

"Don't be goofy. Nat King Cole? Come on. A man like me?"

"We'll find out soon enough. Then your ass will be grass, and the Chief will be the lawn mower." She chewed her lip and grew somber. "I hope."

"Me too," said Alex softly.

"We need to focus, okay? We just need to do our jobs and let the doctors do theirs," Manny pointed out.

"You're the boss, and you're right. It's not that easy for some of us," agreed Sophie.

"You're right, but it beats the hell out of sitting on the sidelines. Stella's right."

"Works for me," said Alex.

"Sophie and I will go to the office. We need to see why the security cameras weren't working and go over everything again. Any visitors, people he put away who had the biggest hard-on for Gavin. Anything or anyone we can think of for a motive that fits this thing."

"We're not going to get a ballistics match unless the docs think they can get that bullet out of Gavin. Might not anyway," said Sophie.

Alex removed his glasses and wiped them on his shirt. "We've been pretty focused on Argyle and Gavin, but we need to face some facts about our other problem."

Manny nodded. "Three murders in three days. That would mean that Lansing has a serial killer, apparently knocking off convicted rapists and sex offenders."

"Buzzy confirmed that all three were recently, like in the last week, released from prison. And these days, it's easy to track when these guys are let loose. Especially through OTIS [Offender Tracking Information System]," added Sophie. "She was still researching the third victim. He wasn't in the Sexual Offender database. He was released after serving time for a couple of white-collar crimes, but she's still digging."

"Let's hope she finds a connection. If not, that means the victims are random ex-cons and that makes it worse." Manny cocked his head, knitting his brow. "The thing is, this killer has come storming out of the gate. I mean two in one night is serious dedication, particularly in different parts of town. Usually it takes awhile to ramp it up like this. This seems to be pure rage. "Something, some stressor, got them going."

"Victim?" asked Alex.

"Not necessarily. It could be the spouse, son, or dad that has snapped because of something that happened to a loved one." The glower on Manny's face grew deeper. "If it is a female victim, we have a real problem. She'll stay at it. Women serial killers don't do it for the gratification of some sexual release, but mostly kill for revenge."

"Well, the first victim's crotch didn't look so good. That looks like overkill to me," observed Sophie.

"I need to get to both crime scenes, and then examine the bodies to verify things are what they look like." Alex let out a breath and rolled down his window. The morning was already heating up. "I never thought I'd say this, but maybe we could use some help."

"FBI help? Josh and his crew?" asked Manny. "Do you think we need them?"

"The budget cuts weren't kind to us, and we're down a few people. Plus, we have Gavin's situation on our plate. I'm just saying."

"Ooooo. Let me call him," offered Sophie. "I have his number on speed dial."

"Does your husband know that?" quizzed Alex.

Sophie grinned. "Hey. It's just work. Anyway, Randy's reaping all of the benefits of my fantasy world, comprende?"

"I thought we agreed on this TMI thing," snorted Alex.

"No calls yet. I need to think about it. They're going to be busy getting everything in order to bring Argyle back to Michigan. I don't want to mess with that," replied Manny.

"Fair enough. While you two are checking out the building, I'm going to get my gear and see what I can see," Alex said. "By the way, why do you think Mike wasn't at the hospital? He *is* Gavin's only kid."

"I noticed that too. They've not been getting along, and honestly, Mike has flat-out been acting strange the last few weeks," answered Manny. "I don't blame him, though."

"Still, it's his dad," said Alex.

"I'm sure we'll see him soon. They were pretty close before Lexy died," said Manny.

He wheeled the red SUV into the parking garage. Two detectives talked with three blues near the building's security door. The two detectives, Kathy Ross and Frank Wymer, saw Manny and Sophie and hurried over. Alex got into his cruiser, heading for the west side of town.

"You two look like you've seen a ghost," said Manny. "What's up?"

"First, let me say we're both pulling for the Chief. We're not as close to him as you two, but he always treated us fairly," said Ross, her long, black hair moving as she shook her head.

"Thank you."

Wymer, a very large man, sported a short, gray crew cut, confirming what the military tattoos on his forearms displayed: *Once a Marine, always a Marine.* He stepped into the conversation. "It's gotten worse."

"What has?" Manny asked, not really wanting the answer.

"We got a call from an apartment complex in the south end, near Davlind Road, called the Royal Life."

He had Manny's full attention. "That's where Mike Crosby lives."

"Mike's okay, but we have another murder. Mike's next door neighbor was shot in his bed. Two gunshots to the chest, according to the first officers on the scene," said Wymer.

This didn't feel good. "So?"

Wymer looked nervously to Ross, then back to Manny and Sophie. "Mike may have been involved. Apparently, people heard them arguing. Something about the guy being registered as a sex offender." The big man sighed. "Mike smacked him a good one in the guy's apartment."

"Are you sure?"

The big detective nodded.

Manny felt like Mike Tyson had just landed a solid one-two punch to his ribs. He fought to catch his breath. This wasn't real. Mike too? His next thought was of Stella. The river was rising, and she had no boat.

"Shit," swore Sophie.

What the hell is happening here? Why had Lansing suddenly become the crime capital of the world?

"Sophie. Make that call to Josh," he murmured. "We're going to need them."

Chapter-27

Dr. Fredrick Argyle sat on the edge of the stained mattress that caused his jail cell to stink like some sewer ditch, slowly stroking the long, purple welt that had risen above his left eye, compliments of one of the over-zealous USVI police officers assigned to make sure he stayed in line, that he succumbed to their pitiful rules.

He had been truly impressed. It had taken that officer much longer to reach the boiling point than he'd anticipated. It took a few attempts, but eventually he'd pushed exactly the right button, provoking the guard to hit him. Twice. He knew it would happen. It was unavoidable. How could they resist getting a piece of someone they loathed so intently? But it was more than that, wasn't it? Fear caused nightmares to spring to life—and these pissy, little men were nothing if not afraid. Especially when he told the guard what he was going to do to his wife, his mother, maybe even his kids—in amazing detail.

"I just don't think we were on the same page," he grinned and touched the bruise again. The billy club had been hard, he'd even caught a glimpse of colored stars as he passed from light to dark and back to light. Through it all, he heard them call him sick, an animal, evil.

Evil? What exactly did that mean? The significance held different connotations for everyone. His time as a psychiatrist told him that was true.

For instance, some welcomed the companionship of a snake. The creatures were pets, seen as having value, personalities. Others could barely contemplate being in the same room with one. Even a small, caged one. Invariably, those afflicted with that phobia—ophidiophobia—associated the snake with devils or demons. Malevolence personified. They even quoted the Bible to justify their fear. If God thought snakes were bad news, then justification came easier.

Of course, if there really was a God, why would men like him be allowed to do what they do? He smiled again. He could teach the Bible-thumpers a thing or two about real fear.

Looking down at the chains running from his ankles to his waist and ending at his wrists, he couldn't help reflecting on how long it would take to free himself. Minutes? Half an hour? No more than that. But that would be too easy, and he wouldn't get to play with the stout, black woman who brought him his meals. No problem there. He didn't really want to waltz with her anyway. There were other people to meet, people who needed to learn what he was teaching.

Once he was transported back to Lansing, the real bash would continue. And as usual, he'd be the life of the party, the star attraction. The masses would simply die to get close to him.

Argyle stretched his back as far as the restraints would allow and rolled onto the swaybacked bed. He could hardly wait.

Chapter-28

Alex Downs pressed the accelerator harder. The powerful engine surged, causing his stomach to do one of those flips. It was like flying down the last steep curve of a roller coaster. A big one.

He flicked a switch, and the red and blue lights swirled into life. Another switch and the siren bellowed out its authority, telling everyone to get the hell out of his way. He was a scientist at heart—in fact, it was what he lived for—but getting to drive a police cruiser, particularly like this, was a rush and not something he thought he'd get to do when he took the job. Perks were certainly in the eyes of the beholder, but this was over the top.

The corner of Waverly and Smith was buzzing with activity, cops and LPD cruisers everywhere. He parked his unit, grabbed his case, and hurried to the center of attraction.

Sarah Sparks, one of his techs (and a damned good one) stood just outside the yellow crime scene tape, cordoning off the body and the immediate area around it, forty feet in every direction. A perfect square. Sparks was concentrating on the camera they occasionally used to create virtual crime scenes. The process was called photogrammetry. It's a technique that combines hundreds of different photos taken at a particular scene then sends them to a computer program that in turn creates a 360-degree image. It was helpful when a crime had been committed in a high traffic, public area, like this one. The images would be on file long after the scene was trampled and forgotten.

Alex cleared his throat, and she jumped. She turned quickly to see who had interrupted her train of thought. Her gray eyes grew larger than her thin face could seemingly accommodate. He grinned; she looked a little like a lemur.

"Easy there, Sparky."

"Sorry boss, a little jumpy. And I'm glad you're back."

Sarah's pretty face was a little more pale than usual. She was a tough kid, and homicides hadn't bothered her up to this point. But she was obviously affected by this one.

"You okay?"

"Yes. I guess so. This one is . . . well, see for yourself." She looked at the fast-food bag in his other hand, then back to him.

"You're going to eat that over there?"

"Of course. I'm hungry."

"But Alex . . ." Sarah's face turned a whiter shade of pale.

He opened the bag, letting loose the rich

aroma of greasy sausage and fried eggs. One whiff sent Sarah to the other side of the yellow tape, where she quickly rendezvoused with gut-wrenching heaves.

"Gets 'em every time," he said to the cop standing near the camera.

He downed the food, and then he took out latex gloves from his case and moved to the body. The tall man lying on the pavement of the parking lot hardly looked human. He'd only been dead for maybe eight or nine hours, but the smell was far worse. The hot asphalt made sure of that. Scorching flesh was never going to be used for aromatherapy. This one definitely had the same bullet-hole pattern to the head and chest as the first victim at the White Kitty. His hands and ankles were bound with black leather, but this time, his clothes had been removed and the acid trail ran from his neck to past his thighs. It concentrated on the crotch area to the point that his willie's stub was barely discernable. There was a small amount of gelatinous tissue welded to his upper right thigh, probably what was left of his testicles. The acid concentration was high, very high. Someone knew what they were doing.

Sarah Sparks crouched next to him. "You did that on purpose, and I have a long memory."

"Bring it, girlfriend."

Her smile beamed like the sun. "Someday, boss, someday." She pointed toward the body. "There wasn't a lot of blood, so this seems to be a dump site. We didn't notice any blood trails or drag patterns, so I think we're solid with the assumption he was killed elsewhere."

Alex nodded. "Help me turn him over."

His back and neck showed the same footprints and strange, deeper marks as victim number one. There appeared to be a bit of bone stabbing through the tattooed skin of his lower neck.

They rolled the body back to its original spot, and Alex stood up. "The damage to the back and neck was done postmortem, but the penis burning session was definitely antemortem." He snapped his gloves off and rubbed the back of his neck. "The unsub is getting more aggressive, more violent. There is a lot of overkill here, more than the first. Okay, Sparky, what else can you tell me?"

"I'd say he was submissive and was into whatever game he and his killer were playing. He's a bigger man, so it would have taken a lot to blitz him and then tie him up like this."

"Good. Anything more?" asked Alex.

"We found a few bits of particulates from his hair and calves. Fibers that might be carpet strands and some black flakes I don't recognize. We'll go to work on them when we get to the lab. The fibers could mean he was transported in the trunk or on the floor of a vehicle," answered Sarah.

"Or—"

"That the game started in the car, making it easier to dump the body. But that would leave copious amounts of blood in the vehicle. Sparks stared at the ground and then looked back to Alex. "Stolen car?"

"That's what I'd do."

"I'll have one of the guys check out stolen vehicles over the last couple days."

"Excellent. Does ol' stubby here have a name?"

"Stubby? Oh man, that's just cold, even for you." She shook her head. "Anyway, his name is Ben Morgan. He just got out after doing two years for white-collar crime: embezzlement from his former company. He was the CFO and apparently thought he wasn't making enough."

"I hope he enjoyed the extra money. It's the last raise he's ever going to see. Get it? Raise?"

"You just have no respect, but it's not hard to see your point."

"Sparky! Good one," he laughed. "Okay. Let's finish up here and let the ME get to work. I've got to get to the north side of town."

"Boss, there's one more thing that is kind of odd."

Alex raised his eyebrows. "What?"

"There was a small roll of paper stuffed up his left nostril."

"Paper?"

"Yes. It had the letter 'S' printed on it." She held up the evidence bag, and the white swatch of paper winked at him, daring him to figure this one out.

Alex's mind swam. He was the science guy. The profiler and detective gig was where Manny and Sophie came in, but he didn't have to be a detective to see that this was a message.

He wiped the sweat from his forehead. In his experience, messages from serial killers were akin to drinking Kool-Aid with Jim Jones--really bad medicine.

Chapter-29

Manny walked into Gavin's office, Sophie trailing behind, and stood silently, taking in the complete and unusual atmosphere of a police chief being shot in his private office. If the top cop in Michigan's capital wasn't safe, was anyone, anywhere?

"Kinda creepy," said Sophie, her voice as soft as a summer breeze.

"That's one way to put it." He scratched the stubble of his two-day growth. "How could this happen? I mean, we have security desks on each floor, key cards and passwords just to get through the door. Not to mention the cops assigned to the lobby."

Manny moved closer to the desk, past the CSU's yellow numbered evidence markers, and stood in front of Gavin's large, oak desk. The front of his tan leather chair was stained a deep maroon. The blood had run off the edge, dripping to the carpet and pooling just behind the desk. There were two vacant patterns in the middle of the stain where Gavin's feet had been, leaving a butterfly-like shape.

To the left of that, on the carpet, rested one of the evidence markers. It was alone, away from the others, and seemed out of place. At first, Manny couldn't see what it was guarding, but bending closer, he noticed a line of small blood drops, most shaped in oval patterns.

"What is it?" asked Sophie.

"It looks like cast off, maybe from the weapon."

"Shooter's blood?"

"I don't think so. It's not much, but it might show how close the perp had been to Gavin when he was shot," answered Manny.

"If the shooter was that near, I mean, close enough to get blood on the gun, then one of two things is probably true," said Sophie. "He was being held at gun point, or—"

"He knew them," finished Manny.

He moved the chair and peeked under the desk, near where Gavin's left leg would normally rest. The emergency button glowed in an intermittent green pattern.

"The Chief didn't hit the emergency button, which lines up with what the officer on watch said."

Sophie bent closer to the spatter. "That wraps it up for me; he definitely knew the shooter."

"Just freaking great. It was someone he knew and apparently trusted. He let them get real close, with no sense of panic or fear."

Sophie puckered her brow. "Another cop?"

She could be right.

Just then, Buzzy Dancer tiptoed to the door. "Hey guys. Good to have you back. I have the security camera recordings, such as they are, for you to look at."

She was looking at the ceiling, trying to avoid seeing anything that remotely resembled graphic. No denying her gift with technology, but blood gave her nightmares.

Maybe we all should be more like Buzzy.

"What do you mean, such as they are?" asked Manny.

"They're all messed up. Come see what I'm talking about, and then I'll tell you what I think."

Sophie and he stood over Buzzy's huge computer monitor and waited as she loaded the video. Her eyes were bloodshot, and she wore almost no makeup, or any of her tart perfume—something Buzzy Dancer never went without.

Manny put his hand on her shoulder. "It's not your fault, you know that, right?"

The pink-clad computer tech stared a hole through the monitor. A small, desperate sob escaped from somewhere deep in her chest. "I should have been here. I left a little early. First night of bowling. I usually stay until 8:30 or so. Last night I left at 8:00. I . . . I could have helped."

"You could have just as easily been victim number two," said Sophie. "Wait, you bowl?"

"Maybe. But I do have a gun, department requirements." Buzzy flexed her left hand. "I carry a 180 average."

"Now that's a wee bit scary," said Manny.

"My bowling average?"

"No, well, that too, but the whole gun thing."

Buzzy smiled, putting her hand on Manny's. "Thanks, both of you."

The screen sprang to life, showing the outside of the security emergency door on the first floor.

"I checked all of the other feeds and what's coming up next happened to them all, at exactly the same time. Notice the time stamp in the corner."

It blinked 8:48, and the screen suddenly went blank, then turned to electronic snow.

"Whoa. That's not good," said Sophie. "What happened?"

"Our security system is CCTV, closed circuit television, which means it transmits directly from our cameras to our monitors in the security room. It broadcasts from point to point, making it much tougher to tap into. It's tons more secure because it's not blasting a signal that any hacker could pick up."

Buzzy slurped her coffee. "I had the system run through a complete debug checklist, and there was nothing wrong on our end or with the software vendor's equipment."

"So this was an intentional jam? Can that be done?" asked Manny.

Buzzy was just getting warmed up.

"There was a study done in Australia a few years back. Some PhD students discovered they could jam the security cameras at the local airport with just a PDA." She grinned at Manny. "Personal

Digital Assistant, to you, detective."

"Learn something every day."

"Anyway, their research showed, with a little tweaking, they could take down a network in a few seconds, and it was virtually undetectable. The system could then be restored in a heartbeat, making it appear that there had been a network congestion problem. That's what our incident report showed, even though we've never had an interruption like that before."

She turned back to the screen, fast-forwarding the video. "At exactly 9:01, the feed returned to normal. Thirteen minutes and, *tada*, it's like nothing ever happened. Weird as Lady Gaga's wardrobe."

"Don't you have to be some kind of tech guru to pull that off?" asked Manny.

"Nope. Internet sites can show you how, and it's not very complex. About a two on a scale of ten."

"So this was a planned hit, and the shooter went the extra mile to make sure no one got a good look at them," pointed out Manny.

"Up and down four flights, with a close-up shooting sandwiched in, all in thirteen minutes, or less. Damn," said Sophie.

Manny ran his hand through his hair. "There's something else here. This looks like the same thing that happened at the White Kitty two nights ago."

"You mean the security cameras going nuts?" asked Sophie.

"Yeah. Remember what the manager said, that it just popped back on, and they couldn't find a problem."

"I also remember her asking about your weapon."

"Really? She asked about your . . . Oh my gosh," giggled Buzzy.

"Stay on task, ladies."

"Okay. Okay. So you think the camera thing might be a connection?" asked Buzzy.

"If it smells like crap . . ."

Sophie shook her head. "If you're right, what links Gavin with the first victim?"

"I don't know, but that could be the sixty-four-thousand-dollar question."

The cell phone in Sophie's pocket rang. She looked at the number. "Josh is returning my call."

"Let me take it."

"Hell no. I'm talking to him."

"Sophie?"

"Manny!"

"Sophie!"

"Fine." She gave Manny a dirty look and slapped the phone in his hand.

"Josh?"

"Not Sophie?"

"No, it's me."

"Has she ever been arrested, like for stalking?"

"Never convicted."

"That's a relief. How's Gavin doing?"

"He's hanging in there, for now. But it doesn't look good."

"Sorry to hear that; he's a good man."

Manny let out a breath. "I need your help. We've got four murders and another shooting. Three are related, so that makes it a serial-killer problem. It's like Lansing's being confused with New York."

"Three? Not good. I have to talk to you about Argyle anyway. We'll have him in Miami by tomorrow. After that, Max, Chloe, and I will be there."

Manny felt his stomach flip when Josh mentioned Chloe's name. He wondered, briefly, when that would stop. "Excellent. What do you mean, talk about Argyle?"

"It seems he'll only talk to you and hasn't spoken a word since he said so. He says he wants to talk about 'the others.'"

"What others?"

"He wouldn't say, but you know he's no altar boy."

"Could be nothing. Typical for his profile. He still thinks he's in control. We'll get to him when the rest of this is over. And Josh?"

"Yes?"

"Bring extra clothes; this thing is going to get worse."

Chapter-30

Mike Crosby sat on the edge of his leather sofa, fingers knitted together between his knees, staring at something on the hardwood floor that only he could see.

Manny touched his shoulder, and Mike glanced upward, arresting Manny's eyes for the briefest of moments. But it was enough. Fear, anger, pain, and confusion were undoubtedly Mike's closest confidants. He'd been through a lot; maybe more than a person should have to go through in this life, but he'd never seen him like this.

Manny sat beside him. "How're you holding up?"

"Kind of a dumb question for a hot-shot detective, don't you think? And why are you here, Williams?" asked Mike. The strain in his voice was as palpable as trees in a forest.

"I asked because I care. I think you know why I'm here."

Mike rubbed his bearded face with both hands, still not looking at Manny. "I didn't shoot the sick prick next door. But I won't lie. I wanted to. Blake Harris got what he deserved."

"Why would you say that? He did his time, right?"

Mike got up and walked to his kitchen table, picked up a DVD case parked beside two empty whisky bottles, and handed it to Manny, still refusing to look him in the face. Manny wondered what he was hiding. It was something more than the clandestine drinking.

"What's this?"

"Open the cover."

He did. There was a pornographic image of two men and a woman on the front, but no title.

"Warped, but probably not against his parole to buy this crap."

"I got it in my mailbox, even though it was sent to him. I was just going to give it to him, unopened, but I knew his background, so I thought I'd check it out."

"And?"

Mike let out a breath. "It's a rape and snuff video."

Manny instantly felt surprise and disgust ripple through his body. He slammed the DVD shut, threw it on the floor, and smashed it with his shoe. "He'd go away for a long time with that in his possession." Manny stood up and moved closer to Mike. "So you confronted him? That's what the argument was about?"

Mike nodded. "He denied it was his. He laughed and then thanked me. He said even if he'd bought something like that, I'd bailed him out by opening it. Then he suggested that I was the one who was a pervert, that all cops have something to hide, and this was my thing."

"Then what?"

"I knocked him on his ass." Mike stood straighter, head still bowed. "He screamed that he was going to sue me. I told him to go for it, kicked him in the face, and walked out."

"What time was that?"

"I've been over this with the blues."

"Just humor me."

"Whatever. About 11 p.m."

"What was he doing when you left?"

"Bleeding and swearing, but he was alive . . . and no, I didn't go back and shoot his ugly ass. He isn't worth going to prison."

"The ME thinks he was shot between 2 to 3 a.m. Did you hear anything?"

"No," said Mike, looking at his feet.

Manny put his hands on both sides of Mike's face, pulling it up so they were eye to eye. Mike started to fight it and stopped. Manny spoke in a hushed voice, one filled with understanding. "I know you're not telling me everything. There's something else."

"No . . . there isn't . . . I . . ."

"Mike, I'm just trying to help, get you out of here, and up to the hospital to see your dad."

The tears welled in Mike's eyes, his face twisting with brief, but powerful, emotion.

"How is he?" he whispered.

"He's hanging in there, but he needs to hear your voice."

Mike broke away from Manny and sat back on the couch, shoulders heaving accompanied by loud sobs that might have been pent up for weeks or months. Only Mike knew for sure. He finally looked up.

"I . . . I couldn't sleep again and was drinking pretty hard. Sometimes the booze gets Lexy off my mind, but then there are the dreams." He wiped the tears from his beard. "Anyway, I thought I heard something a little after two, but I was pretty blitzed by then."

"Heard what?"

Mike licked his lips. "A gun shot, but it could have been anything, so I let it go. A few minutes later, I heard the degenerate's door open and close."

"How do you know it was his?"

"The walls in this place are like paper . . . and maybe I was honed in on him. Hell, I don't know for sure. I thought maybe he was headed out for a good time or something, and I wanted to nail him for a parole violation."

"You thought that, even though you were drinking pretty hard?"

"I know. It sounds crazy, but it's true. It was like instant sober, almost."

"What did you see?"

Mike turned away, tapping his foot on the floor. "A woman. I saw a tall woman walking down the hall, away from his door."

Manny's pulse stepped up a notch. "Did you get a good look at her?"

Gavin's son bit his lip. "The hallway isn't well lit . . . I'm not sure . . ."

"All right. What do you think you saw?"

Mike tugged nervously at his beard. "She looked kind of familiar and then she was gone. So I went out on the balcony to see if I could see her leave. She came out the front walking close to the building, then she moved under one of the streetlamps."

"Familiar?"

"I need a drink."

"No more drinks. Talk to me."

"I could have sworn it was my mom."

Chapter-31

"This is not going the way we thought it would," said the short woman with the powerful body and platinum blond hair. She sipped from her vanilla latte as the two women sat in a secluded booth in Mack's Coffee Emporium. "What do you want to do?"

The taller woman seated on her right smiled. "Things are pretty much going the way we hoped they would. Crosby not being out of the picture is the only thing we've not counted on."

She scanned the other woman's face. "And that will most likely take care of itself."

"And if it doesn't?"

"She'll handle it. Have faith. Remember that we're all in this together, and she won't let us down," answered the tall woman.

"I remember. I just hope Stella does," replied the blonde.

"What does that mean?"

"Let me lay this out for you. He saw her. He knows who shot him. If by some miracle, he makes it, and without brain damage, we're all going away for a long time." She put her hand flat on the table. "Ballistics will eventually match the gun used at each crime scene. Even though we used hollow point ammo, they'll probably still get enough fragments to put it together, which was part of the plan. We want them to think one killer is at work here. Crosby still breathing could ruin all that."

"But won't they think Stella was the shooter?"

"Probably. But because she offed that pervert at the Royal Life, it puts a strain on the time line of the other two we took care of last night. Dropping off a gun to each other is a lot easier than doing these three pieces of shit alone, especially in a five-hour period."

"Four shootings. Don't forget Crosby," added the tall woman.

"Whew. Busy night. But given the locations, the LPD is going to think it was feasible. They'll believe it to be a spree thing," said the blonde.

"Williams might not think that way."

"If not, we'll deal with that if, and when, we have to," answered the blonde. "He's good, but we're better. For example, these wigs . . . better to be safe than sorry."

The tall woman grinned. "Always wanted to be a redhead. I think my ex would have liked it too."

"Men are so easy. A little leg, a little boob, some lace, or maybe leather, and they trip over their dicks to do whatever you want, just to get laid," answered the blonde. "And so far, it's working for us."

The tall woman reached for the hand of her partner. "Be strong and hang onto the vision. Stella was with us from the beginning, and she'll hold up her end. Okay?"

The blonde nodded. "It makes me nervous, that's all."

"All right. Now I have to go drop the gun off at our spot, then go to my dentist appointment."

"What? You still have the gun?" asked the blonde, a trace of panic in her voice.

"Yes. I picked it up after you dropped it off, after you and Stella were finished with your little meetings. What's the problem?" questioned the tall woman.

"What time was that?"

"About 12:30 a.m., during my dinner break. You're freaking me out. What's wrong?"

"I picked it up at about 10:30, after Stella was finished with Ashcroft," the blonde whispered, harsh emotion straining her face. "You've had it ever since 12:30?"

"Yeah. So?"

"According to the police scanner, the first officers arrived at the Royal Life about 6 a.m. The CSU reported that the psycho *she* took care of was killed between 2:00 and 3:00 this morning."

"So what did she shoot him with?—oh shit."

Pointed reality dawned on the tall woman as unavoidable truth slapped her across the face. The two women sat in stunned silence.

Finally the blonde spoke. "They're going to know there are two guns involved in these shootings and two guns most likely means two shooters."

"That's not the worst. What if the gun she used is registered to Gavin or her? They'll know she had access to it."

"Damn it. Let me make one thing clear. I'm not going to prison because she acted like a twit."

"What does that mean?"

The blonde woman sat back in the booth, crossing her legs. "It means, after tonight, there'll only be two of us left."

Chapter-32

"Mike, are you positive? Stella? Your mom?"

"I know it sounds crazy, and hell no, I'm not sure . . . it *could* have been her. But like I said, I was drinking, it was dark . . . it might have—hell, I don't know." Mike shook his head and went silent.

Manny looked at the ceiling as doubt whispered in his ear. He had known Stella for seventeen years. She simply wasn't capable of this kind of thing. In fact, she had a serious disdain for guns, almost a phobia. Gavin had joked that if anyone ever broke into their home, she would talk them to death before she could ever shoot them.

What reason would she have for shooting a man like Harris? How would she know him? That was like Mother Teresa having some dark communion with Charles Manson.

Mike was mistaken. Maybe he felt guilty for not being in his parents' lives the last few months, and seeing a woman that vaguely resembled his mother caused him to jump to some subconscious conclusion.

Nothing like a little pop psychology.

Whoever shot this guy had a beef. When it was all said and done, it would be the mother of one of the depraved jerk's victims. Or maybe even a victim who decided to confront the source of her nightmares. It wasn't Stella Crosby.

But the look on Mike's face forced Manny to consider what he'd said. He raked the thought from his mind.

"Go see your dad."

"So, I'm not a suspect?"

"Not to me." Manny opened the front door to the hall and motioned for the two uniforms to leave. "After you go see your dad and talk to your mother, then head over to the office. It's time to finish the department's psych evaluation so you can get your ass back to work."

"You think I'm crazy? That I'm seeing things?" Mike clutched his hands together. "I'm not having some psychotic episode or whatever the hell it is that people go through from some stressor. It's just that I can't get Lexy off my—"

"I don't think you're crazy, but it's time to get back in the saddle."

His eyes grew moist. "Manny, I don't know if I'm ready. I still miss her so much. Most days, nothing matters, and I see her face everywhere."

"You'll always miss her, but there's no way she'd want you to keep doing this. The man she married was strong, confident, able. Not someone who wallowed in whiskey and pity."

Mike's eyes came alive with anger, and then it left as fast as it came. He sighed. One of those sighs that said *I know you're right, but it isn't going to be easy.* "I don't know . . ."

"One more thing." Manny walked to the kitchen and grabbed the two unopened bottles of liquor standing arrogantly on the counter, opened them, then poured them down the drain. "This is over. No more drinking."

Mike stood, and Manny saw something he'd not seen for months: Mike Crosby and a smile holding hands.

"Yes, dear. But do me a favor. Don't quit your day job to become a counselor; one of your patients might kick the shit out of you."

"No problem there," Manny laughed.

Mike looked like his mother when he smiled like that. Always good to see.

Manny walked out of the room and headed to the car. Sophie had decided that she was tired of being his secretary and had gone to the cell phone company that supplied phones and service to the LPD to get him a new phone, an electronic tether that would bring him to the cutting edge in PDA technology. Great. Something else he had no time for.

She would wait for him to pick her up, and then they would get to the office in time for a meeting with Alex's department. Apparently there was some disturbing evidence concerning the two new bodies. Just what they needed. And how could it get more disturbing than the first victim? He'd be glad when Josh and his crew got here. This was getting crazy, fast.

He ran his hand through his hair, hoping to shake the nagging, persistent words Mike had spoken.

"I could have sworn it was my mom."

Mike had been a great cop and was going to be a good detective some day. He wasn't prone to exaggerations or illusions. However, he wasn't exactly the same man he'd been a few months ago. Manny had seen his share of cops who had lost it—and not just because of booze and drugs. Seeing what cops saw, like the total disregard for life with these crimes, sometimes clouded perceptions of reality.

Still . . .

He pushed at the troublesome pictures in his mind that were forming a portrait of Stella Crosby. This time, they pushed back.

Chapter-33

“Here’s your new phone. Try not to turn this one into electronic roadkill, at least for a few days,” Sophie said, putting both hands on the top of his desk.

“You said it was a good throw,” answered Manny, turning his new smartphone over in his hand.

“I was just trying to be supportive. You’ve lost at least five MPH off your fastball, and I’ll bet the curveball hangs there like a big old balloon, just begging to be hit out of the park.”

“I could still strike your ass out on a bet.”

“You think you can blow three of those little girl pitches by me? Oh, just bring it.”

The talk of baseball reminded Manny that the Williams family had tickets to Comerica Park to watch his beloved Detroit Tigers play against the hated Minnesota Twins on Sunday, only four days away. He couldn’t wait to see the look on his daughter Jennifer’s face when they settled into their seats.

Louise and he had gone about a zillion times.

She had been a big baseball freak before they'd even met. As much as Manny loved the atmosphere of a Major League park, he thought Louise loved it even more. (Another reason she had been the perfect woman for him.)

She knew every Tiger player from the last twenty years and could recite most of their stats, and how good each of them looked in their tight-fitting home uniforms.

The smell of roasting hotdogs and sausages, the vibrant color of the perfectly manicured grass, the indescribable excitement that seemed to spread from the very structure itself was special. And of course, the little boy or girl dressed in his or her Tiger hat, matching jersey, and new glove, standing a seat or two away hardly able to contain themselves: all of this made a trip to the ballpark what it was always intended to be, pure joy. He wanted Jen to get into it too. Time would tell.

"Earth to Williams. Hello?" Sophie said.

"Sorry. Just thinking about the game we're going to on Sunday," he sighed, "if we get this mess sorted out by then."

"You should go anyway. You know how important family time is. And don't give me crap about that whole workaholic thing you've got going on. Just go."

He grinned. "Thanks for the encouragement—I think."

"You're welcome. What are partners for? Oh, and don't think I forgot about that wet noodle of an arm you've got. We're going to settle this on the field when the time's right."

"I don't know what fantasy world you live in—well, a few of them—but that'll be like taking candy from a baby . . . a TINY baby."

"It's a date, rag arm."

"Whatever. Tell me about this thing that I have in my hand—and keep it simple."

"First, let me tell you that all of your contacts have been programmed in, so that's just like before."

"Yeah? Then I'm good to go."

"That's not all."

"It's a phone, right?"

"Yes, but it also—"

"And phones are used for? You guessed it, talking with other people who have phones."

"Manny—"

"I don't need anything more."

Sophie rolled her eyes. "Listen, techno-phobe, this phone can do things to save lives, catch the bad guys we all think so fondly of, and even order dinner, so heads up and pay attention."

"Your eyes really get big when you get pissy. Ever notice that?"

"I'm ignoring you . . . do they really?"

"Yep."

"You're not getting around this."

Manny shrugged in surrender. "All right. Fire away. But this better be good."

"I'll keep it simple. This is a smartphone with a touchscreen. If you touch the screen here, you can get your e-mail. This one lets you download and play videos or music. This one will let you buy certain applications, like GPS or games. Touch it here, and you can surf the web. This has 4G, which means you can search the Internet from almost anywhere. You can check Facebook, Twitter, and all of the social websites you're a member of."

"Yeah. My heart beats just to check those out."

"Don't be sarcastic. This is good stuff."

"And that helps me how?"

"What if you found something at a scene that you didn't recognize, and you thought it was important? Just snap a picture, upload it to your e-mail, like this, and send it to Alex or whomever. A few minutes later, you'll have his input. You can even get ballistic and DNA reports from the lab."

"Great. What about dinner?"

"What?"

"You said it would order food."

"Men. It's all about food, sports, and women, isn't it?"

"What else is there?"

"You ain't right." Sophie pointed to the touchscreen. "Put in the web address of your favorite food joint here, hit the menu, and order away."

"Okay. I might use that. Are we done here? We have that meeting with Alex and—" Mike's statement about Stella came storming back. They'd been so busy with the new phone that he hadn't mentioned anything to her.

Sophie cocked her head. "And what?"

"We have to talk about my interview with Mike. He said something that seemed absolutely nuts, at first. But now I'm not so sure."

"Did he shoot the guy?"

"I don't think so. I believed him when he said he didn't."

"What else did he say?"

Manny opened his mouth to speak when Alex strolled through the door and stopped. He stared at the plastic, yellow tape guarding Gavin's office, shook his head, and moved to where Manny and Sophie stood.

"You two ready? We've got some crazy stuff going on here, and we need to go over all of it. This is getting weirder by the minute, and honestly, it's on the bizarre side."

"How can it get any stranger?" asked Manny.

"Sparky will be here to confirm the other crime-scene findings, but for starters, the small pieces of paper found in the nostril of both of last night's victims. Each had a small letter printed on them. The first victim's note had an 'S'; the second one had a 'U.'"

"Up their noses? Eww," squirmed Sophie.

Manny scratched his head. "Great. A freaking message from a serial killer. Not good."

"That's exactly what I thought," said Alex.

Sophie spoke. "You didn't mention anything like that from Morse, the first vic, right?"

Alex looked at Sophie and then back to Manny. "The body was so swollen, we didn't notice it. I called the ME and she confirmed, after digging for nose gold, that there was indeed a note. It had the letter 'J' printed in the middle. She's having it sent over by courier. Dollars to donuts says it's the same handwriting."

"J-U-S? What the hell does that mean?" swore Manny. He felt his blood pressure rise as the shooter's intent became clear. "This could mean that this unsub is a mission-oriented killer. If I'm right, and he's spelling something here, the murders won't stop until the message is complete." He glanced at Alex. "We're going to have a lot more bodies if we don't nail this guy."

"I think you're right," said Alex.

"It fits the profile," said Manny.

"There's something else. These murders seem to be just an hour or so apart. I know a little about escalation, and this is one busy killer."

Manny frowned. "But what set him off? Starting this fast doesn't fit."

"Maybe they didn't. Maybe they worked on it somewhere else. Not that unusual," said Sophie.

"True. We'll have Buzzy research for similar MOs around the state in the last year."

Sarah Sparks rushed through Manny's door. "Boss, you gotta see this report."

"Slow down, Sparky. What report?"

"I know a guy in ballistics. We dated for a while, until his wife found out, but anyway, I was waiting for my DNA reports to process, so I asked him to rush whatever he had on these shootings." She grinned, still catching her breath. "I had to promise him a couple things, but he came through."

"What things?"

"You don't want to know. Anyway, you know how the department requires every service pistol to have a ballistics profile? Well, Lansing also requires that if an officer owns a second gun, it has to be profiled too. In case the backup weapon is fired, yada, yada, yada. Look at this."

Alex's eyes scanned to where she was pointing. "I'll be damned. Didn't I hear you say that Mike didn't shoot that sick troll in his apartment complex last night?"

"Yeah. He didn't. Why?" answered Manny.

"You need to rethink that. He was killed with Mike's backup weapon."

Chapter-34

"Hey, Mom."

Stella turned to see Mike standing by the elevator, turning his hat in his hands like he did when he was a little boy and knew trouble was on the horizon. There were still faint lines around his nose and eyes that reminded her of that ten-year-old.

Gavin had been a busy man back in those days, and Mike and she were on their own a great deal more than the norm. But the family of an ambitious cop knew what was required. The two of them had done their best to support Gavin and had grown close because of it. She was glad to see him.

"Hey, buddy. Come give your old mom a squeeze."

"I've got some of those."

They hugged, and Mike whispered into her ear. "I'm sorry. I've been so wrapped up in my problems that nothing else seemed to matter."

"I understand, but you're here now." She heard him catch his breath and felt hot tears against her cheek.

"How's the Old Man doing?"

She moved away, looking down to the floor. "He's hanging in there. His heart stopped a couple of times, but they brought him back and he seems stable, for now. They . . . the prognosis isn't good, but he was always a fighter . . . until lately anyway."

Mike knitted his brow together. "What do you mean?"

"Since Lexy . . . well, it took a huge toll on him. He's been withdrawn, depressed, and not around much. He spends a lot of nights in his office, and I spend a lot of them alone."

"I'm sorry, Mom. I didn't know."

Stella smiled that smile mothers use to show their children everything's all right, even when it isn't. "No worries. I've got a strong support group, and I'm getting through it. It's amazing what you can do with the right kind of people around." This time her grin held a double-meaning that Mike would never understand.

"I suppose that's true." He walked to the room where his dad lay between life and death, and disappeared inside. She waited. A few minutes later, he emerged with fresh rivulets of tears funneling to his beard. He was whiter than when he first came through the door.

"I hate all that stuff hooked up to him, it's . . . he'd hate it," he said in a quiet voice.

"I know, but all of that equipment is doing its job." She gazed at her son and felt the anger snake its way back to her. Her son looked like hell, and worse, seemed lost. More to blame her weak, pathetic husband for. If he'd just done his job, professionally and personally, Mike wouldn't be in this state, and of course, Lex would be here. The anger grew, and little dots of rage teased the corners of her eyes.

You bastard, Gavin Crosby, look what you've done to my kid, my life.

Stella put her hand on Mike's, masking what she felt inside. "It'll be over soon, one way or the other. Then life will get back to normal, at least as much as it can."

Puzzlement shrouded Mike's face. "What does that mean? That it'll be over soon."

"I only mean that he'll pull through, or he won't. That's all." She forced her eyes to moisten. "I can't take much more of this whole thing. I just want it over."

Her son hugged her again. "I'll be here, for both of us."

"Okay. Enough of the sappy crap; your dad would have a fit," she said, pulling away from him. "We just have to hang tough and expect the best."

"Deal. God knows I've a got a few other things going on too. There was a man killed in the apartment next to mine last night."

Stella glanced to the floor. "How awful."

"Not really. He was a real scumbag, big-time pervert. I won't miss him."

She watched him twirl his hat around again and suddenly felt uneasy.

"Mom. I think I saw the woman who did it."

Stella's heart dropped to her toes. "Really?"

"Yeah. It was late. I had too much to drink. But I could have sworn—"

"Sworn what?" her heart threatened to pound right through her chest.

"Mom. Where were you last night about 2 a.m.?"

His eyes were clear, pointed, but the little-boy look had returned. He was afraid of her answer. The honest one. She opened her mouth to speak just as the elevator door clanked opened. Detectives Ross and Wymer stepped out with a big, burly, uniformed officer.

Kathy Ross pulled her cuffs and moved to Mike. "Mike Crosby. You're under arrest for the murder of Blake Harris."

Chapter-35

Manny pulled into his driveway, the window down on his Explorer, feeling the heat of the late afternoon sun and wondering where the last two days had gone. He felt like he'd been put through a meat grinder and was spent, physically and mentally.

Josh had called and said his plane would be in about midnight, earlier than first anticipated, but a good thing. Manny told Sophie and Alex to go home, get some sleep, and they'd meet with the Feds back at the station to bring them up to speed, then take it from there. Plus, they were bringing in some help from the Detroit FBI field office. The more the merrier on this one, especially with the forensic processing. Alex and his staff were amazing, but they couldn't be in that many places at once. The Feds seemingly, however, could.

For once, Manny was going to follow his own advice. All he wanted was one of Louise's famous barbequed steaks, a hug from his daughter, and a king-sized nap. As much as he hated shutting down for a few hours, even he was going to be out on his feet if he didn't take care of business.

Every available officer was coming in to shore up patrols for the midnight shift, and his department would be out there too. Maybe with the stepped up patrols and the FBI involvement, they'd get lucky. Maybe not. He'd take anything at this point.

FBI involvement. That fact brought into focus again just how many resources the FBI had—and Lansing didn't. Working for the Feds would have serious benefits, but could he leave the Lansing life? Especially now? What if Gavin didn't make it? And what about the Crosby family? Stella was tough, but how tough could anyone be under all of the dire circumstances involving her family?

He rubbed his eyes with his thumb and forefinger. By now, Mike would be in jail. He'd apparently blown smoke up Manny's ass about what had really happened in the apartment next door. Odd though. He'd never known Mike to lie about anything. Stress does odd things to people, and a night behind bars just might improve Mike's memory.

His new phone rang just as he reached his front door. He did a double take. The caller ID said it was Chloe Franson.

Keeping busy had kept her out of his thoughts, yet there she was again, bigger than life and twice as beautiful. Shaking her image from his thoughts seemed to be getting tougher. He did it anyway. The phrase "Out of sight, out of mind" had helped. Not to mention, these cases would take everything he had . . . and more.

Feels like a damned soap opera.

"Williams here."

"Manny. Chloe Franson. I see you got another phone. I was going to leave a voice mail, but lucky me, I got the real you."

Her Irish inflection caused his stomach to do that thing again. "Ahhmm, yes I did. This one lets me track the hairs on my head, my calories, and when I need to get a physical."

"I have one of those. It also lets the Bureau know where I am every second."

"How's that?" *Were they small talking?*

"It has a special built-in GPS. Big brother's watching."

"Makes sense." *They were.*

The awkward silence lasted only a few seconds, but long enough for him to wander to the color of her eyes. This was getting a little more than weird. She must have felt it too. She jumped back into the conversation.

"Ah, I know that you're busier than an English dentist, but Josh wanted me to call to say we'd be on time, and there would be four other agents coming from Detroit. He also said to tell you that Argyle would be in Michigan in a couple of days, not next week."

"Good. On all accounts. Has Argyle talked yet?"

"Nope. Just wants an audience with you. That's why the brass hurried things up. They want to hear what he's got to say. They're hoping he has no other bodies, just a line of crap. Then get him locked down in the Supermax at ADX in Florence."

Louise came to the screen door, grilling fork in hand. Manny smiled at his wife.

"That works for me. See you tonight." He hung up, not quite understanding why he was feeling the way he was, but glad to see his Louise at the same time.

Manny stepped through the door and kissed her.

"Glad you're home. Who was that and what about tonight?"

"The FBI, and I'll tell you the rest at dinner."

"Manny. It's 5:00 and you've been gone two days. You need to rest."

"There have been three more murders, including one that Mike Crosby might be involved in."

"Three more? Mike? Really? No wonder you look like this."

"Like what?"

"You know, tired, worn out, horny."

"Horny, huh? You offering your considerable talents to fight that cause?"

"Honey, I've got things to offer I've been saving for a rainy day."

"Well, I feel a storm coming on."

She smiled and kissed him. "Later." Louise grew serious. "I feel bad for Stella. It must seem like she's walking around with a target on her back: a big one."

Manny decided not to tell her about what Mike thought he saw. It was probably a diversion to keep the heat off him anyway. "She's got support from her friends—that's something."

Louise looked at the grilling fork and back to Manny. "She does. And she's a tough one. Those Yoga classes we've been taking will help. All this just sucks."

"When it rains, it pours, like they say. I'll see her again tomorrow. But for now, a good meal and a few hours' sleep sounds like Heaven."

"Well, Jen is spending the night at a friend's house. So when you're ready to lie down, I guess, if you're up to it, I can tuck you in." Her eyes sparkled.

"Oh, I think I could handle that."

"We'll see, Big Boy, we'll see," she laughed, turning for the deck and the smoking grill.

Manny watched her walk away and wondered how there could ever be another woman for him. No matter what thoughts Chloe put in his head.

He felt the phone vibrate in his hand just before it rang. There was an incomplete number displayed, and he didn't recognize the area code. "Hello."

Manny waited for the person on the other end to speak. He could hear breathing.

"This is Detective Manny Williams; who is this?"

"You can call me Lucky. Because it's your lucky day. I have something for you."

The caller's voice was masked with an audio

disguiser, making him or her sound like Darth Vader with a cold.

"I don't talk to people who hide behind this kind of crap."

"Suit yourself, but you better think twice about turning down this information."

"How do I know I can use this information, that you aren't jerking me around?"

"Judge for yourself."

"All right, I'm listening."

"I know who is shooting the perverts in this town."

Manny stood straight. The caller had his full attention. The latest murders hadn't reached the papers yet. It wasn't common knowledge that there was more than one victim or that they were being shot. He steadied his voice. "How do I know this isn't some prank? We get these calls all of the time."

"I suppose you do, Detective Williams. But not everyone knows what I know."

"What's so special about what you know?"

"I know who tonight's victim will be."

Chapter-36

The tall woman gazed at her reflection in the mirror, wondering how someone like her had gotten to this point. She was smart, even brilliant, according to her old professors. The shape of her face, her coal black hair, and her big brown eyes added up to stunning. Not to mention, a body to die for. A patient smile formed on her thick lips when she thought about the last part. Men *had* died for her body, hadn't they? More would. A lot more. The pigs always thought with the little head, and that was fine with her. In fact, necessary. If they were thinking about her, what she was offering, then getting them where she wanted them was easy. Child's play really.

She folded her arms together, forming a substantial cleavage, and laughed. A little boob and they would forget everything their mamas and daddies ever taught them about playing with strangers.

But that was how she'd gotten where she was. Flaunting her assets created opportunities, but it also led her to open one too many of those dangerous doors, the kind that got you killed. He had overpowered her and kept her for three days, doing things to her that she only heard about in crime story magazines. Her captor had laughed when she begged him to stop, to let her go.

She wiped absently at the tear moving down her cheek. Eventually, he grew tired of her and was preparing to get rid of her, for good. He told her so during his last perverted frolic. She found herself welcoming death. It had to be better than another day, another second with him. But he'd made a mistake, forgetting, or not caring to make sure the handcuffs were secure. He must have thought her half-dead already.

She waited three hours, quietly opened the door of her demonic prison, found the kitchen, and then his bedroom. She never hesitated, stabbing him forty-eight times in the chest and face, then cut off his genitals and put them in his mouth.

The next day, she left Chicago and ended up in Lansing. Two years later, she was still here. But things were changing, evolving. She could no longer control the anger, the pain, the shame inside, and didn't care to. It was time for all of them to pay up, and she was the cashier.

"Shit happens, but someone has to clean it up," she whispered. Her mother had been right about that one, right up until she died four months ago, lung cancer dragging her into the afterlife—if there was such a place.

It had been good to get two others to join her

cause, her club. And surprisingly, not that difficult. Stella had been more willing than the other. The chief's wife seemed to be traveling down a similar path. But a few nights out and a couple of drinks will do wonders to get people to talk about what's really on their minds. The trick was to get them to put the words, the thoughts, into action. A few sad stories, a little sympathy, and a mutual hate (and make no mistake, hate was as strong as love) proved strong motivators for building and cultivating a state of mind that was already blooming. A few more sessions, and eventually the concept of the JUSTICE CLUB was born. Nothing like a freshly discovered loathing for men to bind women together.

She put on the last of her makeup, picking up the prepaid cell phone she'd used to call Detective Williams, and headed out the door for work.

She hated breaking up the Club like that. They'd grown close. But stupidity wouldn't be tolerated. Stella Crosby would have to learn that lesson the hard way.

Chapter-37

"This grieving wife and mother crap is getting old fast," Stella whispered, looking out the window of Gavin's hospital room. The sun was beginning its trek to the horizon, and she wanted to be out in it. Not here. By God, not here. It was a minor miracle she'd hung around as long as she had. But she had to keep up appearances, at least for a while longer. Williams wouldn't take too long to put things together, particularly once her too-honest son explained that he hadn't seen his backup weapon for a few months. The Firestorm .22 was supposed to be locked away in Gavin's study.

Mike never could keep a secret, not even for his mother. She supposed it was a good thing he hadn't become a pathological liar, but a little white lie once in a while wouldn't hurt, especially to protect his old mom. That wasn't in the cards based on the question he'd asked her, right before he was cuffed and rushed downtown. He had seen her leaving the apartment complex and had probably already told Manny. Not a real problem—

it's just that she wanted a couple more days. No matter. She was ready for what came next. All part of the plan.

She rolled the piece of paper with the name and address of tonight's lucky contestant around in her fingers, then stuffed it into the pocket of her blue jeans. She had a few hours before she had to leave, to dress the way that would get her in the door of his apartment. She'd tell the nurses she couldn't take the visitors and phone calls anymore and wanted to go home for a few hours. They would nod with sympathetic understanding, and that would be that.

Stella walked over to Gavin's bed and glared at his face, felt his helplessness, and wondered if some kind of coherency existed in the secret landscape of his brain, anything that would cause him to remember how he got where he was. She hoped so. He deserved to know, to suffer. Lexy had, and so had she, all on his watch. She couldn't put a date on it, or even a year, but he'd killed what was "them" a long time ago. Stella shrugged. What did it matter? What was done was done. Onward and upward.

She reached out to touch the "we're thinking of you" card that Louise and Manny had sent, and laughed.

After tonight, she would *really* be on their minds.

Chapter-38

"This better be good. It's late, and I'm missing my beauty sleep. You know how I am when I don't get that," moaned Sophie, taking another slug of black coffee.

Manny caught the quick glimpse she threw his way from the darkened passenger seat of their unmarked cruiser. They were parked across the street from the less than high-end Mason Street Apartments where the caller said the next target lived.

"Did you hear me?"

"Yes, dear. I know you didn't get much sleep. But four or five hours is better than nothing. And like I said, for the fifteenth time, I believe the caller knows something, and we have to make sure, one way or the other." Manny's fingers gently drummed on the steering wheel as he glanced at his partner. The faint glow of the streetlamp allowed just enough light to see the outline of Sophie's oval face. He turned the radio down, and the sweet harmonies of Celtic Woman faded away.

"I hope you're right. Otherwise, this goes on

your tab and I AM going to collect."

"Collect what?"

"I don't know, maybe a set of diamond earrings, or an oceanfront condo in Aruba."

"How much do you think I make?"

"You can get a second job as a male escort or something."

"That could be interesting, but not the part where Louise hurts me . . . in all of the right places."

"I still want something for my trouble."

"I'll see what I can do."

He knew she hated the whole stakeout idea. He got that, but after he received the call, plans had to change.

The call. Why? How did the caller know? What was in it for him? He would bet his next paycheck that being Citizen of the Month wasn't on the caller's agenda. But he couldn't ignore the warning that the caller claimed as truth. Not to mention, it *felt* like the truth.

Manny had contacted Avery Buck, the alleged next victim, through his parole officer. After some serious convincing, he had managed to get Detectives Wymer and Ross planted in the spare bedroom of Buck's apartment. There were two other surveillance units, a block east and a block west, parked along Mason Avenue. The blues had a full description of what the perp was to be wearing. That would let them know when, or maybe if, the shooter decided to show up to the party. The caller had said 10:30 . . . only a few more minutes to show time. He prayed this wasn't some wild goose chase, but what choice did they really have? This could be the break that ripped the thing wide open. God knew they needed one.

The radio crackled. "Nothing yet, Manny. Hope this isn't a waste of time."

Sophie snatched the microphone from the dash. "Who is this?"

"Sergeant Wang. Is this Detective Lee?"

"Your worst nightmare. Don't be bothering our asses with small talk. Keep radio silence unless you got something to say. And Wang, are you Chinese?"

"Sorry, Detective Lee. And yes I am. Why?"

"You're giving our people a bad name by acting like a rookie. Got it?"

"I only . . . yes, detective. It won't happen again."

"Better not. Next time, I'm all over you so hard and fast, you'll whine for your mama."

She slammed the handset back into place, crossing her arms over her chest, and then let loose a full belly laugh.

"Done?"

"Yeah, that felt great. Besides, you gotta keep these guys in line." She shifted in her seat. "A little over the top?"

"Not you."

"Sarcasm again. I get it. But it was fun, and it helps pass the time."

He smiled.

"I felt that little smirk. What's so funny?"

"Nothing. Just thinking how lucky I am to have a partner like you."

"You're damn right, and don't forget it. I'm special . . . and you're lying to me, aren't you?"

"That hurt."

"Just answer the question."

"Not exactly, but at least you've stopped bitching."

"That could change if I don't get more coffee." Sophie poured more java from the thermos. "So what's the deal with this Avery Buck character? Sex crimes?"

"No. He was put away for hurting someone while drunk driving. Pretty upstanding guy before that, he even did church work. Just couldn't shake the drinking demon." He ran his hand through his hair. "I can't get a grip on this victimology. Three serious sex offenders, if you count the guy killed at Mike's apartment complex."

"But—"

"I'm just not sure what's going on. It could all be related, or not."

"The guy on the Westside, Ben Morgan, had no record other than embezzlement. The other two were complete reprobates," said Sophie.

Manny grew silent, trying to make sense of what he and Sophie had just said.

"So what's going on in that brain of yours?"

"I don't know. It's like someone knows something about Morgan that we don't. Some skeleton in the closet, same with Buck."

The radio sprang to life again. “Subject matching description approaching from the west.”

This time, Manny picked the mic from its cradle. “Are you sure?”

“Yes sir. Tall, dressed in black, and a hoodie hiding the subject’s face.”

“Got that, Ross?”

“Copy. We’re ready. If I can keep Wymer’s hands out of the chocolate-covered nuts.” There was a brief sound of a scuffle. Wymer came on line. “I’m ready, guys. For the record, they were M&Ms, and I put them away.”

“Yeah, every one of them,” said Ross in the background.

“Just get it together.”

“Yes sir.”

Sophie grabbed his arm. “Look close.”

“There he is. But can you see those shoes?”

The light was better on that side of the street, and Manny did see as the subject of the night’s festivities moved up the steps of the apartment complex.

Reaching for the car’s door handle, he turned to Sophie. “I don’t remember the last time I saw a man wearing four-inch stilettos.”

Chapter-39

Stella moved gracefully to the front porch of the apartment complex across from the park and stopped, looking around to see if anyone had noticed her. There were a couple of cars parked on the street, but that was it. Who would really see her anyway? Not in this part of town, particularly this late. People dressed in black didn't draw a lot of attention on the east side, especially when keeping to the shadows. If she ran into someone, they wouldn't remember. They were too wrapped up in their own worlds. People just didn't give a monkey's ass anymore. Life is all about them and instant gratification, nothing more. It hadn't been that way, back in the day, when neighborhoods were important and neighbors were more important. But times were a changing, as they say, and she'd take full advantage of the new king of society: human apathy.

She tested the grimy door handle and found it unlocked. So much for security.

Standing in the dimly lit foyer, she unbuttoned her silk blouse to her navel, displaying a tanned stomach and a lacy push up, and hiked up her skirt, showing off long legs and black fishnet nylons. Most women didn't look this good at thirty-five, let alone in their fifties. She'd worked hard to get in this kind of shape. But hard work couldn't hide everything that the years had handed her. She'd love to be thirty again, but it wasn't an issue tonight. It wasn't like he was going to see the rest of her. It wouldn't get that far. She patted the gun and the bottle of acid and smirked. "My friends and I have different plans," she said softly.

The steps creaked and the smell of old smoke and lavender disinfectant ran rampant in the halls as she reached the second floor. Apartment 203 was two doors to her right. She stopped, stood tall, and moved to just the right angle in front of the security peephole. The gun felt good as it rested against her thigh. She knocked on the door.

A few seconds later, there was a noise as someone bumped the door. She moved a little closer to the peephole. She felt his eyes do a double-take. Then a third. He was probably racking his brain to figure out what he'd done to deserve what he was seeing. She couldn't wait to tell him.

The safety chain clicked into place, and the door opened six inches. His partially exposed face was unshaven; the eye she could see was bloodshot. His drug addiction seemed to be in full bloom.

"What can I do for you?"

"You can't guess?"

"Makes me nervous when I get a question answering a question. What do you want?"

"I understand you are into certain things—things I need."

He swallowed so loud that she almost laughed.

"Yeah? Like what things, and who told you what I'm into?"

Stella pulled a photo from her purse and eased it through the crack in the door.

"Let's just say a mutual friend said that action like this gets your attention."

The man behind the door grew silent, then spoke. "Are you a cop?" His voice had already grown thick.

"Not in this lifetime."

"You want me to do *this* to you?"

"And more. I'm not here to bring you cookies. My husband thinks I'm sick. He doesn't understand people like you and me. I need to be handled . . . your way. But if you don't like what you see, maybe I've got the wrong guy..."

"No, no. I'm your man, baby. I want to see your face."

"I'll show you everything, do everything, when you let me in."

The lobby door, two floors down, closed with a thud, and she heard footsteps coming up the stairwell. More than one set, in a hurry to boot. She couldn't be seen.

"Now or never," she urged calmly.

The chain rattled, and then the door opened.

She walked in.

Stella took one more step and pulled her purse tight. He was on her like lions on meat. He spun her around and slammed her face-first into the wall, his groin pressing against her buttocks with unbelievable force. Ignoring the pain, she laughed. “Wait. Wait. Let me get ready.”

“Your friend should have told you more about me,” he snarled.

“Oh, she did.” Stella reached back, grabbed his woody, and twisted. The yelp of pain was amazingly gratifying, but he hung in there like a bad hairdo, pressing harder. She twisted again, he screamed, and this time backed away. She pulled the gun, whirled, and stuck the barrel up his nose.

“I think I’ll take over now.”

Chapter-40

Manny crouched on the left side of the door with Sophie to his right. Sergeant Wang and three other uniforms positioned themselves in a half moon behind them. It had been a minute or so since the mystery woman had entered the apartment, but they had heard nothing from Ross and Wymer. He was getting nervous.

There was a sudden thud against the wall followed by excited yelling, and with the suddenness of a Florida thunderstorm, the door burst open.

Detective Ross looked at Manny. "Well, that wasn't too tough. This woman is supposed to be our perp?"

Manny cruised through the door and almost into laughter. Big Frank Wymer was sitting on the worn velour sofa, flabby leg draped over the midsection of a young woman who was half dressed in black lingerie and a short leather skirt. She was handcuffed to his thick right arm. The woman's eyes were wet, but spitting fire, as she struggled helplessly against the leg that must have weighed as much as she did.

"Hey, Manny. Look what I found. Can I take her home? I don't think the wife will mind too much."

His captive started to speak, but was having trouble catching her breath. "Get-t-t that-t thing . . . off . . . me!" she panted.

"Are you going to behave?" asked Manny. "If not, he's got another leg."

She nodded with the enthusiasm of a lottery winner. Manny motioned to Wymer, and he moved his leg. She gasped for air, and then jumped up, darting for the door, forgetting about the cuffs. She was jerked unceremoniously back to the couch, long legs flying over her head. A few seconds later, she was again pinned by the leg from hell.

"That wasn't nice." Manny slid the maple coffee table over and sat close to her. "What's your name?" he asked. "And how old are you?"

"None of your business, and I don't remember. Get lard ass's leg off me, and let me go. I didn't do anything."

"That's not going to happen. What are you doing here?"

She gave Manny a sour look. "What the hell does it look like I'm doing, cleaning the freakin' carpet?"

"I think she broke my wrist," complained Wymer. "Can someone get me some ice?"

"The gentleman that lives here didn't call you, or anyone else. So I'll ask again, why are you here?"

"Some gentleman. I got this one like I get all of my appointments. I got a message from my . . . business associate . . . to be here at 10:30."

"Does this look broken to you?" moaned the big detective.

"How did your business associate get the message to be here?"

"I guess from the bulletin board at the church. How the hell do I know? I just go where I need to go."

Sophie leaned over to Manny. "There was nothing dangerous in her purse, unless you count cherry-flavored condoms and a small whip. I kinda like the whip; it's cute."

"Nothing else?"

Sophie shook her head. "That's it, want to see?"

This was beginning to stink like roadkill on a hot day. He hated it. It was becoming obvious they had been set up. In a big way. But the caller had been right about the time and the place and even what the woman was wearing.

This made no sense.

He stood up and paced to the apartment's front window, then turned back to the young hooker. "Listen, I don't care about the prostitution thing, not tonight. I just need some answers."

"What do I look like, the Internet? I got nothing."

"I don't think I want her after all," said Wymer. "She's too mean. Just like the wife."

Manny ignored him and bent closer to the girl's face. "I wanted to do this the easy way." He turned to Ross and Sophie. "Detectives, take her downtown and book her as an accessory to murder and anything else that you can think of."

The young prostitute's eyes grew to the size of small tires. "Murder? What? I didn't . . . All right, all right." She looked at Manny, and he saw the scared little girl that had become a woman long before her time. His heart broke a bit. He wondered what had happened to her and promised himself to find out, but not tonight.

"Frank, take the cuffs off, and for God's sake, lift that tree stump off her."

Wymer swung his leg off her for a second time and unlocked and removed the handcuffs, rubbing his wrist. "I think a bag of M&Ms would help ease the pain."

"My name's Shannon and I'm . . . seventeen. And I didn't kill nobody. I don't even like to see no dead animals."

"Fair enough, Shannon. Tell me how you got this gig."

"I called my contact and he said he got a call from some woman asking for someone like me, tall and stuff, to show up here, wearing all black, including this hoodie thing, which is so not cool, but he said the trick would be triple my normal fee. I need the money, so it's all good."

She gave Manny a pathetic look. "I'm not gettin' paid, am I?"

"No, but maybe we can swing a good meal."

“Do you like M&Ms?” asked Frank.

Manny gave him a look, and he shuffled over to his partner.

“Anything else?”

“I swear. It was just like always. He calls, I go.” She wagged her head. Then her eyes brightened. “Wait! My contact said the phone number on his caller ID was strange-ass.”

“Strange? Like how?”

“I don’t like giving away this stuff. I could get hurt.”

“I promise, you won’t get hurt. We’ll make sure you don’t.”

“You cops always say that. Whatever. Anyway, like I said, the call came from a strange place.”

“Where?”

She looked at Frank. “I’d like some of those M&Ms.” Then back to Manny.

“It came from the ICU at Eagle Memorial Hospital.”

Chapter-41

Standing on the stoop, outside the apartment complex, Manny's mind raced. They had been set up, of course, but it didn't make sense. Why? What purpose? And why give them the right place and time, but not the unsub? It was almost like a chess game with a third player countering each move. He hated where this was leading. He'd called dispatch to send a unit to Gavin's room, just to make sure he and Stella were safe. Maybe the call originated from the man, or woman, who shot Gavin . . . in fact, that was a sure bet. Manny tried to fight the story that logic was trying to sell him, but the knot in the pit of his stomach refused to allow him to win that fight.

Could what I am thinking even be conceivable?

He wanted to talk to Mike again about his back-up weapon, where it was the last time he saw it, but maybe he already knew that answer.

If Shannon was telling the truth, and he was sure she was, there was no denying the possibility that Stella saw something, or someone, that didn't belong at the ICU. He closed his eyes and gave in to the thoughts.

Was Stella involved?

It sounded alien, contrived, except for a persistent ring of truth.

Stella involved? A few days ago that was pure fantasy. He'd known her for seventeen years. She'd been a great mother and wife. Supportive, witty, practical. She loved her family. Maybe dealing with Lexy's death had been too much. But he hadn't noticed anything different in her behavior. She had changed her hair, lost a little weight, but nothing drastic.

Sophie drove the car to the front of the building, got out, and stood on the sidewalk. "Hey, Ross and Wymer took Shannon out for a late supper and then are going to take her home."

"Good. Remind me to check on her when we get a minute to breathe."

"I know this is tough, but we have to talk to Stella to see if she saw anything. I mean, come on; it was right on that floor. The nurse's station is only fifty feet away," said Sophie, reaching to adjust her leg holster.

He nodded, face tight-lipped, watching her wrestle with the holster. Manny had another thought.

"Do you know what kind of back-up weapon Mike carried?"

"Yeah, I do. We bought ours at the same time. It was a Firestorm .22. Why?"

Suddenly all of the pieces clicked together. His stomach clutched even harder, and a small wave of nausea washed over him. It was becoming all too clear. Hadn't he suggested to Sophie that the person who shot Gavin could be a woman? And all of the victims were shot with a .22.

He took out his cell phone and spoke to Sophie. "We're going to the hospital."

"Okay . . . but . . . oh shit. You don't think it could be Stella, do you?"

Manny didn't reply as he tapped his foot on the concrete, waiting for Stella to pick up. The call went to her voice mail. His angst rose higher.

"Stella's not answering. Let's go."

Sophie flipped on the siren and burned the tread off the front tires, heading for the hospital.

"Mike wasn't lying. Stella *was* the shooter at his apartment complex. But why make the call from the hospital?" asked Sophie, sliding on her NASCAR Victory sunglasses.

"It's almost 11 p.m. Sunglasses? Really?"

"Relax. I got this."

Manny stared at the streetlights as they whizzed past his window. "Yeah. You got the first part. The call from the hospital only makes sense if she wanted us to know it was her. That means one of two things. She wants to get caught, to talk about whatever she's done. Or . . ."

"Or what?"

"Or she's lost it. Hell, I don't know. Maybe something to do with Lexy's death."

"Come on, can that happen? I mean, especially to her."

"I think it could. And to almost anyone, if the

circumstances were right. But I could be pissing in the wind. We need to talk to her."

"What do you mean 'lost it'? Like psycho?"

"It means she might become a second cousin to Argyle."

"Any chance she's just in a bad mood?"

"I wish it were that simple. The thing is, I didn't notice anything different about her . . . but again, I could be all wrong here."

"You don't sound too convincing."

Manny sighed. "I don't feel too convinced."

Sophie adjusted her glasses. "That's just plain scary."

"The mind can convince itself of anything, given the right conditions. Controlled studies show that with enough exposure, people will do just about anything that they have some predisposition to do. They just need a nudge in that direction."

"More scary crap . . . and how do you know this stuff?"

"Sometimes I wish I didn't. Too many books."

Sophie pulled up to the front door of the hospital, and they jumped out of the car, lights still flashing.

"We'll know in a couple of minutes," he said.

They rode the elevator to the ICU and were greeted by the two officers standing in front of Gavin's door. They were talking to the nurse Manny had seen earlier in the morning.

"Could you guys go get a cup of coffee?" he said to the two blues.

They nodded and left.

He turned to the nurse. “Do you ever sleep?”

She grinned. “I might ask you the same thing. I’m pulling a double, or maybe a triple. I forget.”

“We know the feeling. How’s he doing?”

“He’s unchanged, but hanging in there.” She glanced at Sophie, then back to Manny. “What’s going on?”

He let out a sigh of relief. “Nothing. We got some bad info, that’s all. Is Stella in his room?”

The nurse shook her head. “No. She left a couple of hours ago. She said enough was enough for the day. She wanted to be alone.”

Manny ran his hand through his hair. No denying the truth now. “Did she call anyone before she left?”

“She did, about 8:30. She asked to use the phone, saying her cell was dead. I reminded her there was no cell phone use inside the ICU anyway. We’re not supposed to do it, but I let her make the call. It’s against hospital policy, but what they don’t know won’t hurt them. She thanked me and said she’d be back in a few hours.”

“In this case, I’m glad you ignored policy. Can you print out a phone log?”

She reached into her pocket and handed him a piece of paper. “I already did. Tech support brought it up a minute ago. I figured, once those officers got here, something was up. I thought you might need that number.”

“Good thinking. You want a job?” cracked Sophie.

The nurse laughed. "I wouldn't trade places with you guys for a million bucks."

"The feeling's mutual," smiled Manny.

A buzzer sounded, and a blue light flashed furiously outside one of the other rooms. "Gotta go." Then she was hustling down the hall.

"I rest my case. I couldn't do that."

"I see what you mean. But those little nurse outfits are cute. I could get one and cut it really short. Do you think Josh would like it?"

"You mean Randy, your husband?"

"Him too. But I'm thinking about building a better relationship with the Feds. Couldn't hurt."

"You've got issues, you know that?"

"True, but that's another reason to love me."

"Keep reminding me. Put out an APB on Stella—that sounds so damn ridiculous—I'm going to check on Gavin, and then we have to get to the airport. Alex wouldn't be happy if we were late for the forensics meeting. Maybe the six of us can figure out what she's up to."

"I'll wait here for the other guys to come back. Maybe I'll get to see more blue lights."

Manny moved closer to Gavin's bed and wondered what his take would be on all of this. Then it occurred to him what Gavin's view would be.

"The truth," he would say. "Always go after the truth. It might hurt sometimes, but you can't go wrong with it."

He wondered if Gavin could follow his own advice, given that his wife probably shot him at point-blank range.

Turning to leave, he saw a yellow piece of paper on the table beside Gavin's bed. Manny's name was printed near the fold in Stella's handwriting. His heart rate pranced as he reached for the note and unfolded it slowly, reluctantly, like the words would speak a sermon he didn't care to hear, one of damnation and revelation at the same time. He was right.

"**Don't worry about looking for me. I'm in the wind for as long as I want to be. There's another mess that I cleaned up for you. You'll have to find it yourself, if you can.**"

Several blank lines down, written as an afterthought was a three-word warning.

"**Your time's coming.**"

Chapter-42

"We have trouble. She didn't go where she was supposed to, and I think she figured out it was a setup somehow." The tall woman took a long draw from her cigarette and released it. The gray-blue smoke rose and danced in front of her face, then slowly drifted away.

"I know," replied the shorter member of the Justice Club.

"What? It's only 11:30. How in the hell do you know?"

"How in God's name do you think I know? The real question is how did Stella find out this gig was a con?" Curiosity dripped from the shorter woman's voice.

"Oh no. Not me. Let's get this out of the way. It wasn't me. I didn't tip her off. I agreed with you on this one. Remember?"

The shorter woman heard the anger in the other's voice. That was good enough for her. "Fair enough. I believe you. But that's not important now anyway."

The taller woman let out a long breath. "You're

right. If she's gone rogue, we're all in trouble."

"She knows everything about us. What we do. Where we go . . . and what we've done."

"Almost true. She doesn't know *everything.*"

"What does that mean?"

"It means we have a trick up our sleeve," said the tall woman.

"What kind of trick? When we did this, we promised no secrets, and now you're telling me that's not true?"

"Relax. I'm pretty good at covering our asses, and this was a need-to-know thing."

"I appreciate your concern. But trust is trust, and right now I'm not feeling it. So, no more horseshit. What is it?" demanded the shorter member of the Justice Club.

"You're kind of cute when you get pissy," the tall woman giggled.

"I don't feel cute. Get to it."

The tall woman took another drag from her cancer stick and released it. "There's a fourth member of the club."

Chapter-43

Sophie stood near the door of the waiting room, killing time fumbling through her bag until Manny came out of Gavin's room. She wanted to remind him of their busy dance card for the next few hours and that they needed to go, but she suspected he was close to full-bore cop mode and didn't need any reminders—of anything. He was scary when that persona kicked in. Like he was born to pull miscellaneous facts into full-blown pictures that made sense. There were things no one else could see, and leaps no one else could make. Putting together Stella with Gavin's shooting, Mike's gun, Blake Harris's murder, then the setup at the apartment complex had to be killing him on the inside. And she suspected he had it figured out long before he said anything.

She dabbed on a few strokes of lip liner and pulled out a stick of gum. Manny told her once that he had had dinner at the Crosby's place so many times that their home felt as familiar as the rural farmhouse near the town of North Star where he'd grown up. Stella and Gavin had even become somewhat surrogate parents after his parents had died in a car accident fifteen years ago. He and his family had become a real part of Gavin's and Stella's lives, even being a kind of big brother to Mike. Now everything was haywire, nuts, and changed forever. Stella's newfound purpose, or whatever the hell she was thinking, was at the center of it all. Sophie shivered.

How would she handle finding out that her surrogate mother had gone off the deep end, shot her husband, and was murdering men after burning off their johnsons with acid? (Although she'd met a few men over the years that could use the acid treatment: her ex, for one.)

Manny's MO was about to come into play, like usual. He'd suppress any emotional ties and go to work. She admired that trait in him and, although it exacerbated the workaholic addiction he fought so hard to control, it also scared her. How far into the dark would he choose to walk to totally disconnect his emotion from the job? She worried a time was coming when he couldn't make it back, that the dark would be more appealing than the light. But as long as Louise and Jen were with him, she thought he'd be okay. They were his *reason.*

Manny walked out of Gavin's room, a note hanging from his hand and a look on his face that could only be described as hollow.

"Is Gavin okay? 'Cause you look like he just bit it."

"No, he's fighting hard." He handed Sophie the

note.

She read it, and her eyes darted to his face. "Manny I . . . I . . ." She couldn't remember all the times he'd been there for her. The divorce and her remarriage, the affair with Lynn Casnovsky, and everything in between. Always strong, as reliable as the sunrise. It was her turn.

Sophie did something rare for her—she stopped talking and hugged him.

He squeezed her back, and then he stepped away. "Thanks Sophie. This one hurts. Thirty-six hours ago, I had lunch with them. We laughed about Stella's diet-plate special. Now she wants to take me out?"

"You're the brains, but it seems to me we won't know what's really going on until we bring her in."

He smiled. "That's good thinking from the one who says she never does."

"Hey. I have to leave something for you to do. I kind of like having you around."

"The feeling's mutual. But enough of the touchy-feely stuff. It's time to go to work."

He stood up straight, and Sophie watched most of the pain on his face disappear like rain on a desert highway. He was no longer Manny Williams, the surrogate son, the caring man who loved the Crosbys, but Manny Williams, the cop. The transformation was startling and comforting at the same time.

As they reached the elevator, a small smile formed on her face. If she knew her partner—and she did—the bad guys were in deep shit.

Chapter-44

Manny greeted the FBI agents seated around the table, careful to regard Chloe the same as Josh and Max, but he couldn't ignore the tingle that danced in the middle of his chest. She looked . . . amazing.

"Long time, no see," said Manny.

"Too long," pined Sophie, batting her eyes at Josh.

"Ah . . . it's been thirty-six hours, but good to see you . . . both," replied Josh.

"So you did miss me, didn't you?" said Sophie.

"Absence makes the heart grow fonder, detective," smiled Josh.

This time, it was Sophie's turn to wear a slack-jaw expression. Manny watched to see how his loquacious partner was going to react to being put on the other side of the innuendo fence. Before she could respond, Alex came to her rescue.

"Well, well. I'm glad you two cleared out your schedules so that you could join the rest of us, who are up at freaking 12:30 a.m. working instead of sleeping, like normal people get to do."

“Sorry. We got tied up at the hospital,” apologized Manny as he and Sophie sat.

“Besides, it does you good to get your panties in a bunch once in a while,” said Sophie, that infamous mischievous look prancing in her eyes.

“Really? Are you the new department shrink? And I don’t wear panties,” responded Alex.

“Not what I heard.”

“We have work to do and no time for this crap . . . who told you that?”

“I can’t reveal my sources.”

Manny raised his hands. “Whoa. It wasn’t me. Besides, I thought you gave those up.”

Josh looked at Alex. “What kind of panties? The little leopard spot ones with lace?”

“What? I expect this crap from them, but you too?” scowled Alex.

“For the record, I guess I’d need to know too,” said Max, grinning. “You know, for future reference involving any other cases we might work. If panties come up missing, I’d know where they went.”

Alex released a sigh. “Are we done?”

“Hopefully. Those mental images were getting to me,” Chloe grinned, pouring more coffee.

Manny settled back in his chair, looking at the files stacked in front of Alex. “Before we get on to the forensic evidence, we need to talk.”

“We don’t have much to go over anyway,” said Alex. “You all have the reports, and I gave the rest a rundown of the MO from notes-in-the-nose to acid type.”

"Glad I didn't piss off this killer," added Josh. "I've grown fond of the men below."

"Haven't we all," smiled Sophie.

Josh cleared his throat and leaned back in his chair. "When will I learn?"

"Learn what? Whatever it is, I'm a great teacher," said Sophie.

Alex rolled his eyes. "Anyway, the ballistics are weird and Sparky's working on that. It's tough to get a match from the hollow points, but not impossible. Plus, we're analyzing the black leather they were all tied with and hope to know where the straps came from soon. We also figured out the small marks on the backs of the victims appear to be high-heel shoe punctures. More to come."

"Thanks, Alex." Leaning forward, Manny spread his hands on the table and sorted out thoughts he never imagined he'd have.

"I had Mike Crosby released. Stella Crosby is involved in these murders, and I believe she shot Gavin."

His statement resounded like fireworks through the conference room, bringing the lighter mood to a halt and replacing it with something from a darker realm. Much darker.

"Are you sure?" asked Josh.

"One hundred percent." He tossed the note that Stella had written to the special agent. "And that's not all."

Josh read the message, frowning, and then read it again before he passed it to Chloe. "First things first. Why would Stella do that, or be involved in any of this?"

Manny looked to the ceiling then back to Josh. "I don't know. It's been killing me. Maybe Lexy's death snapped something precious in her mind. It could be—no, probably is, a first psychotic episode."

"Brought on by stress, or depression, at least that's what the experts say," confirmed Chloe. "Unusual, but it makes some sense here."

"It does. Lexy was treated so brutally that . . . well, you saw it. We all did our best, but maybe Stella blames us, in particular Gavin and me. God knows we blamed ourselves," said Manny. "I mentioned to Sophie that her behavior fits with that kind of trauma. People react in different ways. This is her response."

"So, she figures what good are you two? She wants to make you pay the price and do what the system can't do, at least in her eyes," nodded Chloe.

"By taking out these other sickos, she thinks she's doing the world a favor," said Sophie.

Manny shrugged his shoulders. "That's my best guess. Stella's turning fantasy into reality. I believe she's swimming in the middle of an ocean of pain that she thinks will never end."

"I'm sorry, Manny. I know you're close," Josh said softly.

The emotion welled up, and it was all Manny could do to keep it inside. Life was constantly changing, that was hard to deny. But changes like this translated into losses that would last the rest of his life. It would take awhile to get his mind around it. Maybe more than awhile. "I'll deal with it later; I just never saw it coming."

"Who would?" said Max.

"I guess you're right, but it doesn't make it any easier."

Josh slid the note back to Manny. "What do you mean that's not all?"

Manny explained the call warning him of another murder and the phone call Stella made from the hospital. "I still believe the information was totally legitimate, that Stella was supposed to be at that apartment, but something went wrong."

"And that she knew you'd find out about the call from the hospital, so you'd come running to Gavin's room, thus the note," said Chloe.

"I do, and she was right."

"But you don't think she made the warning call to your cell, do you?" asked Josh.

"No, I don't."

"Oh crap. That means—" moaned Sophie.

"—that we have more than one killer here. And I think they're women." Manny frowned and finished his thought. "There might be more than two."

"I'll give you that the other shooter could be female. It makes sense. But more than two? Why would you say that?" asked Alex.

"I think the timeline for the murders, counting Gavin's shooting, might be too tight for two people." Manny leaned forward. "If Stella did what she says she did, she left Gavin's office about 8:55 p.m. Mike claims he saw her leaving his apartment complex about five and a half hours later."

"The department called Stella to tell her about Gavin at 3:20 a.m., then picked her up to go to the hospital."

"I follow you so far," said Josh.

"The guy on the west side, Ben Morgan, was killed about 3 a.m., then the victim on the north end, Arlo Becker, maybe an hour later. She couldn't have been involved in either of those attacks."

"True, regarding the times. You're making my head hurt, but true, nonetheless," said Alex.

"But you can't pinpoint the exact times of death, right?" Manny scribbled on a note pad.

"Yeah, not exactly, but there is no doubt Morgan was killed first. The science says so."

"So, the killer would've needed twenty minutes to get to the north side, persuade Becker to let her in, do whatever she did, tie him up, use the acid, shoot him, then dump his body by the shopping center on the north end where he was found about 5 a.m."

"Sounds tight, but it could be done," said Max.

Manny shook his head. "According to the officer who discovered Morgan's body on the West side, he wasn't in that parking lot at 5:30 a.m., but he was there twenty minutes later on his next neighborhood round. So that—"

"—means the second victim was dumped

before the first," finished Alex.

The room grew silent. The implication that three killers were involved was staggering. Getting three people to agree to anything for very long was not an easy task, let alone to agree on some kind of vigilante partnership.

"I think that explains the call I received. And since I got the call after the guy was offed in Mike's apartment complex and since that crime didn't fit the MO of the other three victims, my guess is that the group didn't care for Stella's Lone Ranger act," said Manny, breaking the silence.

"Why? A dead pervert is a dead pervert to them, right?" quizzed Sophie.

"I get it, I think. If the other two thought she was putting their special project in danger, they'd set her up for a fall. But then what?" said Chloe. "What if she spills her guts? They all go to prison."

"Maybe they weren't worried about that. I mean, how would Stella know that she was conned? To her, it could've been bad luck. She'd take the fall. The others would let things cool off, and then, later, finish what they started," answered Manny, sipping his coffee. "Or maybe she was tipped off. Hell, maybe she figured it out. We don't have enough information to be sure."

"Okay. Now *my* head is starting to hurt," groaned Sophie. "That could mean that Stella is out there, doing her own thing, and she's pissed because she was betrayed."

"Actually, I'm not," came the voice from the open door.

Manny turned his head and saw Stella Crosby, dressed in hooker black, blood streaked down her skirt, standing at the door with a gun pointed at his head.

Chapter-45

The fourth member of the Justice Club, calling herself Penny, sat inside the stolen SUV parked down the street just east of the LPD headquarters, window down, inviting the warm air to sit with her. It carried with it the scent of the city, her city, subtle but unmistakable.

The CD player loosened a sound that was elevator music to most, but not to her. Penny loved the old tunes and the men that made them come alive. Not just Glenn Miller, Jimmy Dorsey, and Count Basie, and all that Big Band sound, but Old Blue Eyes, Sammy Davis, Jr., Bing Crosby, and, of course, Dean Martin. Tony Bennett could make her cry, and none were better than Andy Williams . . . except the one singing right now, just for her.

"Unforgettable, that's what you are..."

His middle name said it all. Nat King Cole was the brightest star in the sky, and you were simply a damned fool if you didn't believe it.

"God knows there's a shitload of those out there," she said softly.

Take Stella Crosby for instance. She had come undone. Stupid bitch. The Club had a good thing going, but Stella couldn't keep it together. She'd made things too private, and now they could all sail up Shitcreek without a paddle. And everybody knows how fast that creek can rise.

Penny had followed Stella from the time she left the hospital and knew she wasn't heading to the drop spot to pick up the gun, but had another path in mind. And why not? The so-called leader of their tight-knit killing Club had betrayed Stella. And Stella would never have known about the setup if Penny hadn't intervened. All it had taken was a brief, anonymous call to warn Stella that things weren't looking good for tonight . . . and why. Stella had reacted predictably, took care of the next sick bastard on the hit list, setting things up for this very moment. For Stella *and* her.

King Nat switched tunes and she closed her eyes, taking in every nuance of the King of Crooner's talent. God in heaven, she loved his music.

"Hey."

Penny jumped, but held her poise. Her years involved with law enforcement had taught her well. She glanced over to the source of the greetings. A young uniform was leaning in her open window grinning like an idiot Cheshire cat. She hated cats.

"Hey yourself."

"What are you doing out here this late? Surveillance?"

"Close, more like undercover." The look on his face turned so serious she almost laughed out loud.

"I didn't know . . . does Manny . . . my gosh. Did I just blow it? I'm so sorry. I should keep moving, right? Oh crap!"

"No harm, no foul yet . . . but you're right, move your ass and get into the car, now."

The young officer rushed around to the passenger side, fumbled for the handle, finally made it work and climbed inside, breathing hard with excitement. "Wow. I never thought after only three months, I'd be sittin' in an undercover unit."

"Well, it's not really an undercover unit; I just couldn't afford any witnesses."

"What witness? What do you . . . ?"

She put the .22 Smith and Wesson with the custom suppressor to his temple and pulled the trigger. His head jerked to the right and slammed against the door, then bounced back against the head rest. Warm blood quickly filled the seat, but it wasn't a problem. She was done here.

"Sorry, kid. Life is full of wrong places and wrong times."

Ejecting the CD, she put it in her bag. Then she reached into the backseat and pulled the large attaché case over the seat and got out.

She scanned the area. Satisfied that no one noticed her, she moved across the street to the old brick building directly adjacent to the LPD, with a full view of the LPD's large conference room window. Moving around back, she punched in the security code, closed the door, and moved up the four flights of steps to the fifth floor where she unpacked the M24 Remington 7.62mm rifle and snapped it together in seconds. She loaded six cartridges of M118 Special Ball ammo and racked one in the chamber.

Settling in front of the three-by-three window that gave her the best line of sight, she focused the M3A scope directly on her intended target.

Penny took a deep breath, remembering everything she'd learned in the life before this one and waited.

Chapter-46

"I want everyone to put their hands flat on the table, now. If any of you even twitch the wrong way, I'll empty this clip, and we'll see how many of you are still breathing."

Manny watched as she shifted her weight, eyes growing harder. Not good.

"I said now. I don't have all damned night."

"Easy, Stella. We're doing it," Manny said quietly.

"Don't start that easy-speaking, good-cop shit with me. I've heard it a million times. If you do it again, I'm going to puke, then start shooting."

She closed the heavy door behind her with the heel of her foot, never taking her eyes from the group. She moved a few feet to Manny's right. "At least you're smart enough to do what you're told. Not that it will do you, any of you, any good. You couldn't save Lexy, and you won't be able to save yourselves."

"We did our best, Stella," said Josh.

"Well, that wasn't good enough, was it? She's gone, you're not, and I've hated you all ever since."

Manny saw the tears welling in her eyes. He couldn't tell what was worse, the pain or the anger. He chose his words carefully. "So, Gavin first, then me, then the others?"

"Gavin was even worse than the rest of you. He not only let her die, but he let me die, too. I wasted away on the inside, and he wasn't there for me; he just wallowed in his own pity. My biggest regret is not putting a couple more rounds in him."

She smiled a wicked grin. It reminded Manny of the lunatic they'd taken down on the cruise ship.

"As far as the rest of you go, let's just say I brought a couple extra clips and the acid."

"Acid? Whoa. I don't even have a wong," said Sophie.

"True. So maybe I'll just shoot you a couple more times."

"What? Not in the face though, okay?"

"Stop talking," said Stella.

Manny's mind was racing. She fully intended to carry out her threat. "It's not too late to stop. There are people who can help you."

"Oh, I found help. I found support. Not too conventional, but it worked for me. It took some time, but we decided that if people like Argyle and the perverts we've already taken care of got away with doing what they do, why not us?"

"But cold-blooded murder?" said Sophie. "They did their time."

"You call that justice? They get to ruin the

lives of women, and even little girls, forever, and they get a few years in prison, then get out to do it again. If you think that's right, then you're dumber than I thought. Much dumber. That's why we formed the Justice Club."

Manny had seen the wild, out-of-control look on the faces of others. It hurt to think she'd gone this far.

"So, because we're cops, part of the system, your Club decided we have to go too?" asked Alex, his voice shaking.

"No. Not the Club, just me. You have to go because you let Argyle and Jenkins kill my new daughter. That makes you screw-ups . . . and also you're part of the system. That's enough strikes in this game."

"You're gonna shoot me a couple times? Really?" said Sophie, disbelief in her voice.

"Maybe three if you don't shut up."

Chloe turned her eyes to Stella. "Your Club set you up. Some support that turned out to be."

Stella flinched, her hand tightening on the gun. Manny knew Chloe had hit a nerve. It was a classic technique to throw off her game, hoping she'd make a mistake.

Gavin's wife relaxed and smiled. "Nice try. What goes on in the Club, stays in the Club. We'll work it out . . . because we're not finished."

"Stella, I—"

She put the gun to Manny's head and bent close. "Enough talk. This is over."

"Like hell it is," yelled Sophie, springing from

her chair, lunging for Stella in one motion.

Manny pushed his chair back violently, knocking Stella off balance. He reached for his Glock but never made it. Shots were fired, and at the same time, the conference room window exploded into a million pieces. He felt pain on the back of his head, and his world went black.

Chapter-47

The tall woman nibbled at her chicken salad sandwich while she sat inside the 2002 Chevy Blazer in the employee's parking area. Twelve thirty a.m. had taken forever to get here. She couldn't have taken much more tonight. The ogling, the intended clever remark that was supposed to make her want the man who said it with an uncontrollable lust. But instead of accomplishing the desired effect, the words caused her nausea to rise and her thoughts of murder or suicide to increase. God knew she'd rather die, or watch them die, than to sleep with any of them, even the good-looking ones. *Especially* the good-looking ones. They all had needs better satisfied at a damn zoo.

She drank from her coffee cup, looking down at her long legs. That wasn't the worst of it though, was it? There existed a healthy desire for sex, one that was natural between men and women, one she'd never really experienced, not yet anyway. She was sure it was there. Maybe even the knight in shining armor that wanted to take her away to a different, even normal life. But all she ever noticed in the eyes of her patrons was the evil feeling of depravity that accompanied men in heat as they undressed her with their eyes. She wasn't a woman to them, but a place, a thing that would allow them to act out their most secret perversions. Furthermore, they thought that since she worked where she worked, she was ready and willing to be a part of any sick fantasy they wanted.

All they had to do was hand her an envelope stuffed with money, and she was going to climb on board the ship they were sailing. She shook her head and smiled to herself. The look of surprise when she turned away each request to be treated like a blow-up doll was absolutely wonderful. Their reactions ranged from pure anger to utter embarrassment, and she reveled in it. The pervs would all go out the door wondering why, and she supposed, trying to figure out what to do with a libido raging higher than the Sears Tower.

Another date with Rosie and the sisters.

She finished her coffee and wrapped up the rest of her sandwich. Not everyone was turned away, at least in the last few weeks. There was the money thing, which always helped, but it was much more. There was a certain type that she needed to be with to make her feel alive. Everyone had a button, *the* button, that could send them to the top of the world and perhaps into outer space. When that climax of utter bliss arrived, it was like the soul separated from the body, causing a person to stop breathing because, for the moment, breathing wasn't important, only that feeling, that release.

She was no different. She had needs too, albeit, a tad different than most. She smiled. That just might be the understatement of the year. After all, wasn't that what the Club was all about? Things had gotten a little harried the last day or so, but that was about to be handled.

The slanted headlights flashed her mirror as the 2011 Mercedes-Benz E-Sedan 3.5L pulled up beside her. The driver got out, bending his homely, unshaven face toward her, almost falling through the open window of her car.

"Are ya Cat?" His breath was just this side of putrid.

"Who wants to know?"

He grinned, yellow and black lacing the teeth he had left. "This secret stuff just gets me harder. I be Cooldaddy. We talked las' night."

She nodded. "Any trouble getting the vehicle?"

"Not for me, darling. I've been doin' this stuff for a long time."

"Good. You just got out. I'd hate to see you go back."

"I didn't go ta prison for that. It was somthin' else. I ain't never been caught stealin' a car."

She felt him staring at her breasts and saw him lick his lips, trying to control the trembling.

"I been away awhile, and I'd like to get this party started. I got the car ya wanted, the kind ya said gets you hot, so can we go?" His face contorted into something halfway between a smile and a leer.

This was going to be remarkably good.

"Sure, baby. You get back in the car, and let me get my bag," she said, drawing her skirt up, showing him her red lace panties. "Then we'll go someplace quiet and rid you of those years of suffering."

Sweat popped out on his forehead. He stared another few seconds.

"Mercy," he whispered and scrambled into the Mercedes-Benz.

She checked her look in the mirror and reached for the large black shoulder bag resting in the passenger seat. She did one last inventory of the toys needed for the night's playtime. Her hand brushed the black-leather wrist bindings and the vial of hydrochloric acid as she gripped the .22 and stuffed it into the front pocket of the bag. It wouldn't be good for the founder of the Justice Club to be unprepared. Not good at all.

Chapter-48

The shimmering fog filtered out the light that shone in the distance, and he wondered if he was in a dream. But it didn't feel like a dream. He was sure he could feel his feet and that never happens in dreams. Maybe his ticket had been punched, and the beckoning light he'd read about when people die was what he saw shrouded through the haze, just out of comprehension. So this was how the great mystery started. The journey into the afterlife. He felt a tinge of excitement . . . then a voice sounding far away robbed him of that excitement.

"For God's sake man, answer me. Manny!"

Sophie? He loved his partner, but he wasn't sure he wanted her floating into eternity with him. This was personal. She'd get her chance, probably sooner rather than later.

Another noise brought him completely out of his daze, and his eyes flew open just in time to hear another round of high-powered gunfire explode the computer screen near the front of the conference room. He was now fully awake—and just as aware of the throbbing pain in the back of his neck and his forehead. His head was in some kind of humongous vice, and Godzilla was turning the crank.

"Manny. Are you all right?" Sophie prodded. He turned his head, fought the black curtain that threatened to throw him back into Never-Never Land, and stared into Sophie's anxious gaze.

"Yeah. I guess so." He looked past her shoulder, noticed the FBI crew lying flat, side-by-side, under the conference room table. Alex sprawled to his left. Another shot rattled the corner of the table above Manny's head, turning the wood into so many toothpicks.

Another wave of dark nausea passed in front of his eyes. He waited, hoping for it to pass. It did, taking its sweet time.

Finally, he opened his eyes and grabbed Sophie's wrist. "What the hell is going on, and where is Stella?"

Sophie glanced over her shoulder searching Josh's face and looked away. "She's dead, Manny. The first shot hit her in the back of the neck. She flew on top of you and you hit your head on the table. Part . . . part of her is over there and the rest . . ." She pointed. He twisted his head, more nausea, but it was lessening—and he didn't care anyway; he had to see.

Stella Crosby, his surrogate mother (adopted big sister at least), lay sprawled on her back. Her head was tilted at a severe angle. There was a section of her right shoulder and neck missing, but her face seemed to be untouched. Stella gazed at the ceiling with the haunting stare he'd seen far too often in the last three months. Deep stains of crimson surrounded the upper portion of her body, the bloodied .22 that she was going to shoot him with lay inches from his feet.

Another shot slammed through the chair to Stella's left and hammered the wall. Manny pulled his eyes away from Stella's body and ducked his head.

Odd. He felt a sudden sensation of relief, immediately followed with an awful sense of searing guilt. Relief that it was over, that she wouldn't be a threat to anyone again. But guilt that said he should have been there, should have seen what she was going through. He could have helped.

"Manny. I know that look, that Guardian of the Universe thing. You couldn't have helped her. She'd made up her mind to travel on the dark side of the moon. It was her choice," soothed Sophie. "And there was that other thing."

"I know. I know. But to go like this . . . what other thing?"

"She was going to shoot me in the face. You heard her. That wasn't going to happen."

"That's why you jumped her?"

"Hell, yes. Can you think of a better reason?"

"I thought you were distracting her so I could get the gun?"

"Ah . . . well, okay. That too."

"Can we talk about this later? We have a tiny

problem here," said Josh. "You need to keep your asses down."

"Josh," said Chloe, barely raising her head from the carpet.

"What is it?"

"I've been timing the shots. They were about seven seconds apart, except the last one, which was about twenty-five seconds."

"Reloading?"

"I don't think so. The sniper can't stay there all night. He, or she, has to know help's coming."

"She's right," agreed Manny. "How long since the last one?"

"Over thirty seconds. I think the shooter got the hell out of Dodge."

"Only one way to find out," said Manny. He crawled toward the door, stopping at the edge of the table, and lifted one of the fallen chairs above the table top. He waited.

The only noise coming from the window was the breeze flowing from the late night air.

A few seconds later, Manny dropped the chair and glanced back to the others under the table. "Let's hope this works."

"What are you going to do?" asked Sophie.

"I'm going to stand up."

"Wait. Can't you like raise your hands or arm or something? It'd be better than your melon."

"How long, Chloe?"

"Ninety seconds."

"That's good enough for me."

Manny crawled two yards, took a deep breath,

and lurched to his feet.

Chapter-49

"How's the noggin?" asked Sophie, plopping down beside Manny in the burgundy leather chair. She had to almost yell because of the din inside the conference room. It was buzzing with forensic techs and LPD personnel practically stepping over each other.

He moved the blue ice pack to the back of his neck. "I'll live, but a couple more pain killers could be in my future."

"Mine too, but not for the same reason as you," she grinned.

"Recreational? You?"

"I know. Hard to believe, but how else do you think I keep my edge? Good looks and brains only go so far." Sophie's face turned serious. "I have a question for you."

"All right, but nothing too strenuous for a few more minutes. I have to get these bells to stop ringing."

"I know what you mean. So this is a tough question and no dancing around. I need a straight answer."

"Sounds serious."

"It is." She let out a breath. "Do you think I should get breast implants?"

"What? Why?"

"I think it could enhance my career goals. I might even make lieutenant with bigger ta-tas, say 38DD. Besides, I read a couple blogs and checked out a bunch of porno sites where Asian women with big boobs get lots of action. Men think they're hotter than habanera peppers dipped in jalapeño sauce."

"Seriously?"

"Hey, I don't kid about this stuff. Lots of men have some real kinky itches that only we Orientals can scratch. So yeah, I'm thinking about it."

"No. I mean there are blogs out there talking about Asian women with big breasts?"

She patted Manny's arm. "I need to get you plugged in." Then she moved over to where the FBI threesome was conferring with Alex.

He wasn't sure he wanted to get plugged in, Sophie style.

The new smartphone was growing warm in his hand. He wanted to call his wife and tell Louise that one of her close friends was gone, that she and Stella wouldn't be doing lunch anymore. But each time he pushed the speed-dial button, he hung up just as fast.

He finally put the phone in his pocket. He would tell her face-to-face when he got home. They would sit on the sofa, close together, and he'd be there for her. He'd make the time, somehow.

A minute later, the ME tech rolled the gurney toward the door with Stella's body enveloped in a black body bag. Manny watched her go, realizing his sense of surrealism had never been stronger. Gavin was in the ICU fighting for his life, and now this.

Stella had changed, gone deep into the realm of hatred and fear. He'd never know why, completely, and for the hundredth time, he asked himself why he hadn't seen it. But people mostly only let you see what they want you to see. Mostly. She must have been tortured on a level he never suspected.

For reasons he wasn't sure he'd ever understand, he stood up and stopped the ME tech. He took in a deep breath and unzipped the bag. Her eyes were closed, and she looked almost serene.

He lowered his face and kissed her on the forehead. "Goodbye, Stella. I'll miss you," he whispered.

He motioned for the tech to keep going. Maybe she'd find some peace in the next life. He hoped so. God said it was true.

Manny slid back in his chair, switching the ice pack to his forehead and wondering which way to go next. He didn't have to wonder long.

Agent Corner moved beside him, joined by Chloe and Sophie. "Manny, I know this is tough, but we've got more issues and have to get things in gear. We need you thinking straight. Are you up to it? I mean, I'd understand—"

"I'm as ready as I'll ever be. What do we have?"

He met Josh's even stare with one of his own, and the agent nodded slowly and motioned to the window. "Let's go over there."

Once over to the large, blown out windowsill, Josh pointed to the old brick building across the street. "The shots came from that window on the fifth floor. The shooter was using M118 Special Ball ammo. We found one spent casing. Nasty stuff. Alex and Max went to the lab to give it a once over, hoping to get lucky with a print or something. That kind of ammo can pierce light armor from 125 yards. It's pretty standard issue for military snipers—and contract hit men."

"But you don't believe this was a hit man, right?" asked Manny.

"No. Too sloppy," said Josh.

"We're lucky the sniper wasn't a great shot," added Chloe. "Assuming the shooter was a member of their Justice Club and a woman, which makes sense, she just got a small part of Stella's neck and shoulder, and the ammo did the rest. The other shots weren't close. For some reason, the shooter couldn't hit the broad side of a barn after that. Nerves maybe."

"I don't think so," Manny shook his head. "Ouch. Got to stop doing that."

"What do you mean?" asked Josh.

"Chloe said it was about seven seconds in between shots. So that means the shooter was in a rhythm. Hitting Stella from that distance, through thick glass, means she, if it was a she, knew what she was doing. To miss us after that was virtually impossible. There's something else." He pointed to what was left of the computer monitor. "The shot pattern, after hitting Stella, is a perfect arc from right to left."

"So the next five shots were cover fire so she could get out of the building and escape?" frowned Sophie.

"I think so. She knew help was coming. She would have planned for that, delaying that help could have given her a bit more time to get away."

"That means she wasn't after us. Just Stella," said Chloe. Manny noticed how the light caressed her face as she cocked her head. It was all he could do to not notice too long.

"If you're right, and we have this part figured out—" started Sophie.

"—then we have to answer the why question," finished Manny.

"But that should be obvious. I mean, we already know she broke rank. The Club must have been worried that she was going to screw things up and put them all behind bars," said Josh, his hands gesturing to emphasize his point.

"That's true, but remember what Stella said about working it out, that there wasn't a real problem. And on top of that, why wait until she's in the LPD conference room to take her out?" said Manny.

"Maybe they didn't know where she was?" interjected Sophie.

"We didn't find a cell phone on her or anything

else the Club could track her with, but I'm not buying that. It took time to get set up for the shot, so someone from the Club had to know," answered Manny.

"Okay, smartass, what's the answer?" asked Sophie.

"I'm not sure, but it's almost like the shooter was prot—"

"Detective Williams?"

He turned to see who had called his name.

Kathy Ross, followed by Frank Wymer, stepped through the door, Wymer with a super-sized chocolate shake in his plump hand.

"Frank? A chocolate shake at 1:30 a.m.?" marveled Sophie.

"Hey. Gotta keep up my strength."

Ross rolled her eyes. "Never mind that. We got a problem. In fact, we have three of them."

Chapter-50

"I don't see what's so special about you," snickered FBI Special Agent Jake Rosen as he bracketed Argyle's right side, with Agent Hoover on the left, while they walked through the secured concourse at Miami International Airport. "Just another deranged prick who thought he was smarter than the rest of us."

Argyle stared straight ahead.

"It's ridiculous that we have to shut down this end of the airport and escort your ugly mug to Lansing, wherever the hell that is, just because you're supposed to be some dangerous psycho. But I don't see it. You look like a pansy-ass to me, right, Doc?"

Argyle kept walking. No emotion or acknowledgment that he'd heard the agent. But he had, all too well.

"What? No comment? Didn't your momma teach you to answer when spoken to?" The agent rammed his elbow into Argyle's ribs. "I'm talking to you, murdering piece of shit."

Argyle never flinched as he managed to keep

pace with the two agents, even with the iron restraints restricting his mobility, but he stayed silent. There was a time for everything.

Rosen glanced to the other three Feds some twenty feet behind, shotguns resting across their arms. He leaned over to Agent Hoover. "I hear he has real problems gettin' it up," he whispered. "Am I right, Doc? No can launch the rocket?"

Argyle smiled. "Why don't you ask your wife and mother? They didn't seem to mind. In fact, I'm not sure which one screamed the loudest."

Rosen's mouth dropped open, and then Argyle watched him lose control.

The agent swung the billy club at Argyle's head like he was trying to take one deep into the seats of Comerica Park. Argyle moved as fast as any man in his position could and ducked beneath the blow. The stick nicked the top of his head and landed flush into the face of Rosen's counterpart, shattering his mouth into pieces and setting free a gushing stream of blood and broken teeth.

Before Rosen could draw the club a second time, Argyle moved close and hammered the agent's nose with his forehead, splitting it open and sending him to the tiled floor, blood instantly covering the agent's face.

Argyle heard the other agents coming up behind him, but they weren't fast enough. He dropped to his knees, bending close to Rosen's ear. "How do you like me now, agent? Not so much? Didn't *your momma* ever teach you not to play with things you didn't understand?"

"On the floor, face down, now," yelled one of the Feds behind him. "Or you're a dead man."

"Certainly, agents. No problem. I just need a second." He promptly bit off the top part of Rosen's ear, spitting it on the concourse floor as Rosen screamed in agony.

Argyle moved to all fours and slid to the floor as the rain of blows covered his head and neck. He began to laugh.

Chapter-51

"He took one in the head, up close, and that was it," pointed out Alex, leaning away from the passenger door of the vehicle. "He'd only been a cop a few months. Too bad."

"Damn. I think this is the kid that was going to get married next month," said Sophie.

Manny searched the sky, focusing on the amber moon hanging full in the heavens. A small, dark cloud floated just out of reach of the lunar brilliance, and he couldn't keep from noticing the contrast between the light and the dark cloud. Just like the concept of four murders in the last three hours were almost out of *his* comprehension.

"What kind of weapon?" he asked.

"Small caliber, probably a .22."

"Did we run the plates?"

Alex pulled at his ear. "It was stolen a few hours ago."

"So what the hell was he doing in a stolen SUV less than a block from headquarters during his dinner break?"

Alex shrugged his shoulders. "You're the

detective. I just tell you what's here. But if you're interested in my two cents, it looks like he was in the wrong place at the wrong time."

"Yeah. But what does that mean? He wouldn't have known the vehicle was stolen yet, so I don't think he was trying to bust anyone."

"The blood spatter and his position plus the amount of blood on the seat say he was in the vehicle when he was shot," answered Alex. "Sparky will be here soon with another tech, and I'll put them to work processing this thing."

"So, do you think he knew who shot him?" asked Sophie.

"That or he was forced inside," said Manny. "Either way, one of ours was murdered in cold blood."

"That's just for starters," said Sophie. "We got two more bodies that are probably compliments of the jacked-up Justice Club."

Manny looked to Alex, then Sophie. "What the hell is going on in this town?"

Just then two black Chevy Tahoes pulled up to the curb, a few feet behind the yellow tape, followed by Kathy Ross's LPD unit. Agent Tucker got out of the first vehicle, Josh and Chloe out of the second.

"I contacted the Detroit office and they still can't have people up here until the early morning. Meanwhile, what do you want us to do?" asked Josh.

"We got two more homicides to check out, so that's next," answered Manny.

"If this keeps up, we're going to have to move Quantico to Lansing."

"If this keeps up, I'm going to work for the FBI to get a break."

"Workaholics like you don't take breaks."

"I'm willing to learn."

Josh turned serious. "I want you to know that Argyle's on his way back to Lansing."

"So soon?" Manny raised his eyebrows. "I thought it would be a week or so."

"I pulled some strings and got him extradited here. Especially since he wasn't going to talk to anyone except you. I'm sure there are plenty more charges that your new DA will bring against him in Michigan. Besides, I'm curious about the 'others' he spoke of."

"If he killed others, or even by saying he did, he knows we'll want to find out the truth ASAP. I still think it's a ploy for him to control us. And to think, I'd almost forgotten about him for a couple of days."

"Not to mention the longer he stayed in St. Thomas, the harder it would've been to get him out of there," said Chloe. "Or he could've ended up accidentally dead."

Manny nodded. "There's no death penalty in Michigan. He knows he won't fry here."

"He could plead insanity," said Sophie.

"If he does, he'd still go to a Super Max prison, like ADX Florence. So either way, we win," said Josh.

"Yeah, enough about Argyle. We've got other

things going on," said Alex.

Sarah Sparks and the other woman lab tech, Dana Gary, walked up carrying large black cases and wearing blue, LPD-issue jumpsuits.

"Do you want us to start on the vehicle, Alex?" asked Sparks.

"Yep. As good a place as any. Then see if you find anything on the sidewalk in both directions."

Manny motioned to Wymer and Ross. Frank was making love to a dark-chocolate bar the size of Manhattan. He ran his hand through his hair. "Frank, are you going to be able to pass the fitness test next month?"

"Hell yeah. I switched to dark chocolate because it's got that antitoxin stuff, and they say it's good for my heart."

"But you're not supposed to gobble the whole bar in one shot."

"I don't know, Manny. I look at it like this. The more I eat, the better chance it has to work for me, you know? And it doesn't give me that bad gas like fiber does."

Ross thumped herself on the forehead. "See what I have to put up with? Can I shoot him, now?"

Manny sighed. "You two stay here. I want you to go door-to-door at the condos on this street, then hit any of the bars and restaurants still open. Maybe they saw something or someone. Then get a hold of the owner of the building where the shooter was and get a list of people who have access to the building's security code. Make sure we have a couple of blues here with the CSU techs."

"The rest of us will break into teams and each check out one of the other murder scenes."

Sophie stepped close to Agent Corner. "You're going to need one of us locals to go with the Feds. Josh and I will team up." She batted her eyes at the agent.

Agent Corner adjusted his tie and moved a few feet away. Sophie followed.

"Okay, but Alex is going with you to protect Josh. Which one do you want? The stolen Mercedes with the spread-eagle body on the hood, or the dickless corpse on the merry-go-round at the park?"

"Ooooo. Never been in a new Mercedes. We'll take that one."

"Chloe, Max, and I will take the other. Keep in touch and get back ASAP so we can compare notes. We'll have Buzzy put our findings and thoughts in a spreadsheet and see if we can get more insight. We've got to figure this victimology out before tomorrow night."

"You think they'll keep at it, with all the heat they've stirred up?" asked Josh.

"I think they believe we can't catch them. And if they do have a mission, they won't stop. In fact, they may accelerate the attacks."

Chloe frowned. "I think he's right. Nothing matters to them except finishing what they started."

"Hard to argue with your logic, especially in

light of what's happened here," agreed Josh.

"Okay. Let's go. I'm driving. Josh can ride shotgun," urged Sophie, hooking Josh's arm.

"OH NO! Not Bobby. Oh my God. NO!"

Manny whirled toward the stolen SUV and watched as Dana Gary slipped to the ground, sobbing wildly. Sarah Sparks tried to catch her, but they both went down in a tangled heap.

"What's wrong, Dana? What is it?" yelled Alex, rushing around the vehicle.

Manny scrambled to the other side.

Dana continued to sob, then finally pointed to the window where the bloodied dead rookie leaned. She began to speak, but couldn't. Her eyes rolled back in her head as she shuddered and passed out.

Sarah clutched Dana close, looking up at Alex and Manny.

"What it is it?" Manny repeated.

Sarah cleared her throat. "That's . . . that's Bobby Foster. Her fiancé."

Chapter-52

The third member of the Justice Club heard the other cell phone ring, and she sensed trouble before she answered. No one calls at 3 a.m. to tell you good things. Besides, there were only two people who knew this number. Neither one was calling to tell her she'd won the lotto.

She looked down both sides of the lighted street and saw that none of her coworkers were in view. She hurried into the alley. She was greeted with the special smell garbage dumpsters share in hot weather. Rancid.

"Why are you calling me?"

"We need to meet, now. Things are coming undone," said the caller.

"I know," she answered, not caring for where this was going.

The silence on the other end was deafening. "What do you mean, you know?" said the caller.

"Just that, I know," she repeated.

"How could you? It happened only an hour ago."

"A little bird told me. Did you forget what I do

for a living?" She switched the phone to the other ear. "Why do we need to meet? The plan is still good."

"It's not good. Whoever killed Stella shot up the LPD headquarters in the process. I don't know what Stella might have said, but I think we need to talk about cooling it." The caller's voice was labored, tense. "You did it, didn't you?" she stated.

"Did what?" asked the third member.

"Killed Stella, and shot up the place."

"Use your damned head. I was working." The third member could almost hear the wheels turning in the caller's head. She saved her the trouble. "It was your secret member of the Club, wasn't it? I mean, who else knew what was going on? Not to mention, she killed a cop."

"I . . .I . . . Shit. Yeah. It makes sense. But I thought she was just going to follow her, make sure she didn't bury us," said the caller.

"And take Stella out if she needed to, right?"

"Yeah. But she was supposed to let me know first so we could talk it over."

"I guess she didn't want your opinion." The third member shifted her feet, her mind already running to the next step. "You're right. We do need to meet, and you'll have to make sure your mysterious fourth shows up. By the way, who is she?"

"I don't know her name. I met her like I met you two. She said to call her Penny, and all I've got is her cell."

"I don't care how you get her there, just do it.

We have to end this now."

"You want to get rid of her?"

"Do you have a better idea? She's not exactly playing for the team here. She's like Stella. We don't have a choice."

"Don't forget who runs this Club, and I'll make those decisions."

"Yeah, well, make one fast because prison's not my idea of a good time. I'll be at the usual spot in thirty minutes." She hung up.

Looking to the sky, the third member of the Justice Club stuffed the cell phone in her pocket. She had to come up with an excuse to get away for an hour. Her boss would buy just about anything she had to sell, so that shouldn't be a problem.

She lit a cigarette and leaned her shoulder against the building. This wasn't supposed to work this way. This was a zero risk proposition, at least for her, but Stella had screwed that up. And the unknown member of the Justice Club had made it worse, a lot worse, particularly with Williams and the Feds snooping around. This had to stop. Maybe both Evelyn and "Penny" had to go. That seemed the only rational thing for her to do. She'd find ways to have the evidence point to them and away from her.

I mean. Who could do that better than me?

"Well, fancy meeting you here."

She whirled around.

"You seem a little jumpy."

The voice was familiar, but she couldn't quite place it. The dark shadows and the hoodie concealed the face. "Hello. You startled me, for sure. My head was somewhere else."

"I suppose it would be, based on what I just heard. It's probably far away and dwelling on things that couldn't be good . . . for me."

"How . . . how long were you there?" But she already knew the answer to that one. Her pulse picked up the pace.

"Long enough."

She reached slowly for her sidearm. Then stopped in mid-motion as she felt the barrel of her visitor's gun press against her temple.

"Not a good idea, especially for you, to try that. You see, I plan to live a lot more years." The visitor leaned closer and spoke in a low tone. "A lot more than you."

The third member suddenly recognized the voice. Her mind pounded with contradiction. *How could this be? It's crazy.* "Does he know what kind of woman you are? What you've done?"

"I could ask you the same question, but I won't."

The visitor pressed the gun even harder to her head.

She yelped, then started to cry.

"No, he doesn't know. And he never will," whispered the fourth member of the Justice Club.

Chapter-53

The FBI's sleek Gulfstream G-V banked around Detroit and continued a shallow descent to Lansing's Capitol City Airport. The moon's bright reflections danced off the portside wing in rhythm with every shimmy and shake of the plane, causing the moonbeams to act as if they had a life of their own.

At least that's what Dr. Fredrick Argyle thought. He sat in the seat closest to the rear of the plane, shackled to its infrastructure in four different places. The manacles offered him no mobility, other than moving his toes and fingers, and of course, his eyes. Not to mention the mask that was strapped tightly across his jaw and mouth. Apparently biting off the ear of an FBI special agent was a no-no, even if the agent was a total ass.

The Feds don't seem to have much of a sense of humor about such things.

The thick, white plastic restraint allowed him to breathe and speak, but he could barely move his jaws. No matter. He had nothing to say, not yet, but the time was coming.

He glanced up to the three armed agents aligned in a semicircle to his right. None of them had wiggled an inch during the flight from Miami. They wanted him to move; even a small twitch would suffice. He smiled to himself when he thought of the famous line, "Give me a reason." Not that they needed much of one. He was truly fortunate that all FBI candidates had to pass extensive psychological testing. If he'd stayed in St. Thomas, he'd probably already be in the morgue.

Still, for them, he imagined, cleaning his blood and brains off the window and wall appeared to be an acceptable alternative to letting him stand trial in Michigan. He'd have to watch his manners. The agent on his left was particularly vigilant. He was also the one who had made sure the mask was going to be a source of pain.

I don't think he likes me.

Argyle noticed the agent's wedding ring. When he was through in Lansing, he'd make it a point to stop by and see what the agent's wife thought of his . . . appetite.

But for now, he would play by their rules. He'd speak how they wanted him to speak, sit where they wanted him to sit, and piss where they said to piss.

After all, he had a rendezvous or two to keep.

Chapter-54

Manny checked his watch as he leaned against the Fed's SUV, then squeezed his phone tighter. Gavin was still hovering in the same status. "Hanging in there" the nurse had said. But did anyone really understand where "there" was? He didn't think so. Just a phrase to use when saying "I don't know" or "it's really not good."

He reached for the coffee sitting on the hood and downed what was left. Agent Corner, Sophie, and Alex would arrive in the parking garage any minute and none too soon. The quicker they compared crime-scene information, the better chance they had of running down the others involved with the deadly Justice Club's vendetta—and Stella's killer.

The crime scene at the playground was staged like the others, but there were some subtle differences, as if the killer had run out of time or maybe had some place to be. The victim was shot an extra time in the head, at close range, based on the black-powder residue. The wrecking of the body was even more extensive, especially the genitals. Sick stuff.

Max thought the victim was killed around 11 p.m., about the same time they had left the Mason Street Apartments, where they'd been misled by the young hooker.

The note Stella had written told him to find the mess she was going to handle. Mission accomplished. He ran his fingers through his hair. Stella's journey to Psycholand was still more mystery than fact. He'd have to accept that for now.

The elevator chimed, and Chloe emerged. Max was nowhere in sight, and he knew instantly that was by design. She moved directly at him, never taking her eyes, those beautiful green jewels, from his.

Here we go.

Looking to the floor, his stomach did flip-flops at a world-record rate. He'd always been able to throw distractions under the bus, to ignore everything that had nothing to do with the current investigation. But this woman, this captivating woman, had put a huge monkey wrench in his tool box.

Each step she took echoed through the parking garage like thunder claps, and his temperature rose. She was five feet away when his body, somehow, became still more alive. Not with her perfume, or even her body language, just her. He'd felt this same exhilaration a few times dating Louise, but never this intense, this . . . alluring.

I'm in deep trouble here.

Chloe moved to within a few inches, searching his face. "Hey," she said softly.

"Hey yourself."

She stood silently for a moment, then touched his hand. "Manny. I . . .I've never felt quite like this about someone. Especially for a man I've only known a few days. A married man, no less. But the first second I saw you, I knew I was in over my head."

"Chloe—"

"Let me finish. I told myself that as long as I didn't see you or work with you again, I'd be fine. As you can see, that didn't work out so well. And I was lying to myself. I think of you every minute." She took a deep breath.

Manny closed his eyes to ignore the way her breasts rose and fell.

Really not good.

Chloe swallowed hard. "I know you're feeling something too. This profiling thing can be a bitch of a two-edged sword. You did a great job, for the most part, hiding your body talk and even your eyes, but not *that* great."

"So I can't lie about the distraction you are? The way I get flustered around you?"

She smiled a sad smile. "Not to me, Big Boy."

When Chloe used his wife's nickname for him, his mind raced to Louise's face, the curve of her lips and the shape of her nose. How she laughed. The way she held him had always felt like they fit together. Like God had ordained it.

"I'm married to a wonderful woman. She's the

best thing that's ever happened to me. Not to mention, I said some vows I meant. In front of people I care about and God."

"Wait. I'm not asking you to break those vows or leave your wife, especially after three days. Really. I only want you to know that . . . that if something happened . . ." her voice trailed off.

She straightened her jacket and smiled. "Or if you decide to get rid of that Boy Scout thing, I'm here."

Manny put his hand on her warm shoulder and just as quickly, removed it.

Really, really, not good.

"Chloe, that's the best offer I've had since Louise said 'yes' to me."

She reached up and kissed his cheek. "I meant every word."

"So did I." He grinned. "Okay. Are we good?"

"For now, and as long as you don't touch me again. You've been warned."

"It's a deal."

Chloe stepped back as the elevator door opened, and Max strode toward them from the interior. Just then, the other SUV screamed around the corner and slammed to a searing stop just short of where Manny, Chloe, and Max stood, sending them scrambling.

Sophie jumped out of the driver's side. "Wow. These things can move. I gotta get one."

Josh and Alex got out, both as pale as the walls of the parking garage.

"Never again," said Alex. "And I mean it this

time. She's crazy."

Josh laughed. "We need to hire her to train our other agents. I never saw anyone drive like that, text her husband, and put on fresh makeup all at the same time."

"Yeah, well, if you'd been in the front seat, I would've shown you one more dimension of my multi-tasking skill," Sophie proclaimed, winking at the special agent.

"I bet you could."

The stink of burning rubber and puffs of gray smoke still emanated from the tires of the SUV Sophie had parked. Manny motioned the others away. "Damn girl. That unit's going to need new rubber."

"No problem. We got a little money," said Josh.

"I've heard that. So, anything different about the Mercedes murder?" asked Manny.

Alex shook his head. "Not really. He'd been dead maybe two hours. Same desecration of the groin area. Three shots in the chest, one in the head. Black-leather bindings. The body posed in similar fashion as the others." Alex leaned against the truck. "I did notice a couple places that looked like stab wounds, so we'll check that out once we get into the lab. Other than that, we collected hair samples, fingerprints, a cosmetic fingernail, and anything else that looked like it could help."

"Wait. We think we figured out how the first victim might have been dumped behind the White Kitty, but not really dumped," said Sophie. "There was a lot of blood on the hood, but even more in the back seat."

"So the first victim, Morse, could have been killed in a car and then dumped behind the garbage bin?" asked Max.

"Yeah. That's what we think."

"Makes sense," said Manny.

Alex held out his hand showing a small piece of paper in an evidence bag. "Of course, the obligatory 'note up the left nostril' had to be extracted. The letter 'I' was on this one."

Josh looked at Manny. "How about you? What'd you find?"

"Nothing different than you. I think this was Stella's last victim, and she seemed to be a little more in a hurry. But the MO was identical except for the back-stomping part."

"We got the letter 'T' out of Boogerland," added Max.

"Boogerland? Uck." snickered Sophie.

"Wait. You got an 'I' from his nose, we got a 'T'. The other three letters were 'J-U-S', right?"

"Yeah they were," said Sophie.

"That's the first five letters of JUSTICE. My God; they were going to kill enough men to spell out the Club's name."

The implications left the others silent, contemplating the possibilities.

Manny ran his hand through his hair. "How did this get so nuts? Gavin, Stella, Dana's fiancé, and five other murder victims, all within a couple of days. That's six months worth of homicides for Lansing."

“This shit is getting deeper and deeper. We need to stop them.” Alex threw up his hands.

Just then, Manny noticed the other small evidence bag in Alex’s right hand. He bent closer, squinting in the florescent lights of the garage. He’d seen that style of cosmetic fingernail before.

“Alex. Open that bag.”

“What? I can’t do tha—”

“Just open the damned bag, now.”

“Okay, okay. Hold on to your shorts.” He pulled a latex glove out of his pocket and then Alex unzipped the seal as the others squeezed closer.

“You and latex . . . I just don’t know,” said Sophie.

Manny took the nail from Alex and rotated it in his fingers. Even though it was cracked, the teal background contrasting the tiny star and moon shapes running vertically up the nail were unmistakable.

“I know who this belongs to,” said Manny.

“Who?” asked Sophie.

“Don’t you remember?”

Sophie frowned, the wheels turning. Then her face lit up like a Christmas tree. “That belongs to Evelyn Kroll. The manager of the White Kitty.”

Chapter-55

Frank Wymer waddled out of the twenty-four-hour convenience store with an extra large soda in one hand and an open bag of cheesy twist puffs in the other. It had been a long night so far, and only two things were mandatory when he was up late: eating and more eating.

He stuffed a handful of twists in his mouth and washed it down with a long draw from the soda. Better.

Ross had been on his case, really on his nerves, all day so he suggested they split up and cover more ground. But he really just wanted to get away from her and knew she felt the same. He wasn't sure which of them was more irritated, the bitcher or the bitchee. Either way, the break was necessary. He hated it when she got like this. He didn't think it was him this time. She'd been more on edge lately, probably fighting with that loser boyfriend of hers. People went through things, he got that, but enough of the moody-ass personality for now. Besides, they *were* covering more ground. Ross was faster, but he moved pretty well for 320 pounds, at least his wife said so.

One more drink drained the soda, and he tossed the empty snack bag in the trash, wiping the yellow-orange residue on his slacks.

They needed to be cleaned anyway.

He continued down the south side of the street, looking for any lights coming from the windows of the above-the-store condos. So far, he hadn't gathered much. The three condos he'd visited weren't any help. All of the residents claimed to have heard and seen nothing. Two young ladies were freaked out that a cop was knocking on their door, and the other one, a drunk male, told him to get a warrant and slammed the door. He'd remember that one when this was over.

Neither of the two storeowners he'd spoken with saw anything out of the ordinary, although one had seen a hot-looking chick hurrying past while he was out having a smoke. He admitted he was too busy watching her walk away to notice anything else. Best walk of the shift.

She may have been carrying a case, but he just couldn't remember. He said it wasn't all that unusual for students from the law school up the block to show up at anytime, toting anything you could imagine.

Frank knew that the law school's library was open twenty-four/seven, so it seemed a logical place to go next.

He turned the corner heading west and stopped as quickly as someone like him could stop. A woman was walking toward him from across the street, moving at a fast pace. Too fast. When she flashed under the street lamp some thirty yards away, he noticed she was on the phone, her light-colored hoodie coat flapping behind her, with something red streaked down the front.

Squinting his eyes as she moved under the next light, he zoned in on the woman's jacket again. His eyes got bigger. No doubt, this time. The splatter pattern could be blood.

But whose?

Frank drew his Glock .40. "Hey. Stop right there. I want to talk to you."

The woman, only ten yards away, spun on her heels and turned back the way she'd come, sprinting all out, and dropping the cell phone in the process.

"I said stop! Now!" he yelled. He broke into a run and stopped ten steps later, breathing like he'd just run a quarter-mile sprint, sweat popping out on his forehead as he put his hands on his knees.

Maybe Manny and Ross are right. Maybe I need to lose a couple pounds.

He looked up just as the woman disappeared around the corner of the next block, heading away from downtown. Closing his eyes, he tried to remember everything about her: her height, her hair, her posture, and her shoes. It wasn't like having her in cuffs, but it would have to do.

The phone's screen reflected light from the

mercury lamp while the added reflection from the setting moon gave it an eerie glow. He took out a slightly stiff handkerchief and grunted, plucking the phone from the sidewalk.

The black casing had web-like cracks running up one side, leaching over to the screen. He touched the power button and nothing happened. Damn it. He'd have to get it to the CSU. The CSU could pull the memory card and see if it was any help. The phone was exactly like his partner's, like Kathy Ross's phone, and it had a memory card.

Just like Kathy Ross's.

The sick feeling in his stomach crawled up to his throat as he turned the phone over and read the initials "K.R." monogrammed into the lower corner of the casing.

"Shit," he whispered.

Frank scanned the street, up and down both sides, and started to move. "Ross! Kathy Ross! Do you hear me? Kathy, where are you? Talk to me girl."

No sign of the partner he'd sworn to protect, to always watch her back. Nothing but silence. The damning kind.

Running in the direction he'd seen the woman go, he let the adrenaline take over. No stopping this time.

After a block and a half, he reached the alley on the side of the street where Ross had been canvassing and stopped. The opaque shadows covered one side of the dirty half-street. The other basked in the late-night moon's silver glow.

The alley is a perfect place to . . .

His imagination ran wild, not something a man like Frank Wymer allowed to happen. But this was different, like the night was speaking to him in a voice born of pure fear.

Taking out his phone, he called for backup, pulled his gun, and began to move into the alley. This was crazy, but what if she was hurt? He couldn't wait.

"Kathy, you there?" he asked. Voice quiet, shaking.

He moved two steps. "Ross? Answer me."

Frank took three more steps before he remembered the small, powerful flashlight in his back pocket. Taking it out, he flipped it on and watched the shadow side of the passage come to life. His eyes darted to both sides of the alley, then fixed on rapid movement. His skin started to crawl.

Huge brown rats scurried away from the light's accusing aura. He jumped back in something just less than panic.

Good God. I hate those things . . . in particular, the big ones.

As he took another step back, the flashlight's beam ran across a sheet of dirty cardboard that wasn't just dirty. It was the color of dark blood.

He swallowed hard. There was something under the remnant, something stirring.

"Ross? Is that you?"

Inching closer, he watched the cardboard slide away in slow motion, revealing its hidden secret.

Ross's right arm materialized from beneath the covering. Not hesitating, he tore the rest of the cover away.

The cheese twists rose up through his gorge, stopping just short of splattering onto the alley floor.

The siren from the LPD cruiser wound to a stop, and two doors opened and closed in rapid succession.

Wymer barely heard the two officers call his name. He was far too busy kicking at the hungry rats gnawing on his dead partner's face.

Chapter-56

"You're sure she's not there? What time? Got it, you'd better be right." Manny clicked off his phone.

"The security goon said Evelyn left for her supper break and never came back. He was all pissy because she was supposed to help him clean up and then lock up at 3:30. He said her car was still there, though." Manny grabbed the safety grip dangling above the SUV's door, knowing what was coming next. "He said he'd wait for us."

Sophie hit the gas screeching around the corner onto Cedar. Alex pounded the door with a thud.

"Hey, the Feds are following us, take it easy," complained Alex. "And now I'll need surgery on my rotator cuff."

"Damn. You're such a sissy. Relax. I taught Josh a thing or two. And what did the guard mean by 'clean up'? Like in the theater?"

"Yeah. I suppose so. Why?" asked Manny.

"Ew. I don't think I want to know what that means."

"Oh man. Me neither," said Alex.

"Concentrate on driving. I still want to get to the White Kitty in one piece."

"Have I ever let you down?" Sophie glanced at Manny and smiled. "Don't answer that."

"Just get us there. We need to get a good look at her car."

"You think it may have been used in the first murder?" asked Alex.

"I believe there's a chance. If she did what we think she did, she may not have known what would happen when someone bleeds out. She probably did her best to clean up."

"One of my best friends will be able to tell," said Alex.

"You gonna get more latex gloves out of your pants? You seem to spend a lot of time in those pockets."

"What? No, I don't. And I meant Luminol. It's a CSI's go-to magic potion. And why all the cracks about latex gloves?"

"Hey. You've been keeping them closer than your wife since the cruise. Never mind the conversation you and Max had in St. Thomas. I think you're a closet latex groupie. You get off on how smooth it feels, don't you?"

"You're a sick wench, you know that?"

"Hell, yeah, but at least I admit it."

"As much as I'd like to hear the rest of this conversation, we're here," said Manny. "Whip in the back. Should be empty this early in the morning."

“A little creepy with Evelyn being involved,” said Sophie.

“Yeah. I think so too. But who sees more depraved men than someone like her?” He thought about the day they interviewed her. She had played her role perfectly, fooling them both in the process. He couldn’t help but wonder what kind of stressor she had experienced to send her down this path. But he also knew people, if they really wanted to, could justify anything. Stella had. And it bothered him to think he almost understood how it could happen. Maybe he understood too well.

Sophie slammed on the brakes, sliding sideways just enough to position the bright headlights in a perfect direction. The girl was scary, but good. The truck’s beams basked the White Kitty’s security guard in artificial daylight as he stood between two vehicles. The security guard was even larger than Manny remembered.

Manny got out just as the second SUV arrived.

“Thanks for waiting.”

“I didn’t do it for you. I did it for her. I don’t like cops; and I need to be here so you don’t finger her for something she didn’t do.”

Manny frowned and moved closer. “Why would you say that? I didn’t tell you we were investigating her for anything.”

The guard blinked and looked away. “Why else would you be here?”

“You think she’s involved in something, don’t you?” asked Manny.

"You're freakin' nuts. Just do what you gotta do so I can get the hell out of here."

Manny leaned in close and whispered. "If I find out you knew something, anything, you're going to like me a hell of a lot less."

The guard stepped away, his defiance replaced by an uneasiness Manny recognized. It had to do with people hiding something.

"Which vehicle is Evelyn's?" asked Alex.

Manny pointed to the Chevy Blazer.

Alex reached for the passenger handle and looked surprised that it was unlocked.

"I don't think I'd leave it unlocked in this neighborhood . . . not in any neighborhood these days," Max said.

"I had spare keys, so I unlocked it," said the guard.

"Did you touch anything inside?" asked Manny.

"No. Just pushed the remote so you clowns could get inside. Do what you gotta do, and then you can leave her alone."

Max went around to the driver's side back door, and Alex opened his case, taking out a flashlight and two small glass spray bottles.

Manny was always fascinated at how fast Alex could turn on the CSI thing. Max was a mirror image in concentration. If there was something there, it was as good as found.

Josh moved beside Manny. "Sophie said you think this could be the first murder scene."

"Maybe. If she didn't know how shooting

someone played out in the physical, she may have messed up."

"Got something here," said Max, ducking out of the back seat. "These look familiar?" He was holding up two black-leather straps.

"Same stuff used to tie the victims?" asked Manny.

"We'll check them out at the lab, but I say yes to that."

"That ain't all. We've got blood on the seat and carpet. Lots of it," said Alex. "And these."

Alex was holding a Blackberry PDA and a DVD in a clear plastic case. "I bet, when Buzzy tears this PDA apart, it's the device used to jam the cameras at the White Kitty and at headquarters. God knows what's on the DVD, but I bet it'll be interesting."

"That's enough for me. Let's impound this unit, and you and Max can tear it apart," said Manny. "Make the call, Alex."

Sophie walked up to the muscular guard, weapon drawn. "Time to start talking, or I'm going to kick the shit out of you. I'm Oriental, and you know what that means. I could Kung Fu your ass in about three seconds."

"Easy there, Black Tiger," urged Manny.

He turned to the guard. "Last chance. Here or at the station."

The big man sighed. "Okay. I don't know anything for sure. She's been acting strange since we found the first body three mornings ago."

"Like how?"

"Leaving for a few hours at a time, acting more bitchy than usual. I figured PMS or whatever until . . ." His voice trailed away.

"Until?"

The guard shifted his feet and then looked directly into Manny's eyes. "Until a couple of nights ago when she said something kind of scary."

"Go on."

"She said the world would be a better place without the pervs that come in here. I laughed, but she didn't. I don't think she was foolin' around. I never saw that much hate in anyone's face before." He met Manny's gaze. "I don't like you people. I suppose I even loathe some of you, but not like that."

Manny nodded. "Anything else?"

His shoulders slumped, and Manny thought he looked like he'd just sold his mother to Satan. "No. Can I go now?"

"Yes. Don't leave town, though."

"Good thing you cooperated. You would've had to eat from a straw for a month when I was through with you," sneered Sophie.

"Whatever." He climbed into his pickup and left.

"We need to find Evelyn. I'll send a couple of units to her house, but I'm betting she won't be there," said Manny.

"Good bet," agreed Josh.

"So we know there were at least two members of the club. But the way Stella talked, there were more," said Josh.

"The question is how many . . . and who?" asked Sophie.

"This killing club thing is usually no more than three, in rare cases, four. The psychology of group dynamics says it's safer, more intimate with a low number. Three to four falls in the arena of a group profile," said Manny, running his hand through his hair.

"If you're right, then we have at least two other not-well bitches?" asked Sophie.

The ringing of Agent Corner's phone interrupted the conversation. He looked at the screen. "It's Chloe calling from the CSU research lab."

"Yes?"

Manny watched as the agent's face evolved into a "you gotta be kidding me" look. He shook his head and hung up without saying goodbye.

"What?"

"You're right; your town is going damn crazy." Josh blew out a breath. "There's been another shooting . . . it's one of yours."

Manny's heart hit the ground. "Who?"

"Wymer found Kathy Ross's body in an alley, shot four times."

Chapter-57

The jail-cell door slammed shut. A brilliant vibration rang throughout the tiny basement facility, right through the very roots of his teeth. The guards walked away, laughing at their juvenile attempt at humor. Juvenile to Fredrick Argyle. But he knew from his days as a practicing psychiatrist that boys would be boys, and he was accepting of their behavior—for now. But soon he'd be laughing, and they'd be quaking in their black shoes.

Argyle rubbed his jaw where the too-tight mask had resided. They thought they had things under control, him under control. The mask, the cold iron shackles that still restricted his movement, and, of course, the sedative they'd administered, were all supposed to calm the savage beast, slay the dragon, and send him to La-La Land.

Wrong. So VERY wrong.

They'd emptied the cell block to make room for him, akin to a dangerous animal prepped for a new zoo exhibit.

No one wanted distractions when they brought him food or when his lawyers came to call. His counselors would invariably recommend that he plea-bargain for a life in a super security prison instead of an extradition to another state that could cost him his life via lethal injection or by someone's version of Old Sparky. The lawyers didn't understand either. They were all products of the same convention that governed mortals. But he didn't fit that convention. Gods couldn't.

Fools.

They all frolicked in a fantasy world that didn't exist for him. But their awakening was coming. They'd see the light just before they died.

He stood up and shuffled to his cell door, manacles clanging in soft rhythms. The first red rays of the early morning sun streaked through the window in the adjacent cell like probing fingers, allowing the jagged Lansing skyline to silhouette against the night. He remembered an old saying.

Red at night, sailor's delight. Red in the morn, sailors be warned. How appropriate.

"It's always good to be home among my people. Always. And I'm so looking forward to the reunion," he whispered.

He threw back his head, laughing.

Chapter-58

"What the hell are you doing?" Evelyn Kroll said in a low tone. "You killed Stella, then you shot Ross, not to mention you killed a rookie cop, all in about three hours. You trying to get us fried?"

The two women sat in the back corner booth of Kewpee's all-night restaurant, away from prying eyes and ears. Penny savored another bite of cherry pie, put down her fork, and looked back at Evelyn with a puzzling gaze. She liked Evelyn. The girl had a story, and it had struck home with her, enough to have her throw away more than a few lifetime perceptions and embrace the type of justice Evelyn preached. But she sensed the girl was getting weak. Weak wasn't tolerated.

Looking at Evelyn and her fear, Penny realized just how strong she had become. How willing Penny was to take care of whatever she deemed necessary to keep her life, her other life, safe—and at any price.

"Stella and Ross were putting the whole Club in a bad place. Stella was reckless and dangerous.

Ross was thinking about doing us both. I could tell by the way she talked to you on the phone," Penny answered. "Because of them, I almost got caught by Ross's partner. It's a good thing Wymer weighs more like a rhino than a gazelle. And frankly, dying or going to jail isn't on my list of things to do today." She stared into Evelyn's face. "How about yours?"

Evelyn looked away without answering.

"That's what I thought."

Evelyn sat up a little straighter. "I started this thing, and I still believe those perverted bastards should pay. I just didn't think any of us would die. Maybe worse, get soft. You're right. We need to keep on track. I think we're safe for now. But I need to get my car and then not go back to work at the White Kitty, ever."

"That's probably a good idea. Someone could've seen you, or maybe one of the other employees doesn't like your work habits."

Evelyn stretched out her hands on the table. "What's next? Do we lay low?"

Penny looked at Evelyn's hands. The cosmetic fingernail was missing from the index finger of her left hand. "For now, I think that's best. Maybe get you into a motel or a flophouse for a few days. But there are a couple of real sick pricks being released tomorrow, so . . ."

"You're probably right," sighed Evelyn.

Penny shoved her empty plate forward. "Lost a nail, huh?"

"Yeah. Not sure where. But I was in such a

hurry to get to work. I probably didn't get it on before I left home."

Penny nodded. *Or you lost it where someone could find it and ID your stupid ass.*

"Let me give you a ride back to your car. We'll talk some more later today, after we both get some sleep."

After Penny left a twenty on the table, they exited Kewpee's, putting on leather gloves before they climbed into the stolen Mustang liberated from an all-night parking garage.

They rode the first ten minutes in silence. Then Evelyn started to cry.

Penny rolled her eyes. More wood to fan the fire. "What's your problem?"

"I was just thinking of what my sister would think of me if she knew."

They twisted down a side street, drove a block, and parked under a large, silver maple tree. Turning to Evelyn, she smiled. "She probably wouldn't clap her hands with joy, but if she's any kind of sister, she loves you no matter what."

"Do you think so?"

"Yes, I do."

Evelyn let out a breath. "You're right. Listen, the White Kitty is only a few blocks away. I'm going to walk and clear my head. I'll talk to you later."

Evelyn got out of the car and started walking along the pothole-lined street.

Penny's hands gripped the wheel so hard she felt the leather imprint in her fingers.

What would my sister think? The bimbo is going to cave. That won't do.

She started the engine and swung the Mustang around, lights shining bright on Evelyn's tall frame.

Evelyn turned to wave and then kept walking.

She slammed the car in gear and stomped on the accelerator.

That won't do at all.

***

The red Mustang smashed into Evelyn, sending her over the hood and off the left side of the windshield. She felt her leg shatter and something go terribly wrong with her hip. Her head throbbed, but she held onto some semblance of consciousness.

Somehow, she found a way to raise her eyes as her world became as bright as any noonday. The lights were mesmerizing, but not as paralyzing as the stark realization that accompanied the light. She really had no time to be afraid. Evelyn grasped the gold cross around her neck and held tight.

The last thing she saw was the wide, black tire inches from her face.

Chapter-59

Manny stood outside the yellow tape, arms crossing his chest, staring at the flashing blues and reds emanating from the squad cars, wondering how things could get worse. Two cops in one night: one with a bright future, the other living her dream of being a detective. Each one snuffed at the whim of a heartless killer riding an agenda every cop dreaded: vigilantes-r-us.

He'd sent Wymer home with a couple of blues and ordered them to watch him until the department shrink could get there. The man was such a mess that he hadn't eaten in an hour.

Frank had sat on the curb in front of the alley mumbling and apologizing over and over. "Manny, I'm sorry. We broke protocol. It's my fault. It's my fault. She's dead and it's my fault . . . those rats, those damned rats."

He'd heard very few people as distraught as the rotund detective. His despair was the kind that ran just the other side of spooky. Detectives had quit the force for less, much less.

Max and Alex were in the process of taking

apart Evelyn Kroll's car while Sophie, Chloe, and Josh were headed to Evelyn's apartment to see what they could find that would add more light to the twisted past three days. They were all to meet him back at the forensics lab where Buzzy Dancer had been called in to decode Ross's cell phone's memory card. Maybe the call that the woman was on before Frank interrupted her would lead to something, someone. Too many pieces to the puzzle, leading to everywhere and nowhere. And how did Ross's murder fit into all of this?

But that is the question, isn't it? Was Ross killed because she got too close to one of the Justice Club members, or was it some random coincidence?

Sophie and Agent Corner respected his wish to spend some time away to think. He worked better when he could step back and escape the hurricane.

For the second time that night, he watched the ME roll away the body of someone he cared about. Ross hadn't been close to him like Stella, and there would be no kiss this time, but she'd worked hard to climb a ladder still regarded as men's work: a legacy she'd leave for other women cops to follow. Legacies were sometimes all folks had, if they were fortunate.

Manny ducked under the tape and walked slowly down the alley. He stopped at the place where her gnawed body had been discovered.

The CSU's other team had done its preliminary processing, but wanted to come back in the morning to finish when the light was better.

They'd found no bullet casings or guns, but would give it the microscopic treatment in a few hours. Meanwhile, they'd left the large portable floodlights to drive away some of the darkness, at least on the outside.

The dark-red splatter was evident against the pale bricks of the building where Ross must have been standing when she was shot. The pattern climbed the wall a few feet, indicating a high-powered weapon or that the source of the shot came from a lower angle. That evidence, and based on the first entry wound at her temple, indicated the killer was shorter than Ross. That ruled out someone as tall as Evelyn Kroll and jived with the description Frank gave—although Manny guessed Frank would have agreed that the woman was orange if Manny had asked.

Closing his eyes, he tried to conjure the scene that took place just before Ross was killed.

She must have been up against the wall, the gun at her head, and standing at an angle that would cause a blood spatter pattern like the one on the wall.

He moved to the blood-covered bricks and stood about where she would have. Ross would've had to look straight ahead while the killer stood at a forty-five-degree angle on her right. He moved into the shooter's position, trying to squat about the right height.

Stepping away, he guessed the killer was about five-foot-six. And he got a sense—for no particular reason, other than he felt it—that she was strong, in shape. A gym addict?

Stella had worked hard to get in great shape over the last few months, and it was obvious Evelyn stayed in condition. Maybe there was something there. He made a note to investigate Stella's gym.

If it checked out, and Stella and Evelyn worked out at the same place, maybe that's where things got started and someone might recognize others in the Club. It was worth a shot. Then again, maybe it was a coincidence. The old saying about throwing enough shit against the wall and some sticking came to mind.

He stood scanning everything in the twenty-foot lighted area like an eagle looking for a trout. After a few minutes, nothing jumped out to say *hey, look at me* . . . until he turned to leave. One of the biggest rats he'd ever seen strolled leisurely from the pile of junk and garbage on the opposite side of the alley into the edge of the searchlight. It stood on its hind legs, and he swore it winked at him. Hanging from the rodent's mouth was Ross's small handbag. The strap had been torn and hung limply to the ground, looking like it had been dragged to hell and back. He crouched on his haunches and studied the animal; it didn't back away, but stood still, sizing up Manny. A little weird for a rat to be this composed, but then again, they could be as aggressive as a caged tiger, and for no apparent reason.

He was suddenly struck with one of those feelings that he'd grown to trust.

"I need that bag, buddy."

The rat dropped to all-fours and backed up two steps, purse still clenched in his teeth.

"We can do this the hard way or the easy way," said Manny, pulling his Glock from the holster.

The rat seemed to sense the danger and stood again, baring its teeth, dropping the bag.

Manny took two steps toward the monster rodent from the Abyss and yelled. It scurried away, out of the light's range. He started to reach for the bag, then realized he needed latex gloves for two reasons: evidence and rat saliva.

Where is Alex when you need him?

Looking around, he placed an old rusted pot on top of the purse and went back to the patrol car where two officers guarded the entrance to the alley.

Borrowing a pair of gloves, he pulled them on and returned to the alley.

As he picked up the bag, something fell out, and the object sent his thoughts in a different direction.

Why did Kathy Ross have two cell phones?

Chapter-60

"We didn't find her," said Sophie, slapping the forensic lab's conference table. "It looked like she'd been there, but the place was pretty neat and clean. I hate neat and clean."

"Why? Because that means she's organized?" asked Manny.

Her face soured. "That too, but I can't keep my place picked up, mostly because of my husband, so I'm thinking of booting his ass." She winked at Josh sitting across from her. "Are you a neat freak? I bet you are."

"Can we stay on task here?" said Manny, shaking his head. "What else did you three get from her apartment?"

"Not much," said Josh. "We took her laptop and an e-book reader, but the CSU will have to send out another team."

Alex rubbed his stubble. "Yeah, like we don't have anything else to do, even rougher with Dana out of commission."

"There are two Fed teams coming up from Detroit this morning to help out for the day, so that will let us take a step back and look at what we have," said Max.

The group around the table looked tired. Talk about *déjà vu* all over again. It reminded Manny of the cruise ship investigation. But they were a tough bunch, and Chloe seemed to fit right in. "Not to mention, we're all running on no-sleep mode."

"That too," said Josh.

"Tell him about the clothes," said Chloe.

"OH MY GOSH," blurted Sophie. "How could we leave that out? I'm so jealous. The girl must have spent everything she had on that stuff. Designer skirts, bags, jeans, and what a rack of shoes. Pumps, stilettos, flats, even jogging shoes that cost $150 a crack. The wench!"

"Did any of you geniuses think about bagging the heels because of the tap dancing on the victim's backs?"

"Of course," said Josh, a little indignant. "They're on a table in the lab. All ten pair."

"We've saved the best for last, though. Alex, this is for you," grinned Sophie, flipping something like leopard skin at the CSI. "This should go with your collection."

Alex held the thong panties up with both hands and stared.

"She had the finest collection of underwear and lingerie I've ever seen," said Chloe. "And Sophie thought no one would appreciate it more than you."

The room grew as silent as a morgue, then

Max started to snicker. Chloe and Josh followed suit. Sophie covered her mouth with both hands and swiveled away from Alex.

Manny felt his lips tremble, strangled his composure, and then it happened. He started to laugh, and then roared. Sophie fell out of her chair, clutching her stomach. The Feds lost it. Like they were prompted by an unseen conductor.

He watched as Alex's lip began to quiver. The CSI dropped the panties, laying his forehead on the wooden table's surface. Then he began to howl, his laughter louder than the rest.

After a minute, Manny sent the tissue box around the table. Nothing like mass hysterics to create bonds.

"Okay. I needed that," said Alex.

"We all did, I think," agreed Manny. "Now, let's get back to work."

"Before we do, I need to tell you that Argyle's here and locked down in your county facility."

"That was fast, but the sooner the better."

"They put him on the basement level in isolation, still shackled, and guards at every exit and entrance." Josh grinned. "We did the overkill thing because we're the Feds and we can."

"Does he still want to talk to me?"

"Don't know. He still hasn't said a word since he bit the ear off one of my agents in Miami."

"What a warped bitch," said Alex.

"We'll worry about him later," said Manny.

He called Buzzy in, and she plopped down, wearing her customary pink, this time a skirt with two layers and enough jewelry to start her own store, smacking a large piece of fresh bubble gum.

"What'd you find on Ross's memory card?"

"Let me just say first that I'm going to miss her. I didn't know her too well, but she was always nice to me. I know you guys worked with her, so I feel your pain."

"Thanks, Buzzy. We'll miss her too, but for now we need to find out who did this and why. So . . ."

"Oh, yeah. Okay. I found lots of stuff. It wasn't too hard to pull the numbers because there wasn't much damage to the micro SD card. One of the other techs had a phone exactly like hers so I swapped 'em out and said the magic words."

"What does 'lots of stuff' mean?" asked Manny.

"I ran all of the phone numbers she'd called or that had called her against the report generated by the recovery software and eliminated the ones that had anything to do with the department. Then I got rid of any texting that didn't need to be there. I cleaned up some other numbers, like to her family, and was left with nine numbers. They are probably pay-as-you-go jobs, so I started calling them."

"Won't they know the call is from here?" asked Manny.

"No, we swapped cards, remember? Anyway we got no answer on the first five. Here's the weird part. I jumped to the last number called from her phone, the one at about 3:38 a.m., and the PDA you brought in from the White Kitty lady started to vibrate. And *voilà*, the number on that screen was the one I was calling from."

"So that proves the caller and Evelyn were linked," said Josh.

"Yep. But there's one more thing . . . well, actually two more things." Buzzy stood up, unable to conceal her excitement.

"Easy girl. Pretend it's the last frame, and you need a strike to hit the mystical 300 game," said Manny.

"You mean take a deep breath?"

"I do."

"Got it. Whew! So I compared the next-to-last call, and it went to the same number, only about eight minutes earlier."

Manny shifted in his chair. Not caring for where this was headed. "So either the killer called twice—"

"—or Ross knew Evelyn Kroll," finished Sophie.

"Say Manny's right, and the killer called Kroll twice. Here's the second thing, the phone Manny brought in from the alley, the one covered in rat spit—which I had to clean, thank you very much—had been used a few times in the last twelve hours. There were only three calls on that one. The first two were made yesterday. I tried them, and no one answered. But here's the kicker, I recognized the third one. That one was made about 10:02 last night." Buzzy lowered her eyes, then sat down. "That one went to Kroll's phone too."

"Damn it." Manny leaned back in his chair.

"So Ross was part of this Justice Club thing?"

"If not, she knew Evelyn and didn't tell you," said Josh. "That makes it a problem."

Manny's gut twisted from one side to the other. If it looks like a duck, quacks like a duck, it's a damned duck. "She was involved. No doubt in my mind."

No one disagreed.

"So Stella, Ross, and Evelyn were in this psycho Club. Is that all?" asked Sophie, her face as somber as Manny had ever seen.

"We'll know when we find her."

He turned to Buzzy. "I need you to do whatever it takes to ID those other numbers from both phones. Contact the carriers that issued them."

"Once you ID what companies assigned those numbers, tell them the FBI will subpoena all the records, if they have to," said Josh. "Usually they want the warrant, but sometimes we get lucky."

Buzzy stood up and saluted. "I'll get right on it."

Alex pushed his chair away. "Max and I've got a ton of shit to go through, including ballistics, fibers, blood types, particulates, and I'm hungry as hell, so I'm ordering out for breakfast and doughnuts."

Max followed Alex's lead. "I heard that, and you're buying."

"I like the breakfast idea, then we need to keep looking for Evelyn. We put the APB out for her, but she's going to be hard to find," said Josh.

"Maybe not," said Manny. "She may not know

that we know she's a Justice Club member."

"Unless that goon at the White Kitty got hold of her," said Sophie. "You should have turned me loose on him."

"I don't think he wants any trouble. I say he's in the dark, at least some."

"You might be—"

Buzzy's yelling from outside the room interrupted Josh. "Hey, who are you? You can't just go in there."

Two men dressed in black suits and ties entered the room.

Manny recognized one of them from St. Thomas.

"What are you two doing here? You should be at the jail watching Argyle," said Josh, scowling.

The one that Manny recognized spoke. "I don't know how it happened, but—shit—Argyle's gone."

"What the hell do you mean *gone*?" asked Manny grabbing the agent's jacket with both hands.

"He . . . ah . . . is not in his cell. He escaped."

Chapter-61

Louise Williams fell into bed exhausted after putting Sampson outside. The dog loved to sleep on the deck in hot weather, and who could blame him?

She'd stayed up late, waiting for Manny to call. He didn't. She worried. Then, he finally called to check in. He said he would be home in the morning, and they'd talk. That was either a very good thing, or he was hiding something from her. She bet on the latter.

She hated when Manny worked the all-night shift, and he did it far too often to suit her taste. He was a good man, but whipping that workaholic thing was never really going to happen. She knew that going in. He wasn't going to be just *her* white knight; she was going to have to share him. She supposed there were worse things.

At least tonight's situation was understandable. All the local TV stations were ranting about the serial killer and the victims, and no way was Manny going to leave those investigations alone, not even for a minute. He'd die first. That thought made her stomach dance with butterflies.

So damn noble.

Before he'd left last night, she sent Jen, their daughter, to spend the night at her friend's. That was no problem. Teenagers would always rather spend the night away than stay home anyway.

It had been a busy night, like always, when he was working. She cleaned, washed, rearranged, got something to eat, and then back at it. No rest for the weary. She sighed, pulling the sheet around her neck. Or like her mother used to say, no rest for the wicked.

Her eyes closed as she thought about what that really meant. She decided she preferred the weary adage.

Louise turned to her side and was almost gone when she heard the ringing, then the barking. Both sounded far away, like a dream. Then both started again. She grasped it was the phone and Sampson. Her eyes blinked open and she thought about ignoring it, but realized it was probably Manny. Not to mention she'd better get the dog in before every neighbor on the block threw a hissy fit. But she was so tired.

Finally, she reached for her robe, leaned out of bed, and shuffled to the phone.

"Good morning, Louise. You're looking as tasty as ever."

Louise Williams froze, clutched her chest, then turned to run. But getting away wasn't in the cards.

Argyle pulled her close and covered her face with the chloroform-laced cloth. His laugh haunted her mind as the world went dark.

Chapter-62

"She's not answering," said Manny, hanging up the phone. His heart resided somewhere near his ankles as he rushed out of the room.

"Wait, I'm coming with you," yelled Sophie.

"Me too," said Alex.

Manny heard the scrape of chairs behind him, but it didn't really register. He had to get home, now. Argyle escaping only meant one thing: he was going to finish what he started on the *Ocean Duchess.* His words echoed over and over in Manny's mind as he raced down the steps and climbed into his SUV.

I want you all to suffer the way I did, to walk a mile in my shoes.

He reached to start the vehicle—and there were no keys. "Shit!' He slammed his fist on the steering wheel just as the passenger door swung open.

Sophie tossed him the keys. The engine roared to life, and he tore out of the parking garage, allowing a fast-moving Alex just enough time to shut the back door.

"I'll keep calling," said Sophie, cell phone glued to her head.

Manny nodded and said nothing. His thoughts raced to a Bible verse he memorized as a young man.

God protects us from evil . . .

He needed, prayed, the verse to be true this morning because Argyle was evil embodied. Maybe worse.

Manny turned the corner of his street and saw lights flashing from three cop cars. He floored it again. The Feds had sent cars, but this didn't feel good. The fact that no one had radioed him made his angst climb a higher wall.

Pulling up in front, he leaped out of the truck and rushed headlong into the house, ignoring advice from the three Feds standing on the stoop. Their warnings raised his panic to a level he'd never experienced.

What don't they want me to see?

He burst through the living room, past the kitchen, and ran squarely into one of Lansing's finest, a woman officer named Molly Holt.

"Molly, what's going on; where's Louise?"

"Manny. We got here first. The front door was cracked open a few inches. We entered and secured the house and didn't find anything . . . ah . . . until . . ."

Her eyes darted to his chest than back to his face.

His panic escalated. Then he started for the bedroom.

"There's no one in the bedroom, except your dog. He was howling like . . . well, you know the sound, so we put him in there and that seemed to calm him."

"You didn't answer my question," said Manny.

Sophie and Alex stood off to the side staring at their shoes.

"There's a body in the family room, behind the sofa. But Manny—"

"A body?" He spun on his heels, feeling nothing and everything. Surreal didn't cover it but neither did dread. His mind seemed to be trapped between reality and the unperceived, the impossible, and was in danger of staying that way.

Not Louise. Please God, not Louise.

The old familiar out-of-body encounter held his hand as Manny stepped through the arched doorway and onto the carpet, his eyes fixing immediately on the woman's blood-smeared feet protruding from behind the burgundy sofa. From the back bedroom, Sampson let loose a spine-chilling howl.

The four Feds moved out of his way, parting like the Red Sea at Moses's command. He swallowed hard and took an unsteady pace toward hell on earth.

What will I tell Jen? How will I explain to my daughter that my chosen profession had . . . had?

One more step. He hesitated. If he took the next stride, his world would surely forever change. If he didn't, insanity would embrace him and never let him go. The second option seemed better, safer. But he'd never worked that way. It was too late to change now.

Sergeant Detective Manfred Williams took the next step.

Chapter-63

Josh stood in the dewy yard outside Manny's home, his body language speaking volumes. The corpse inside the house sang a song Josh had hoped he'd never have to hear. It was bad enough this was happening to his good friend, more than bad, but to fly where Manny was flying right now was unthinkable. An image of his own wife came to him, and he shuddered.

Turning to the agents, he spat questions at them fast and furious.

"How in God's name did this happen?"

"We don't know. He was there after one security check, and a half-hour later, he was just gone. His cell was open, and his shackles were lying on the bed. The door had no damage, like he had a key or something," said Paul Pridemore, the agent in charge of Argyle's transfer.

Josh's eyes narrowed. "A key?"

The agent shrugged. "There was no evidence of tampering, of attempting to pick the lock. The door is old, but well kept. It's like the damn thing just swung open for him."

"Security cameras?"

"The one in his cell wasn't being monitored because we were in the block so often. The others showed nothing."

"I'm lost here. Say I can buy into him somehow getting out of the restraints and even some brilliant scheme to get out of his cell. How in the hell did he get out of the facility?"

"There's an emergency door at the other end of the cell block and he just walked out."

"I told you to put guards at every exit and entrance."

"We did. One of the locals had that one covered."

"Damn it. Why didn't the alarm go off?"

Pridemore looked to the early morning sky. "It couldn't."

"What?"

"The county deputy said it has a manual switch and someone must have inadvertently turned it off."

Josh rolled his eyes. "The worst psychopath this city's ever seen and you don't have your shit together. Unbelievable."

Chloe motioned for him to come with her. Her face grave, even for a special agent who's seen a thing or two.

"What?"

"There's something not right here."

"You think?"

"That's not what I meant. The time frame is messed up."

"What do you mean?"

She inhaled a controlled breath. "Say he got out of the cell and out the door within five minutes of the half-hour checks, and that's being generous. The jail is five miles from here. So he would have had to steal a car. Assume he didn't want to be seen in his orange jumpsuit, so a change of clothes was in order. Then get here to . . . to . . . do what he did and then leave. The first units arrived four minutes after the dispatcher call."

The way Chloe said what she said sent a fresh supply of dread to the very center of his bones. He looked up from the moist grass. "Not much time."

"Not only that, it's 6:35 and getting lighter. This street has been canvassed by three teams of cops and agents. How come no one saw a car in front of the house?"

"You know what you're saying?"

"Yes. I do. I think he had help. It's the only thing that makes sense. If there was a car and clothes waiting for him, he would have gotten here at least fifteen minutes sooner, which would've given him time to pull this off and then hit the road, barely. And might explain why the emergency door's alarm was off."

"Shit." What Chloe said rang true the way those truths do when you try to ignore their incessant nagging.

He frowned. "But how would his helper know when he was going to get out?"

"I'm not sure. Maybe they followed the wagon

from the airport. Some previous plan? Hell, I don't know."

"Police band radios could have picked up something, I suppose. Or the helper was a cop."

"Or that," agreed Chloe.

"Pridemore said it looked like maybe he had a key, or something. We need to—"

Chloe elbowed him as Manny emerged from the front door. Head down, holding something in his hand. Josh caught the look in Chloe's eyes, and he thought she was going to lose it. But then again, he wasn't far from Heartbreak City either. In fact, he was at the check-in desk.

This job does things to people, good people. Manny, and at an even higher level, Louise, doesn't deserve this.

Sophie and Alex were close behind Manny, both wearing puzzled, despondent looks. Max moved over from a group of agents and stood near as the three Lansing cops stopped in front of Josh, Manny turning the object in his hand over and over.

"What can we do for you? Just name it," said Josh, struggling to control his voice.

Manny looked up. Remnants of tears stained his handsome face.

Josh watched as Chloe fought to maintain her poise, losing the battle; Max cleared his throat and turned away. Josh felt the world crash around his shoulders, his mind screaming. Manny's face softened. He put his hand on Josh's shoulder and, with the other hand, held the object, a folded piece of paper, out to him.

"It's not Louise."

Chapter-64

Argyle stepped on the accelerator of the year-old Chevy Corvette and quickly hit eighty. He hadn't driven a vehicle like this in over six months, and the feeling was amazing. He reached ninety, and the mile markers on eastbound I-96 blurred past. At 120, he let off the gas and dropped to the speed limit. He'd hate to kill a cop this early in the morning, but it would make the day more interesting. Not as interesting a morning as Detective Williams and the rest of his clueless associates were experiencing right now, but a good one nonetheless.

He wanted and needed to see the look on Manny's face when he realized the body wasn't his wife's—which he'd do as soon as it was safe to tap into the camera feed coming from the Detective's living room. They might find it before he got that opportunity, but he doubted it very much. And there was always the note to spice things up. The dead deputy had been useful, she'd even been pretty good in the sack, but all good things must come to an end . . . for her, at least.

He rolled the window down and welcomed the warm, late-summer air that carried a hint of fall. It was good to be in control, to have the world, especially the law enforcement realm, dancing on a string. Several strings actually.

What had they expected? Had they really thought that putting me away could be that easy, that I had been that sloppy? I've always been ahead of them. It was like taking candy from a first-grader.

A sparkling red convertible BMW Z4 pulled up alongside the Corvette and slowed to match his pace. The fortyish blonde smiled, raising her cup of coffee, toasting his choice in vehicles. He smiled and tipped his imaginary hat. She laughed, did the universal sign for call me, and then sped off, most likely expecting a chase.

On another day, the pleasure would be his, not so much hers. But he had places to be and a few details to wrap up before he returned to Lansing to finish what he'd started.

If only I had more time . . .

Williams's wife was only the first step on a stairway that went for forever. He knew the game, this chase, couldn't last an eternity, but each moment, each hour he caused them to fear, to worry, hell, to hate, was like dope to a junkie. He'd relish every ounce of emotion he created. And no one could do it like the Good Doctor. No one.

The time would come to end this and to move on to the next game. The question was, would anyone be ready for him—and when? He grinned.

Not in this lifetime.

Looking at the clock on the dash, he realized he was ahead of schedule. Maybe he did have time to play.

“Lucky you, my fair maiden,” he sang, pressing the pedal to the floor. “Lucky you, indeed.”

Chapter-65

"What? Not Louise? I don't get it. Who is it?" said Josh, mouth hanging open.

Manny flipped open the note. "I'll read this in a minute. The body belongs to a county deputy, who was also a former patient in Argyle's practice. She was the one guarding the emergency door. He shot her in the head with her own weapon."

Manny sighed. "Since Argyle was employed by the State to work in the prisons, sometimes he would have law enforcement folks assigned to him who had traumatic situations come up in the line of duty. Apparently, this one was more than grateful for his counseling."

Chloe looked at Josh. "That confirms what we were just talking about. We felt like he had help."

Manny raised his hand. "I still don't know where Louise is, but if the note is telling the truth, she's not . . . well, she's alive."

"Read it," said Josh.

"Okay."

DETECTIVE WILLIAMS,

YOUR ATTEMPTS TO PLAY OUR GAME ARE PATHETIC. THIS COULD HAVE BEEN YOUR LOVELY WIFE, BUT I'VE DECIDED TO EXTEND THAT INDEFINABLE PLEASURE FOR ANOTHER TIME. NOT TO MENTION YOUR DAUGHTER AND YOUR PARTNER, AND OF COURSE, THE PRETTY AGENT FRANSON. WHEN I'VE FINISHED PLAYING WITH THE WOMEN, YOU'LL BE NEXT.

P.S. CAN YOU GUESS WHERE LOUISE IS HIDING? I'D START IN LOW PLACES.

"Just let the asshole try it," said Sophie, "I'll put his nuts in his nose with just one kick."

"Stay focused," said Manny. "What do you think 'low places' means?"

"Do you have a basement?" asked Josh.

"Yeah. But she's not there and not in the garage either."

The group grew silent, but the angst didn't. Big Sampson came out and sat at Manny's feet.

The morning was warming, another hot one, and Manny felt the sweat breaking out on his lip like a sudden attack of hives. Hell, maybe it was hives. Stress did strange things to the body. Bad things.

He searched the faces of his five friends hoping to see a spark that would help him figure out what Argyle had done with Louise. Nothing. The black Lab nudged him and started to whine. Manny put his hand on the dog's head.

If Louise were okay, if she'd been spared like

he said (and psychopaths rarely lie; they are too narcissistic for something so trivial), they had to find her now. Just because she was alive at this moment didn't mean that Argyle hadn't added a twist to his game. She could still be in danger. Sampson grabbed Manny's hand gently in his mouth and began to tug. He pulled his hand loose and started to scold Sampson, then the truth whispered in his ear.

Start in low places.

"Oh, man. He didn't."

Manny turned, Sampson at his heels, and sprinted into the house, rushing to the spare bedroom across from his and Louise's room. The black Lab rushed after Manny, never missing stride, barking excitedly.

By then, the others had reached the room, but not in time to help him rip the large area rug from the floor. Sampson began scratching at the surface. Manny pushed him away and started feeling along the hardwood.

"What are you doing?" asked Sophie.

Manny spoke as he continued to feel along the floor. "When we bought this place, there was a part of the house, this room, that had a crawlspace because the basement didn't come over this far. A design flaw. So they built this trapdoor with a little catch-spring latch that would—"

A small section of the hardwood floor popped up about an inch above the rest. Sampson barked even louder, as Manny flipped up the door.

Louise lay in the dirty trench underneath the wood. She blinked up at Manny, then the others. She was bound and gagged, a purple bruise raised on her cheek, tears streaming from her eyes.

But she was alive.

Chapter-66

Manny quietly closed the door to his bedroom and moved to the dining room where Sophie, Alex, and the three FBI special agents waited. The five friends had been patient. Good thing, because he wasn't sure he ever wanted to let Louise out of his sight again. He held her until she fell asleep. The sedative from the EMT had helped, but he liked to think she felt safe because he was there for her, at least this time. Maybe it was just the opposite. Maybe she was stronger than he was. Maybe she wanted to make sure he was okay, and then she could sleep. That seemed right.

It was hard to fight off the guilt-ridden feelings he thought he had mastered, even controlled. Not this time. They'd touched the right button and opened the door.

He had always been able to justify his workaholic propensities as something he owed the people he'd sworn to protect. To explain away the fifteen-hour workdays, missing some of Jen's school events, not all, but enough to send mixed messages to his family.

He spent hours on end talking about family and how important it was, but then hid behind the Guardian of the Universe syndrome.

What a hypocrite.

He'd been blind to what Stella was going through, and to a great extent what was going on with Gavin. Now, one was dead, and the other could go any minute.

Way to watch over your loved ones, asshole.

Seeing Louise in that pit had done things to him in a split second that being a cop for seventeen years never had. He wasn't going to go through that again. Ever.

Sophie stepped close and grabbed his hand in both of hers. "How's she doing, partner?"

The emotion caused his throat to tighten, and he had to wait a few seconds to answer. "A hell of a lot better than me," he croaked. "Especially after finding out that Stella's dead, on top of this other junk." Manny ran his hand through his hair. "She's got a bruised cheek and her wrist hurts, but it could have been worse. If he'd had more time . . ."

Sophie released his hand and then sat down in the oak kitchen chair.

He'd never felt this tired in his life. It was more than the lack of sleep. It was this screwed-up cop life. What good was he really doing? Shoveling shit against the tide was the pure definition of insanity. And he was nothing if not a dedicated shoveler.

Josh sat down beside him, slapping a cup of

vanilla cappuccino on the table. "I've seen that look a few times, and I don't blame you for what you're feeling. I've been there."

"Next, you're going to tell me it's going to pass, and I'll be ready to hit it again in an hour or tomorrow or whenever, right?"

"I won't have to. You'll do it yourself. It's who you are."

"Did you see her in that freaking damned crawlspace?" Manny snapped.

Josh was silent, but his gaze was steady.

Manny looked away, staring at his hands, turning them over. "Maybe it's time I redefine who I am."

"Maybe, but what happens when things settle down and you don't like the new you?"

"It has to be better than the old me."

Alex sat down on his other side, grabbing Manny's coffee. "Will the new you be drinking this sissy coffee? If not, I could use some more caffeine because I've got a damned job to do."

Manny felt the blood burn through his veins as he stood. "What the hell does that mean?"

"What? You need someone to explain it to you?"

"I think you should slap the piss out him for that remark," Sophie said.

Alex ignored her. "No one ever said this would be an easy gig. There are only two people on earth that love your wife more than you and your daughter—that's Sophie and me. If you don't know that by now, then you're thicker than I thought."

"Wait, you can't talk to my partner like that." Sophie pointed a finger at Alex. "If you aren't going to slap him, let me do it." She took a step in Alex's direction.

Manny put his hand out and held his partner at arm's length.

Alex stared at the coffee. "It killed us to see her like that. I'll never forget it either. I don't have to tell you what Argyle's doing, do I? You know how these guys work better than anyone I've ever met. He's hoping he's messed you up so much that he can do whatever he wants, that he's already won. I think it's part of the reason Louise is still alive. He wants you totally on the run. But if we don't get up off the floor and stop this son of a bitch, who's going to?"

The silence in the room took on a life of its own. Manny scanned the faces of his friends and saw the same expression on each one of them. The look that said *it's your call.* But this life had never been his call. God had made him this way, and everyone knows God doesn't make mistakes. It didn't mean he had to like it. And right now, he didn't. In fact, the only thing he liked less was Argyle. He hated even the *idea* of Argyle's type. Manny had never wanted to see someone pay more than the doctor. Hell was too good for Argyle. Maybe Alex was right: if not them, then who?

Letting out the tense breath he'd been hoarding, he released his grip on Sophie's shoulder. "Okay. Go ahead. You can slap him now."

Josh snickered. "That's more like it."

"You're right, Alex," he said, turning to his good friend, "but when this is over, I've got some things to think about."

"Fair enough."

"Maybe you just need a vacation," said Max.

"Yeah, remember the last one we took?" said Manny.

"Okay, no cruise vacations," said Josh.

"So what do we have?" asked Manny, running his hand through his hair.

Chloe cleared her throat and flipped open her notepad.

It dawned on him that she was feeling things a little deeper than the others, but he knew she'd get over it; they both would. They had to.

"Argyle is probably gone. There was a Corvette hijacked and the owner beaten unconscious two streets over. Apparently, Argyle got him just as he was going to work. We have an APB out, but that was over two hours ago, so no telling where he is now," said Chloe.

"Not to mention he probably didn't keep it all that long," added Josh.

"Good taste in cars though," said Sophie. "So, Josh, do you own a sports car?"

"Minivan."

"A sexy one, right?"

"Anyway, he's done this disappearing thing before. It looks like he wanted to get back to Michigan, throw it in our face, and then keep us guessing at what's next," continued Chloe.

"Any more on the deputy he killed?" asked Manny.

"Not really. Divorced. Kind of a loner. Definitely a former patient and probably a lover. She was in contact with him from time-to-time. According to her cell phone records, she got a couple of calls from that reporter's phone, the one that Argyle skewered," said Josh.

Chloe gave Josh a sour look. "Skewered?" she asked.

"Well, that's pretty accurate," said Max.

"Then there was this." Chloe held up a tiny surveillance camera with wires dangling like disjointed legs.

"Where'd you find that?" asked Manny.

"Just inside the rubber tree near your TV. It was pointed directly at the door leading to the living room."

Manny shook his head. "He wanted to watch my face when I found out the body wasn't Louise?"

"That's what I think," said Chloe.

"I'm going to bury him."

"And we'd like to help," said Josh.

"Changing the subject," said Sophie. "How'd he know about the crawlspace? Not a feature in every home."

Manny nodded. "Back when this subdivision went up, maybe twenty years ago, the builder built a ton of houses in different areas of town. The first couple hundred had this design flaw so they put in the trapdoors for free. It wouldn't take much effort to find out if ours was one of them. Then he used it to his advantage. At least that's how I think he knew."

"Makes sense," said Josh.

"Now what?" asked Manny.

"We've got hundreds of officers and locals looking for him statewide. I think we've got a shot at nailing him." Josh shifted his feet. "Did I just say that?"

"Glad you woke up. The chances of finding him without his allowing it are thin, at best," said Manny. "But at least he knows the heat is on."

The front door burst open and Jennifer Williams sprinted directly to her dad, latching on like she would never let go, sobbing the way teens do. "Is . . . mom doing . . . all right?" she asked in between heaves.

Closing his eyes, he held her close. "Hey baby, Mom's okay. She's tough."

"Tha-that's what the two officers said. Are you all right?"

His heart broke that his daughter would think of Louise and him instead of how she was feeling. It made him think they'd done something right in raising her.

"I'm fine. But the question is; how are you doing with all of this?"

She let go of her death grip and wiped her eyes. "I wasn't tied up by some lunatic, and I don't make a living chasing psychos, so I'm good. Just scared a little, I guess. Can I go see her?"

"She's sleeping and Sampson is lying in front of the bed, but I can't think of anything your mom would like better than for you to climb in there with her."

Giving him another hug, she left for the bedroom.

Head down, he let his heart slow to a normal rhythm and captured his AWOL poise.

"Definitely tougher than her old man," said Josh.

"A hell of lot cuter too," said Alex.

Manny grinned. "Right on both accounts."

One of the blues, Officer Wang, who had canvassed the neighborhood, poked his head into the room. "Sorry to bother you all, but they found a hit-and-run victim over on Washington. Real mess according to the first on the scene. Looks like she'd been backed over a few times."

"What's that got to do with us, Wang?" said Sophie.

"There was an APB out on her."

"Shit," said Alex. "Let me guess, Evelyn Kroll, right?"

"Yes sir. They're wondering what you want them to do."

"Call the lab and have them send out one of the FBI's CSU crews, and let me know when the body is at the morgue."

"Oh yeah, almost forgot why we're here," breathed Chloe. "Almost."

The frustration of losing their best lead and top suspect in the Justice Club murders was palatable. They still had a serial killer running around Lansing, one who had turned on and killed her own club members, and Argyle was now free, like a fox in the hen house. Could things get any better?

Finally, Manny spoke. "It'll take them a few hours to get the site processed and Evelyn's body transported, and it'll take Buzzy some time to finish the phone tracing. I don't see much sense in processing our house; we know all we need to about what happened here."

Manny unfastened his holster and put it on the table. "I'm going to go spend some time with my family and get some sleep. After that, if it's okay with everyone, I'll see you all in the office at four this afternoon. You should all get some rest too. We're going to need it."

Chapter-67

Manny and the others spent the next two days trying to decipher all of the forensic information gathered by Alex's crew and the FBI's loaner staff. All the while, they hoped the phone would ring to say that Argyle was back behind bars, or better yet, being measured for a casket.

The mutilation slayings had stopped, but that didn't mean the Justice Club was out of commission. Someone had flattened Evelyn Kroll, literally, and Manny knew it wasn't a random incident. The cell phone records that Buzzy had subpoenaed tied Stella, Kathy, and Evelyn together. They each had purchased a pay-as-you-go, registering them with dummy e-mails and AKAs. The fact that they had all called each other from time to time solidified the assumption that they had all killed at least one victim, based on times and locations of the calls pinged at individual towers. But they had been unable to unwind the identity of the fourth number. The user had been very bright and only called from locations that were heavily used. The times of the calls helped some. However, there was nothing that linked the fourth number to any of the murders, with the exception of Stella's last victim. The phone had been nearby that location at about the same time as the murder was committed. Manny suspected that the mysterious fourth member of the club had been following Stella and took her out in the conference room. The big question was why?

The .22 that had been used to kill Dana Gary's fiancé and Kathy Ross was not the same gun that had been used in three of the mutilation murders. That one weapon was still missing. The other two victims and Gavin had been shot with Mike Crosby's handgun, the one Stella had taken from the family safe. The victimology tying the five victims together had been hard to put together, until they'd dug deeper. The three degenerates' histories were a matter of public record, but Morgan and Becker hadn't had any such record—until the crime lab played the DVD that Alex had taken from Evelyn's car. The disc revealed that both men had unsavory appetites for underage girls. Alex wasn't sure how Evelyn got the footage, but it could have been staged to see if the men would take the bait. They had.

Manny sat at his desk, hands cradling his chin, reading more reports, and then felt the impulse to look out the window. The sun was setting on the last Saturday in September, and it was beautiful. Not like the last six days had been. Not at all.

Gavin was still embedded deeply in his coma. His son Mike had somewhat recovered from the truth about his mom and had grown a different set of priorities, namely not leaving his dad's side. He'd begun the tough journey to recovering from Stella's death, as much as could be expected, and now was going to be there for his dad. Nice to see.

Josh, Chloe, and Max were getting ready to leave. Josh's boss had decided that it was time for them to get back and on to something else. Josh had reluctantly agreed. Things had settled to a dull roar, and there was no telling where Argyle was. So until he surfaced—and they knew he would show again—it was time for the Feds to go. Manny felt his people could handle things from here on out. Besides, he had a couple of new contacts, including the head of the ERT department in Detroit. He'd use them if he had to.

Sophie interrupted his thoughts. "Hey. What's up?"

"The sky."

"Smartass."

"Seriously, the sunset is beautiful."

"Yeah, okay. Anything about Argyle on the wire?"

Manny shook his head. "No. No e-mail updates either. I did get an e-mail that offered me a new bra if I had trouble finding double D sizes. Does that count as an update?"

"Great! Forward that to me. My boobs are going to get real big, real soon."

"You're lost, you know that?"

"Yes, yes I do. But that's why I need you around."

She moved to the corner of the desk and sat down. "How are Louise and Jenny doing? This police protection thing has got to be getting old."

"They're doing just fine. They know it's for their own good. And I promised no more than a nine-hour work day."

"Damn. You're going to need drugs to get used to that."

He smiled. "I know where to get them if I do."

Josh walked around the corner, followed by Chloe and Max, travel bags—all the same dark-blue FBI-issue—over their shoulders.

"So did you all go shopping at the same travel store?"

"Hey. I know it looks weird, but free is free. Besides, the department got a good deal on them," smiled Josh.

Manny reached his hand out to him.

The agent's grip was pure, strong. "I'll be in touch. I know this week was mean, but I want you to consider my job offer."

"Thanks for all of your help, and I'm not sliding anything off the plate right now. We'll talk," said Manny.

He shook Max's hand and Chloe's next. She had great hands too. He moved on a split-second later. "Good seeing you again Max, and good working with you, Chloe."

"Thanks Manny," responded Max.

Chloe grinned. "The pleasure was mine. Call

me if you need help with some profiling, or anything else."

He hoped no one else saw the tiny wink.

"To heck with the handshake." Sophie grabbed Josh and hugged him. Then stepped back. "Been wanting to do that. And what Chloe said: if you need anything, and I mean anything, call me."

Josh grinned. "I'll be sure to remember that, Asian Fox."

The Feds walked out, and Sophie elbowed Manny. "Did you hear that? He wants me."

"That might be news to his wife."

"I won't tell." Sophie leaned against the desk again, turning serious. "Are you thinking of taking that Fed gig? Because if you are, I'm not sure—"

"Wait," Manny interrupted. The emotion on her face was more than she usually allowed. "I'm more concerned with my family, my cop family included, to think about that now. Let's just see how the next few weeks or so play out with Gavin, this investigation, and Argyle. But I won't lie. If I think the best thing for Jen and Louise is to get out of Lansing, we're gone."

"I get that, of course, just realize that I'm coming with you, got it?"

He started to grin and then realized she wasn't kidding. "I got it."

Alex came in, brow knitted in a hard V. "Got what?"

"It's a secret, and we ain't talking," said Sophie, folding her arms.

"Rumor has it that you won't be able to do that

after Christmas."

"Do what?"

"Cross your arms. Your boobs will be too big."

"Yeah. Maybe. But you won't get to see 'em."

"Thank God. Anyway, I came in here for a reason."

"What reason?" asked Manny.

"You know that number we've been trying to reach on that fourth cell phone?"

"Yes. In fact, I've got it memorized."

"Somebody answered it about five minutes ago."

Chapter-68

Penny reached into her purse and plucked the phone from the inside pocket as she wheeled up to the STOP sign. She put the phone to her ear. “Hello.”

The static was intense, then abruptly cleared. “Hi. Who is this?”

She froze. The voice on the other end was familiar.

But why was she calling me?

Penny pulled the phone from her ear and swore. In her haste, she’d answered the wrong phone.

Damn it.

She quickly hung up, resting her forehead on the leather steering wheel. That was close. She’d almost given away everything. And she’d worked too hard for that. Maybe loved too hard was the better statement. She’d protected the man she loved and would do it all over again.

If she were caught, no one would ever understand how things were for her because of him. How could anyone comprehend?

The horn honked impatiently behind her. She exhaled and drove through the intersection. No worries. She had a good teacher.

Chapter-69

"Someone answered? Who? Where?" Manny rifled questions at Alex.

"Let's see. Don't know. And we'll find out, but it may not be until Monday."

Alex shifted his feet, a mannerism Manny knew well. It indicated Alex was going to talk . . . maybe a lot.

"Buzzy came in for a few hours and had the number sitting on her workstation. She decided to call it and a woman answered. The woman said something you don't hear in church, then hung up. Buzzy had no idea who she was, but it was definitely a woman."

"That makes sense, but why would she answer the phone?" asked Manny.

"Buzzy thinks she caught her by surprise."

"Say you're right. Why would she still have that phone?" asked Sophie.

"It might represent some kind of important event for her, similar to a milestone or an accomplishment. It could even possess some kind of talisman or good-luck charm," answered

Manny.

"She thinks she's invincible as long as she has it?" scowled Alex.

Manny shrugged. "Who knows for sure? It might even symbolize the defeat of an enemy. Kind of like scalps to Native American tribes or headhunters taking the head of their conquered enemies."

"So she kills three members of this idiot club and hangs onto the phone as a keepsake?" asked Sophie. "Man. I thought I was screwed up."

"You are," said Alex. "There is another possibility."

"That there might be another member of the group?" asked Manny. "I don't see it. It really pushed the psychological dynamics of the group to have more than three. Five is out of the realm of any killing group I've ever studied. Too many character differences and chances are high that there will be more than one alpha type in a group that size. Besides, it doesn't feel like that."

"So your feelings seal the deal?" asked Alex.

He knew how Alex felt about intuition, especially given that science was his life. But there was no escaping history. "When was the last time one of my 'feelings' was wrong?"

"I know. But I don't think it's a feeling at all. I think you subconsciously gather information, piece it together, draw the most logical conclusion, and call it a feeling."

"You know that nonbelievers will end up in hell, right?" said Sophie.

"Yeah, Yeah. So I've been told."

"You said we'd have to wait on the tower info. Why?" said Manny.

"We can't get the records until then. They will still be able to triangulate the location by the strength of signal from tower to tower, but we won't be able to get the subpoena until Monday."

"That kind of sucks, what if—"

His phone rang, it was Louise. He snatched the handset from the cradle. "Hey. Is everything alright?"

"Yeah, we're fine. Well, sort of."

"What's up?"

There was a quiet, almost pleading silence that was beginning to make him a little nervous.

"I don't know how to say this any other way, so I'll let it go with both barrels. I'm staring at the tickets we have for the Tiger game tomorrow, and I think I want to go. So does Jen."

"Louise. I don't think that's a great idea. I mean—"

"I know. I know. The son of a bitch is still out there, but he won't know where we are, right?"

"It's not a good idea. There are too many things that could go wrong."

"I'm not stupid. I know that. But you'll be with us and—"

Manny heard (maybe felt was a better word) her emotion well up and knew that she was trying to hold back the tears.

"I really need this. He took my normal life away and replaced it with fear. I can't beat that fear on my own. I need to get back to normal. I need this . . . please."

How could he say no to that? Besides, maybe *he* needed it, too. Maybe this is where beating Argyle started. "Okay. You're right. Let's do it."

"Thank you. I'll see you for dinner and . . . I love you."

She hung up.

Manny sat down and tapped the computer mouse. No new messages. No update on Argyle. No new homicides. No more leads to chase, for now. Hell, no more spam telling him how much he needed to grow his manhood and how big it could get. He clicked the calendar and Sunday began to pulse. The Tiger game notification came to life.

Must be an omen.

"You know. I've got Tiger tickets for Jen, Louise, and me for tomorrow, and we're going."

Sophie punched him on the shoulder. "Is that wise?"

"Probably not, but Louise really needs to take a stab at getting back to normal. I think all three of us do."

"Do you want any security?"

"No!" He turned to both of his friends. "We're going as a normal family. Understand? I can take care of them."

His two friends scoured the floor like scolded children. He threw up his hands. "But I guess I can't do anything about you two going to the game, now can I?"

Alex grinned. "You know, Barb's never been to

Comerica Park."

"Neither has Randy," said Sophie. "He loves cotton candy and beer."

"Just keep yourselves out of sight. Just in case. And I mean it."

"Yes sir. Damn," said Sophie. "Grouchy old bastard."

"That's the nicest thing you've ever said to me," he grinned. "Now. I'm going to stop by and see Gavin and Mike and then go home to tell the women in my life about tomorrow's plans."

Manny turned off his computer and walked out the door. His pulse raced with the prospect of just the three of them, together at Comerica Park in Detroit, eating hotdogs, buying souvenirs, and laughing like families do.

At that moment in time, things seemed right, perfect, in fact.

But in less than thirty world-shattering hours, his life would change forever.

Chapter-70

"Did you get the tickets?" asked Louise.

"Yes ma'am. I took them off the refrigerator magnet clip thing and put them in my billfold."

Louise was dressed in a Magglio Ordonez jersey and white shorts, Jen in a Brandon Inge tee-shirt and jeans. She liked Inge because he was hot, not caring what position he played.

He tugged at the blue and orange cap lettered with the Old English "D." It traveled with him every time he'd gone to a game in the last few years. He had even taken it on the cruise in June. Nothing like familiarity to breed comfort.

"Let's get this show on the road. We might even get to see some batting practice," said Louise.

"And just how tight the players' pants are," grinned Jen.

"Well, that too," agreed Louise.

"You two have been hanging out with Sophie too much." He grabbed the keys off the microwave and headed for the front door. "Okay, you perverts, in the car. We're out of here."

Louise turned to Sampson. "Watch the house,

big dog."

Sampson did the patented three turns and stretched out on the floor.

Manny shook his head, "I guess he's got it covered."

They hustled out the door, waved at the unmarked car across the street, and zoomed off to the land of Major League Baseball.

An hour and a half later, they were seated behind the third-base dugout, four rows up, and cheering with the rest of the other 30,000 fans.

Looking around, he noticed every type, every color, and every size person one could imagine. Families, excitement radiating from each face; men laughing and drinking with their friends; women giggling with their daughters; grandparents pointing things out to wide-eyed grandchildren. Amazing.

The cares of their private world had become just some hazy recollection that reality wouldn't reveal until they all returned home. For now, the pure ambiance of a baseball game, America's pastime, was sufficient to send folks halfway up the steps of Heaven. He wasn't sure why a game like baseball had that kind of mystic effect on the masses, but he was glad it did. Maybe it was the smell of freshly mown grass or the intoxicating aroma of a well-grilled Italian sausage. Whatever it was, the game experience was akin to a family reunion on a nuclear scale.

The umpires came out, the Tigers ran onto the field, and Jen slipped her hand into his and squeezed. The perfect day had begun.

The game was a slaughter. Detroit hit three home runs in the first inning, and the rout was on. By the time the seventh inning ended, the Tigers were up 16-0, a perfect score as far as Manny was concerned.

Louise stood. "I'm going to the powder room."

"Me too," said Jen.

"I'll go with you."

"No. Just stay here. We'll be fine."

"Are you sure?"

"Hey. You can't go in with us anyway."

He pondered the edge in Louise's voice. She was telling him to leave the cop thing out of this. No reminders of Argyle or any other case allowed.

Damn workaholic demon.

No-brainer here. "Okay. Hurry back. We still have two more innings to go."

The girls left. He watched until they were out of sight, fighting an irresistible urge to follow. He waited three minutes, then stood up, craning his neck to see if they were on their way back. He knew it wasn't nearly enough time, especially to get through the line in the women's restroom, but his anxiety was winning the battle.

He glanced back to the field as the crowd cheered a great play and then was suddenly hurtling in midair over the empty seats in front of him. The sharp blow to his back registered as he landed on the seat's armrest full on his left ribs, while his arm and thigh tangled with the underbelly of the seat. The pain caused him to see red, but adrenaline pulsed through his body as he struggled to free himself.

A burly man two seats over helped him to his feet. “You okay?” he rumbled.

The pain in his side was brilliant, but Manny was already searching for the source of the blow that had sent him reeling.

Ten rows from the top, he saw him. The tall man in the Panama hat and white suit was taking the steps two at a time.

He’d recognize the man’s build anywhere.

Argyle.

Chapter-71

Manny rushed up the steps holding his ribs and trying to catch his breath. The pain was intense, but he didn't care. Argyle was all that he saw. He reached the top of the concrete stairs, clutching the handrail, and scanned the direction he thought Argyle had gone. Nothing. He turned the other way and saw the hat, as Argyle disappeared around the curve of the concourse. Manny raced another twenty steps and bent over, pain and labored breathing causing bright motes of flashing lights to dance in front of his eyes.

Not this time, you son of a bitch.

He gritted his teeth and took off, running harder than before. He passed a security guard and slammed on the brakes. He pulled his wallet, showed the guard his badge, told him what Argyle was, and what he was wearing.

The guard's eyes grew as large as Chinaware. "Seriously? A serial killer? Here in the Park?"

"Yes. And if you keep talking to me, he's going to get away."

The guard reached for his radio.

After catching his breath, he took off again. He dodged several fans, and a couple of hotdog and souvenir vendors, and almost caused an already-happy patron to drop the two beers in his hands.

Just when he didn't think he could go another step, he saw them. Four guards had Argyle pinned on the concrete, cuffed and restrained as two more guards arrived.

The pain vanished. Argyle had finally screwed up. The cruise ship capture was by design but this one, well this one . . .

Damn.

Manny felt the wind leave his sails. It became painfully obvious to him that this was another part of the game. There was no way Argyle would get himself into this kind of situation. His plans always left a way out, always. He'd let Jenkins die on the ship, just a pawn in Argyle's twisted, fantasy world. He'd used his death as a diversion from the truth. Manny had that same feeling of revelation now.

Argyle was arrogant, but too smart to let this happen.

Manny limped up to the man in white and motioned to the guards.

"I'm Detective Williams," he labored. "Roll his ass over."

By now there was a huge audience of bystanders, despite the efforts of security to get them to move on. Manny motioned again. The guards turned their captive.

Shit. This is getting real old, real fast.

The man was similar in height and build to Argyle, but that was about it.

He was balding and maybe five years older. His beaked nose and protruding chin gave him an Ichabod Crane look. There were fresh wounds on both and not from the scuffle with the guards.

He peered into the man's close-set eyes and saw fear, wild fear.

"My name's Al Forester. You got to let me go. He said he'd kill them if I didn't get back in thirty minutes."

"Whoa. Easy. Who will kill who?"

"The man who has my wife and mother."

Manny felt sick. Would Argyle kill them? He hated the answer to that one.

"He . . . he said, if I got caught, to have Detective Williams call the number in my coat pocket."

Manny reached for the pocket and fell back on his haunches as the pain ripped up his left side.

"I'll get it," said the voice behind him.

He turned to see his wife and daughter standing beside Sophie.

Sophie shrugged. "Randy really wanted that cotton candy. And there was no way I was going to let you come here without us."

"I know. I would've done the same thing. Where's Alex?"

"He'll be here in a minute. He's calling the Feds."

"We'll talk later. Get me that phone number."

Sophie reached into Forester's pocket and

handed the piece of paper to Manny without speaking.

He glanced at his wife. She was burning holes in the concrete floor, but said nothing. That was worse than chewing his ass. Another family trip gone to hell in a handbasket because of what he did for a living, and what his profession meant to men like Dr. Fredrick Argyle.

Manny started to dial the number when Forester interrupted him. “Detective. He said to use my phone.” Forester started to cry. “Will he kill them?”

Manny didn’t answer, but he knew that Argyle already had. The psycho bastard never intended to let them live. Argyle counted on Forester getting caught. Another way to show he had control.

Sophie got Forester’s phone, and Manny dialed the number. The pain in his side could never match the pain in his soul.

The phone rang once, and he felt the silent evil on the other end. “Argyle?”

“Detective Williams. You are two minutes faster than I thought you’d be, and you are speaking like you’re in pain. I’m so sorry; you were supposed to be on the way to a hospital.”

“Yeah. I’m full of surprises. How did you know where’d we’d be?”

“Calculated certainty. I saw the tickets on the refrigerator when Louise and I had our . . . date, and I surmised your guilt would lead you there. You’re not as full of surprises as you think.”

Manny ran a hand through his hair. He hated

how the Good Doctor sounded so confident. "Why this? Why more innocent people?"

Forester released a horrible wail.

"My dear detective, there is no such thing as innocent. Only strong and weak. You know that. Or are you just a slow learner?"

"Just say I'm wrong."

"But you already know you aren't. The wife was good sport. I especially enjoyed her neck. I saved her for last. If it's any consolation to you, the old woman felt no pain."

Manny grew quiet. "I'm going to kill you and bring flowers to your damned funeral. Do you understand?"

The insane cackle exploded in his ear. "Temper, temper." The doctor's voice hardened. "You have a rather high opinion of yourself. And who knows the future? But you'll not see me until I've squeezed every ounce of sanity from your mind. Just imagine what that means . . . and what I enjoy the most."

The phone went dead and so did another fraction of Manny's heart.

Chapter-72

Midnight found Manny sitting at the kitchen table in the semi-dark. His mind was never a quiet place, but tonight was as bad as it got for him.

Talk about all dressed up with no place to go.

Thoughts continued to ransack his psyche and spied on his sanity like an expert voyeur hoping to get an invite. He had come dangerously close to allowing insanity to visit. But he didn't, couldn't. He had a wife and daughter to take care of.

Today should have been a perfect day, especially given the incredible start. But perfect days and he were fast becoming mortal enemies, thanks to this job . . . and Argyle. Hell, even Sophie and Alex had known the baseball game was a bad idea. But he didn't listen.

He gritted his teeth in frustration. His pride could have killed his family. He wouldn't make that mistake again.

Shifting in his chair, the pain in his side bolted both directions and caused him to gasp like he'd stepped into a cold shower. The emergency room doctor had said there was nothing truly broken.

He had a tiny hairline fracture in the fourth rib and a large contusion that would disappear in a few days. Still, there would be no elephant-lifting contests for the next couple of weeks.

Sampson huffed and changed positions as he lay a few feet to Manny's right. The dog almost never went to bed until Manny did.

Who is guarding who here?

The cops and the Detroit FBI office had sent out another APB on Argyle after they had gone to Forester's home to verify a scene Manny hated to think about. Argyle had done what he'd claimed, and Al Forester would be shattered forever, his wife and mother embedded eternally in the violent, psychotic legacy of Argyle.

The agent in charge told Manny he'd never seen anything like it and never wanted to again. The walls had been painted in blood to taunt law enforcement, Manny in particular, and to make it clear Argyle could do whatever he wanted. The agent could barely speak about Forester's wife, how Argyle had posed her at the dinner table. The man was in tears, and Manny told him to stop. He needed no more fodder for nightmares.

Of course, the Feds hadn't found Argyle, and Manny was beginning to wonder if Argyle had made a pact with the Devil, the real one.

Louise had driven home and barely said a word. She was usually so supportive, so *"let's get to the next thing"* like. But not today, and it wasn't only today.

He'd seen her change little by little since they'd

returned home from the cruise. The breast cancer scare had taken a toll, but she had let that go as a non-issue. When she had seen the rose petals that Argyle had somehow gotten in her purse, something changed. She'd become more internal, more sullen. She confessed to him one night after they had made love that she didn't think anyone was really safe from people like Argyle. He tried to reassure her. She kissed him and turned over.

Maybe she was right. No matter how hard he tried, he might not be enough to keep the demons away, particularly of the human variety.

Jen had sat in the back, staring out the window, occasionally wiping away tears. He had hardly been able to stand it. No physical pain would ever match that moment. He promised that he would never see his daughter like that again.

"So, Sampson, what should I do?" he whispered.

The black Lab raised his head, lifting his ears at the same time, giving Manny his best "*you're on your own*" look, and then flopped back down.

"Thanks, Buddy."

Manny got up and moved gingerly to the third bedroom and pushed open the door without turning on the light. Argyle had invaded his home, and in the process, violated his wife in a way that was akin to rape. It could've been worse. But Argyle wanted Manny to know he was in no hurry, that he would operate on his own schedule, and Manny was helpless to stop him.

The anger began to boil, but wasn't that what

Argyle wanted, even fed on? He pressed the anger down. It wouldn't help matters, and the emotional yo-yo would only delve deeper into the brain screw Argyle wanted to administer. Besides, becoming angry, out of control, wasn't why he was here. He needed reassurance that what he was going to do tomorrow was the right thing. Nothing like a little visual reinforcement. Not to mention, he was curiously drawn to the crawlspace. It spoke to him, even condemned him for not being a better husband and father, and he wanted to face his accuser.

He stared at the area rug, waiting for the self-persecution to begin, but something halted the voices before they began.

The throw rug was usually lined up directly on the door over the crawlspace. Manny frowned. It wasn't lined up properly, not centered. He pulled the carpet to the side, grimacing. He dropped to his knees, felt for the latch, then pushed the door. It popped up about an inch. He pulled it open, resting it gently against the hardwood floor and stood up.

He stared into the blackness. His wife's unholy prison stared back. It mocked him, speaking with a voice that seemed to come from the very walls and floor themselves.

You let this happen in your own house. What a piece of shit husband and father you are.

Some Guardian of the Universe. You can't even protect your family.

Sending the voices scampering away wasn't

the problem; the truth was another matter completely. He started to reach for the trapdoor and realized all of the voices hadn't been stilled, that the pit had something else to say. He felt it. He kneeled to get a closer look. Not at all sure why, just that he should. There! In the damning black, he noticed a tiny glint of light reflecting through the blackness. He blinked, did it again, but it was still there.

What the hell?

He went to the kitchen and pulled the large flashlight from the pantry.

Returning to the entranceway of the crawlspace, Sampson at his heels, he dropped back to his knees, leaned over, and shined the powerful beam in the direction of the fairy-like glimmer of light.

Chapter-73

Alex struggled out of the thick recliner and turned off the fifty-inch-wide plasma screen. It was good to catch up on the shows he'd DVR'd the last week. However, it had kept him up later than he intended. Still *Bones* and *Criminal Minds* were worth it, even if it was just to laugh at how forensic science was portrayed. He wished, in his world, that things would move that fast. That particulates would stay rooted in a bone cut for months. Or that DNA testing only took less than a half hour. But he supposed Hollywood had to put everything together in less than forty-five minutes, so he let some of it slide. Good water-cooler stuff just the same.

Walking to the kitchen, he pulled out a tablespoon, scooped a glop of peanut butter, and sucked it clean. He then turned to the refrigerator, grabbed the milk jug, and took a monstrous swig to wash down the peanut butter. His wife Barb would kill him if she saw the swig. But she was sleeping, so he was safe.

Reaching for the light, he took one last look at

his badge and gun sitting on the shelf above the dishwasher. They were constant, real reminders that he was a cop. It still gave him a bit of a thrill to have that fact register. Not bad for a kid who grew up afraid of everything. He wasn't like Manny, but he did other important things to save lives, and that worked for him.

His thoughts channeled to his good friend. No peace seemed to be his MO.

Sophie had called him to talk about the incident at the ballgame and to see if they could help, but he told her that Manny had assured him there was nothing else they could do and had instructed them to stay home. The ladies and he were fine, he had said, and he would see Alex and Sophie in the morning. Sophie hated no for an answer, but respected Manny on this one.

A nondescript feeling of unrest tapped him on the shoulder. Alex wondered where this was all headed. Maybe Manny really had more than his fill of the detective life. More uneasiness. He didn't want that to be true, but only time would tell.

The phone rang just as he flipped off the kitchen light. It sang again, and he swore. Late-night calls were never good, ever.

He looked at the caller ID. It was from the office.

"Hello."

"Oh my God, oh my God," Buzzy Dancer was in full geek mode.

"Slow down, kid. What's going on?"

"I . . . I . . . well, you know that other phone

number? Oh my gosh . . . holey moley . . ."

"Buzzy! Stop. Take a breath. I don't know what the hell you're talking about."

"Okay. I forgot my laptop, so I came back to the office to get it and decided to see if I had anymore e-mails or stuff, and guess what . . . oh my gosh . . ."

"How many Red Bulls?"

"What? Only three . . . oh, I get it."

She took a deep breath, and let it out slowly, in the vein of winding down near the end of Yoga class.

"Better. Anyway, I had a message from the pay-as-you-go phone company. They ID'd the coordinates of that call from the other day. So I found that location. Very weird. Then they did one better. They traced the GPS in the phone. So I triangulated the towers based on that info and found the closest address to where the phone is now."

"Great. But can't this wait until tomorrow?"

"No. Good Lord, no. I'm going to pee my pants. No. Wait. I think I'll be okay."

"Buzzy, spit it out."

"The first set of coordinates had the phone no further than twenty or twenty-five yards from . . . your house."

"What? My house?"

"Yep, but I thought that it could be a coincidence. So I checked the other triangulations and boom . . . three other calls came from somewhere near your house."

"So, the killer's one of my neighbors?" said Alex, angst building in his voice.

"I don't think so because of where the phone is now."

"Come on, Buzzy!"

"The phone seems to be in Manny's house."

Chapter-74

The beam from the flashlight danced from the hard dirt to the long, black case and then to the half-opened shoulder bag that leaked the cell phone's LCD light. Manny took two more steps in his crouched position and touched the case. No mistaking what it contained. He'd seen a sniper's rifle a time or two and knew how they were packaged.

The large, gray handbag contained more than just the phone. Much more. There was a black leather ensemble fit for any hooker on any street. But that wasn't the worst thing. The four-inch stilettos had traces of a dark-red, almost black substance that he already knew was blood. The metallic smell sealed it.

There was something else in the bag, the grand prize: a .22 handgun.

He touched his throbbing ribcage and felt his mind, his imagination, swirl out of control.

What's the rifle doing here? What's any of this doing here?

Not wanting to taint evidence, he scooted back

to the opening and lifted himself out. He had to call Alex and have him bring his kit. The secret identity of the last member of the Justice Club lies in that crawlspace . . . in *his* house. The world *was* going crazy. Even worse was where his thoughts were rushing.

Brushing off his khaki shorts, he turned the overhead light on and the flashlight off.

What the hell is happening here? How would someone get that gear down there without Louise or me noticing?

There couldn't have been anyone home. Not to mention, it would've been placed there after Louise's ordeal, so it couldn't have been there longer than sixty hours. Unless . . .

His mind sprinted to where it logically had no choice but to go.

Louise? How ridiculous is that? My wife?

But Manny couldn't rid himself of that feeling of denial basking in a truth he didn't want to acknowledge. It attacked like a hungry wolf, and he had to clasp his hands together to stop from clenching them. He hated how his brain worked, but there was no denying the logic.

Hasn't she been acting a little off her game the last few weeks? Who would hide this stuff in our house but her? Her reaction to Stella's death was less than emotional to boot.

The pain in his ribs disappeared as he paced back and forth.

My wife a member of the Justice Club? A cold-blooded killer? The woman I've spent more than half my life with? My Rock?

He stopped his mind from racing and took in a calming breath. The facts didn't support his wild dive into the deep end of the pool. First things first: he knew people and he sure as hell knew her. Next, there was a matter of being able to handle a rifle like that. Not on her resume. She'd also need opportunity, and he'd called her the night Stella had died. She'd been home.

Rubbing his face with both hands, he wondered how long he'd have his balls if she ever suspected the forbidden land where his thoughts had traveled. Probably about as long as it would take to get the words out of his mouth. Maybe right after she gave him that *"your elevator doesn't go to the top"* look.

The feeling of uneasiness came racing back. Elevator metaphor notwithstanding, someone had brought that bag and rifle into his house. Who else besides him and his family had access? He and Louise needed to talk.

Suddenly he felt eyes watching him. He spun around and . . . Sampson was looking at him, head cocked, with that look dogs universally coined as theirs: he really had to take a leak.

Manny patted the dog on the head and let him out the back. Then he went to the bedroom, opened the door, and stared.

His wife usually slept like she was in a deep trance, but this time she was wide-eyed and blanketing his face with a look that melted his heart.

"Manny. What is it?" she whispered.

"I need you to come with me, okay?"

Silently, she picked her robe off the bedpost, their bedpost, and followed him into the spare room. It took everything he had to control the turmoil slapping his heart around.

Louise moved a couple steps toward the trapdoor and stopped, taking his hand. He frowned.

She is afraid to go closer, yet . . .

"What do you know about what's down there?" he asked, almost inaudibly.

"You mean my piece of mind? A piece of hell? A piece of my soul?" she was getting angry.

"I found a sniper's rifle and a bag of bloody clothes, along with a cell phone and a handgun. Someone had to put it there after we got you out."

She let go of his hand and moved in front of him. "What are you talking about? Have you been drinking? There was nothing like that in there and how would I know what a sniper rifle ..." His wife's eyes grew large. An angry, hurt smile creased her beautiful face. "Manfred Robert Williams! How could you think such a thing? Me? What the hell's wrong with you?"

"Louise—"

She stomped out of the room, then stomped back in.

"Are you flipping nuts?"

"Louise, I just—"

"Just what? The evidence led you down this path? I'm not a damn evidence path; I'm the woman you've been sleeping with for seventeen years."

He grabbed her and pulled her tight. "Stop. I know you aren't involved. I just wanted to ask if you had any idea how this stuff could've gotten here."

"Oh." Her gaze softened, and she put her hands on both sides of his face, pulling him within an inch of her nose. "If you found what you found, then we have a problem because apparently our house is some kind of Grand Central Station for deranged killers. I also have no idea how that stuff got down there, and that scares me. But you almost had a worse problem because I was going to kick your ass for thinking I could be involved in those murders. A sniper's rifle?" Her eyes narrowed. "You never thought that, right?"

"I—"

Then out of the blue, it hit him like those sudden bursts of truth do. "Shit. Sniper rifle. I should have put that together."

He kissed Louise and ran to the phone.

"As usual, I don't have a clue what just went though that head of yours, but you don't get off that easy. That minefield for a brain isn't getting you out of answering my question."

He turned and kissed her again. "I'm an idiot, but I'm your idiot, and I love you."

"Okay. Maybe you're digging yourself out a little. I'm going back to bed." She patted her backside. "You're not getting this until you answer my question, got it?" Then she turned and disappeared into the bedroom.

Manny grinned. He'd explain himself later and hope it worked. Reaching for the phone, he noticed the display said 12:57. The man wasn't going to be happy, but maybe by this time tomorrow night, everyone would be sleeping better. He was sure that he was going to be.

He dialed the first five numbers before the knock on the door got his attention. He stopped dialing. It was probably one of the uniforms checking in because the lights were still on, per his instructions. He took the phone with him and finished dialing as he moved to the door. He grabbed his Glock with the other hand. The number continued to ring as he cradled the phone to his ear. He unlatched the dead bolt and pulled the door open.

Chapter-75

Alex and Sophie stood on the small, brick stoop leading to the front of his house. Manny didn't care for the look on their faces. This felt wrong. "Out of whack" was an understatement. He opened the screen door. "What's going on, you two?"

Alex fidgeted. "We need to talk. Can we come in?"

The nervous look Alex shot Sophie did little to ease the warnings going off in Manny's mind. "Of course, but you didn't answer my question."

The shadow to Alex's right came alive, mimicking some creepy science fiction parody. There was no one there, and then there was.

Sarah Sparks, Alex's right hand tech, lifted the M9 military-issue Beretta, fitted with a customized suppressor, so that he could see it clearly. "Hello, detective. We're all going to have a little chat in your front room."

He glanced across the street to the squad car. Sparks noticed.

"Oh, they won't be of any help. I couldn't afford

to be interrupted."

Her smile reminded him of Eli Jenkins, the serial killer they'd taken down on the *Ocean Duchess*. Not a good thing.

"You don't seem to be too surprised to see me. Did the great Manny Williams figure things out?"

"Why don't you just put that thing down and–"

"Shut the hell up and let me see the other hand, slowly." She put the gun against the back of Sophie's head. "Very slowly."

"Hey heifer, watch the hair. This cut cost more than you make in a week," said Sophie.

Sparks pushed harder. "Shut up, bitch. I'm tired of your mouth."

Manny wanted to make a move, only she never took her eyes from him. But then again, Special Ops were a talented bunch. He raised his hand, the Glock pointing down.

"Toss it."

He did.

A minute later Sophie, Alex, and Manny were lined up on the sofa in his family room. The silence was crawling with a tension Manny recognized and hated. Someone was going to die.

"Sparky," said Alex, breaking the choking silence. "Why are you doing this?"

Manny watched her dark eyes soften like a lovesick teenager. "You don't know? Really?" She leaned closer to him, stroking his chin with her hand. "I'll explain everything soon. Just know it was for you. Always you."

She turned to Manny, her look reverting back

to reflect her daughter-of-evil character.

"Before I kill you, tell me how you figured me out."

Manny shrugged. "I remembered your résumé when Alex showed it to me. Not many women make it to a Special Ops level. I know you finished your sniper training before you tore up your knee and were discharged. Your determination was a big part of the reason Alex wanted to bring you aboard."

She looked at Alex with that puppy-dog look again, and Manny knew they were running short of time. She was in love with Alex and wanted to finish what she started here, then run off with him to places unknown.

Pointing the gun at Manny, she stepped back, just out of his reach. "Impressive, detective. I had no idea you saw my credentials. And for your information, I didn't hurt my knee. I was set up by two officers and booted to keep my mouth shut."

Her eyes grew wilder, darker, if that were possible. "They didn't like it that a woman was kicking their precious men-troop's asses in just about every category, particularly the sniper thing. I could hit a four-inch square at 200 yards nine out of ten times."

"So why didn't you say something?" asked Sophie.

"Because I was a soldier. I wanted them to know I was as tough as any of them. And I told you to shut up."

More hatred sprang from her face. "But the

men in charge saw that I wasn't broken, wasn't going to give up. So they put drugs in my footlocker. I had two choices, their terms or the brig."

"I'm sorry that happened, but—" started Manny.

"I don't need your idiot sympathy. I just want men like them to disappear, the hard way."

Alex seemed to catch on to her mental state. "Sparky. You are the best tech I've ever had. Just give me the gun and we'll—"

"I can't do that. I'm going to finish what we started."

Their best shot at getting out of this was to keep her talking. Manny did. "So why hide the guns and clothes here?"

"I couldn't bear to part with them. Every time I looked at those things, it made me feel like I'd made a difference. I hid them here while you were at the ballgame. There was no one watching the place, and Sampson and I made friends at that cook-out you had last month. Besides, if anyone would've seen me, I would've said I was working. But you really should get a less laid-back dog. Not that it's going to matter." She spread her feet a little wider and shifted the sidearm to her right hand.

"It was a perfect hiding place. Who was going to look there? I didn't think you'd find the rifle and bag before I got rid of you and your family. Or before Buzzy could get a GPS fix on the phone."

"Why us? Me, I get . . . but my family?"

"Because once this stuff is found here, your wife will be the prime suspect, so no one's going to be thinking of me, especially with Alex to back me up. You'll all be dead, and, well, I'm home free."

"What about Stella and Kathy? Why them?"

Her impatience was growing, but her narcissism was stronger. She wanted to impress Alex with her story. More time to sort her out, Manny hoped.

"After Gavin was shot, I knew Stella had done it and that she was coming after all of you. I couldn't allow that, certainly not my beautiful Alex." She smiled at him again. "So I followed Stella and set up across the street. You know the rest."

"How did you all get together?"

"Oh, girl talk, a few drinks, a hatred for men, particularly perverts, goes a long way. You'd be surprised what truths people can agree upon."

Sparks frowned. "I hadn't been officially introduced to Kathy and Stella before all hell broke loose, so I decided to take things into my own hands. I followed Kathy to talk to her and introduce myself, but heard her tell Evelyn that I needed to go. Hey, I'm a survivor. I wasn't going anywhere. They're the ones that went."

"But there was one thing I hadn't counted on." She went starry-eyed in Alex's direction. "No one ever treated me the way you did, Alex. Kind, considerate, patient. The men in my life were never like that. Hell, neither were the women. I knew right away that you loved me. A month later,

I'd fallen for you. I never thought that would happen to me."

"So you killed Stella to protect Alex?" said Sophie. "How sweet."

Sarah took two quick steps and put the Beretta between Sophie's eyes. "What the hell would you know about love? You're just a shallow smartass. I'd do anything for him, and he'd do anything for me."

Alex nodded. "So you hung out near my house to be close to me?"

"Of course. There's no other place I'd rather be." She backed away from Sophie, touching Alex's cheek, and Manny knew it was time.

"We'll have to get rid of your wife, and I have a plan for that. Then we can be together. Forever. But more on that later. Let's get this over with."

"No, wait," said Alex.

"Shhh. Don't worry. Let me handle this. It'll be over before you can blink."

It was now or never. Manny gathered himself. He was going to be killed trying, but he couldn't just sit there and let Sparks send them out of this world.

Sarah racked the slide. Then all hell broke loose.

"What are you doing?" yelled Louise from the kitchen doorway.

Sarah spun to see who had interrupted her private revelry.

Manny leaped off the couch as the pain in his side rose to just this side of black-out. He hit

Sparks in the middle of the back, and she flew through the air. The gun went off as she hurtled forward. He scrambled up her back desperately reaching for the Beretta. She elbowed him in the nose. More stars than he could count shot past his eyes, but he held on and grabbed the hand holding the gun. She tried to move it away from him, and another shot bellowed through the room.

Manny grabbed her hair and slammed her face into the hardwood floor. She screamed, and the gun skittered across the wood, hitting the TV stand. He raised her head again, and slammed it down with all his strength. He felt her body go limp, and she stopped struggling. He rolled over on his back, breathing hard and wondering if there was enough pain medicine in the world to quiet the storm in his side.

A second later, Sophie had Sparks in cuffs.

Somewhere in the distance, he heard sirens. The blues in the car outside his home hadn't checked in, so here came the cavalry. It was okay with him; he'd had enough of this shit for the night, maybe for the rest of his life.

Except it wouldn't be enough. Destiny wanted more.

"Manny! Come quick." The pure panic in Alex's voice caused the hair on the back of his arms to raise straight up.

He sat up, looking in the direction of Alex's voice. That's when he saw the blood. Louise had been hit.

Chapter-76

He cradled Louise in his arm, putting his hand on the hole in her chest, trying to stem the crimson flow that wouldn't take stop for an answer. It took only a few seconds before he was covered in his wife's warm blood. Somewhere in another world he heard Alex yelling into the phone, telling whoever was on the other end to hurry.

"Come on, baby. They'll be here soon. Just hang in there," he begged.

He pressed on the wound harder, and the bleeding slowed. He yelled for Sophie to get a towel. She ran to the bathroom to get one, her face as white as Louise's. The coppery odor from her blood reminded him of how many scenes like this had been carved into his memory. Except this was his wife, the love of his life. He shivered and pushed a little harder.

"Not one of my good ones," gasped Louise, her eyes flickering open.

"I'll buy you new towels," he said, trying not to cry.

"You . . . you say that now . . ." she trailed off.

He heard another door open, and a second later, Jen rushed into the room. It had taken the shouts to get her attention because she always slept with her headphones on. The look on her face would be one he'd take to his grave. Maybe beyond.

"Mom!" she screamed.

His daughter sprinted to them, tears already streaking her face, and crowded close.

"Is she okay?"

He nodded furiously. "She's going to be all right. We just have to stop the bleeding until the EMTs get here."

"What can I do?"

He didn't think it possible to be prouder of his little girl than he was at that moment. Just like her mom.

"Put your hand on mine and hold tight."

She did.

A few moments later, Louise laid her hand on top of Jen's, touching his. She felt so cold.

"I . . . I love you two," she whispered.

Jen spoke for both of them because Manny couldn't, hard tears stealing the youth from her face. "We love you too mom, forever."

Louise opened her eyes and tried to smile. Manny felt every emotion the two of them had ever shared in the split second it took to glimpse the light in her eyes.

"Take care of each other," she breathed.

Then Louise Williams left this world.

Chapter-77

Manny felt the sun peek over the top of the tall maple on the east side of his yard as he sat on the front porch of his home. The sun and the warm cup of coffee resting in his hand reminded him that he could still feel something, at least on the outside.

It had been thirty-two days since Louise's funeral, but it might as well have been thirty-two seconds. The pain in his gut felt like a dull, two-edged sword had run him through.

There was no sleep. Nothing tasted or smelled good enough to eat. He picked a little here and there and made dinner each night for Jen, but mostly they stared silently at whatever was on their plates. He sensed they both felt the same way, that Louise would have used her magic to put her own special touch on the entrée, making it incredibly special. But that wasn't going to happen ever again. There would be no more late night raids to the fridge to ravage a piece of her famous cherry pie or some of her unbelievable fried chicken.

There were other late night things he was missing. The way she'd move close on a cold night. The gentle rhythm of her breathing that would rock him to sleep after one of those awful days that made him wonder why he'd become a cop.

The times when they couldn't sleep and would make love, giggling about making too much noise so Jen wouldn't hear. Forever gone like fog in the wind.

He sipped more coffee. The day was turning into a classic Indian-summer day for Michigan. It would get near seventy-five degrees and it was odd to see the reds and golds of transformed leaves basking in that kind of heat. Maybe another hot day would help melt away a little more of the numbness he felt. He'd always heard time made things better.

Please God, speed it up.

At least he had Jen, and she had him. He knew that sometimes teenagers who lost parents would become silent, withdrawn, sullen and angry at anything that was still living, especially the surviving parent. The worst fear haunting him was that his daughter would blame him for what had happened to Louise. But that hadn't happened. Jen had been the picture of grace, a tower of strength that would make her mother proud. She seemed to have taken to heart Louise's last request.

Jen was determined to take care of him, and he would return the favor.

Then there was big Sampson. The dog was the

best natural psychologist in all of creation. Manny or Jen would talk; the dog would listen better than any PhD making $150 an hour. Then he'd come close and rest his head on the nearest body part, knowing just how long to stay.

There was some good news. Five days ago, Gavin came out of his coma. The next day, they performed the six-hour surgery to remove the bullet near his aorta, and he came through with flying colors. He'd have some balance issues and some short-term memory problems, but he was going to make it.

Mike sounded so excited when he'd called, then he'd grown sullen. Gavin had remembered how he'd gotten in the IC ward, only he didn't want to talk about it. Who would?

Manny had gone up to see him, and they were both truly glad to see each other, but neither mentioned the other's pain. Soon enough.

Taking one more sip, he decided to go for a warm-up of coffee. As he stood, Sophie pulled into the driveway with Alex riding in the back. He hadn't seen them since the funeral.

Of course, if he'd gone to work, he would have. But that hadn't happened either. Maybe it never would again, at least not as a cop.

Alex and Sophie had called a few times, sent a couple of e-mails, and so had Josh, Max, and even Chloe, all leaving messages to offer their support. Whatever he needed, they were there. The problem was no one could bring back Louise and fill the indefinable hole in his soul.

Sophie and Alex had someone with them whom Manny didn't recognize. Alex got out of the back and leaned against the car sporting shorts, a tee shirt, and sneakers.

Sophie was a different story. She was dressed like he'd never seen her. She was wearing a San Francisco Giants baseball cap, a Barry Bonds jersey, and baseball spikes. She had a bat draped over her shoulder with a baseball glove wedged on the end. The new baseball was too big for her small hand. She looked like she was headed for her very first Little League game.

The young lady with them was dressed in pink sweats and matching cap. She walked a step behind Sophie, looking at the ground, like she was embarrassed or shy. Manny guessed a little of both.

"Hey," Sophie said.

"Hey yourself. Going to a Giant's game?"

"Hell no. Better than that."

"Can't be a Tiger's game. They didn't make the playoffs."

"Better than that too."

Manny shrugged. "I give up. Tell me. But first, who's your friend?"

The young lady in pink stepped closer, took off her hat, and looked him square in the eyes. "You don't remember me?"

He smiled a tired smile. Maybe the first one since the funeral.

"Hi, Shannon. I like this look better than the hooker thing."

She nodded. “Me too.”

“Are things working out with your foster parents?”

“Better than I could have hoped for, thanks to you.”

He shook his head. “I just made a call. They’re good people.”

Sophie reached down, grabbed his hand, and pulled him up. “Come on. We’re going to the park. We have a bet, and you’re going to pay up.”

“What bet?”

“Remember when you said you could whiff me? Time to see if your mouth wrote a check your ass can’t cash.”

Manny released her hand and backed up the steps. “Sophie, I appreciate what you’re trying to do, but I’m not ready . . .”

He turned and started up the steps. Shannon flew past him and stood in front of the door.

“Sophie says you live to help people. I don’t know about others, but you went out on a limb to help a messed-up, drug-using hooker, angry at all of the bad breaks the world had thrown her way. You helped me when dying seemed like the best way to stop the pain. Let us return the favor.”

He looked in her face and saw Jen in a couple of years. Way too close to home. “I don’t know . . .”

“Please. I think I need this. Besides, Sophie says you have a rag arm, and it’ll be the easiest hundred bucks she ever made. You gonna take that?”

Just then, Jen came around the side of the

garage, her softball glove in hand. Not only that, Manny's baseball spikes and his old Al Kaline glove in the other. She moved in front of Sophie's SUV. "I . . . I think I might need this too, Dad."

More conflict welled up inside. The last conversation he had with Louise, he came within an inch of accusing her of being a member of the Justice Club. He didn't deserve to feel better.

Somewhere deep inside, he knew neither statement was really true. Just excuses to stay checked out.

He watched the drops of coffee in his mug swirl from one side to the other. Quietly, the memory of what the old timer, John Eberle, who had identified Argyle on the *Ocean Duchess*, had said to him forced its way into the middle of his grief.

There ain't no reason to die until you're dead.

The old man had lost his wife, but somehow found the strength to go on, even enjoy life.

He turned to face Sophie. "Did you bring your checkbook?"

***

Three hours later, Jen and Manny returned to the house exhausted, but glad they'd gone to the baseball diamond. He'd watched his daughter, at least temporarily, throw away burdens a fifteen-year-old should never have to bear. He'd ditched one or two of his own.

Even though he'd lost the bet, he'd gained much more. His friends had made him realize that life would go on, for both of them. They weren't over the hump, not even close, and maybe they'd never be, but they'd taken the first step.

Jen went to her room to get ready for dinner when he noticed the two messages on the answering machine.

He pushed the play button.

Josh Corner's voice came to life. "Hi, Manny. Just checking in to see how you're doing. Never mind, stupid question. Anyway, I want you to know that Max, Chloe, and I are all thinking about you, and when you're ready, and if you want, we can talk about the position I offered you. Obviously, take your time. No hurry. Hey man, if you ever want to talk, I'm here. Day or night."

Josh hung up. Good man, maybe he would call him soon. But not about a job.

The second message started.

"Detective Williams."

Manny stood still.

Argyle.

"I'm so sorry to hear about your wife. I wanted that pleasure. But it does my state of mind a great service to think you're suffering . . . your daughter, too. Imagine how it will feel when she goes next. I think about her often. What she will be like as she begs me to kill her? Until then, remember detective: one never knows."

Manny yelled and then ripped the phone from the wall, smashing it against the kitchen floor with such force that it shattered into so many pieces.

Jen flew out of her room and rushed into the

kitchen, eyes wide.

"What happened?"

He reached for his daughter, hugging her fiercely. "Nothing baby. Just one of those moments."

She squeezed him back. "It's okay Dad; I get those too."

Thank you so much for reading this book!!

Please go to www.rickmurcer.com to visit me.

Emerald Moon

Following are the first four chapters of Emerald Moon . . . another Manny Williams Thriller.

I hope you enjoy it.

Chapter-1

She fastened the last button of her silk blouse and reached over to pinch his nipple. "Time to get up, sleepyhead. We have to get this done in the next hour, per instructions."

"Yeah. I'm up. Well, I was."

She giggled. "And you will be again soon. I promise. But I mean the 'get dressed and come with me' up."

Who said that working with the love of your life could ruin the relationship? Granted, not many husbands and wives did what they did for a living. But they truly cared for each other, and spending the kind of time they did with one another was a rare bonus. Besides, it was impossible to ignore sex that brought her body to the brink of explosion . . . every time.

"Has the money been transferred?" he asked, pulling on his slacks.

She ran the brush through her long black hair. "Yep. Just like the last time and with the bonus he promised."

He nodded. "You know how we agreed to never

look for anyone who hires us?"

"Yes. Bad for business."

"This one has me curious, though. Not just that he wouldn't tell us who turned him on to us, but the jobs. I mean . . . cruise ship employees?"

"You're right, on both counts, but we make beaucoup bucks by not asking questions, and I'd like to keep it that way." She reached up to straighten his tie, catching the look in his big, brown eyes. She smiled. "I love you too."

He pulled her close, cupping her cheeks with both hands. "You're the most beautiful woman in the world, and you're my wife. Win-win for me."

Their kiss was the tender, long, drawn-out kind. She loved how his touch made her spine do that little shiver-slip. Not to mention, the way her insides twisted like a hot pretzel when their lips met . . . even with his clothes on.

"Win-win for both of us," she said. "You can whisper more sweet nothings to me later. It's almost midnight. Let's go to work."

They left the posh Miami Hotel and walked, hand-in-hand, to the new Lexus LS parked on the side street next to the river.

She waited for the traffic to clear before checking the back.

The streetlight revealed the owner of the LS stuffed diagonally in the trunk. The scarlet bullet hole between his eyes added an eerie dimension to his permanent expression of surprise.

"Just checking to make sure you're still with us." She grinned and slammed the trunk.

"So, how's he doing?" her husband asked.

"Oh, he doesn't smell so good, but he looks comfy."

"It was thoughtful of him to let us drive his new baby."

"It was."

Fifteen minutes later, they stepped from the car on Snapper Creek Drive in South Miami. They removed their gloves and cleaned the interior with bleach wipes.

He moved a few steps away, wound up like an All-Star pitcher, and hurled the keys into the canal. "Dos keys sleep wit' da fishes tonight," he said in his best New York mob voice.

She laughed and kissed him on the cheek. "You're so talented."

Holding hands once again, the couple walked north for five minutes, located the house of their next target, and waited. It never hurt to be too cautious. Satisfied they were undetected; she led him to the small, stucco ranch facing west.

After moving up the first two steps of the stoop, she saw the dim light glowing through the tiny, front-door window. She waved at her husband, standing just out of the light's arc, and then knocked on the door. The custom .40 caliber Glock 22 in her hand was hidden behind her tanned leg.

She licked her lips and felt her heart begin to pound. It happened each time. There was no rush like this one, not even making love to her man. Not even that.

Chapter-2

Security Chief Craig Richardson pored over the two case files for the hundredth time. Photos and reports covered his oak kitchen table like a new tablecloth. A couple of the pages had inherited coffee stains from a cup gone wild, but he barely noticed.

Each folder contained details of the recent murders of two of his security staff from the *Ocean Duchess*. Puzzling shit. Both victims were found at home, shot between the eyes at close range, their throats slit from ear to ear, postmortem. It seemed the neck butchering served no other purpose than to shock whoever discovered the bodies. No apparent witnesses were found. Each victim was killed around 1 a.m.

Just as confusing was the fact that the forensic evidence was almost nonexistent, other than a few stray fibers and the ballistics report confirming a .40 caliber bullet in both cases. The rifling on the slugs was close enough to think it could've been the same weapon. The barrel may have been retooled between shootings, but the

CSU couldn't be sure. Retooling was rare, but not unheard of. Either way, there was no match in NIBIN, the Feds' ballistics database. It looked like a professional job on every level.

He'd seen a few execution-style slayings in the Big Apple, but usually the mob or gang connection was clear. The reason for these murders was as clear as the Mississippi River during spring rains. Nothing made any sense.

He'd ordered the full routine regarding background searches, and both of his people had come out clean. There were no shady connections that would expose either of them to such a gruesome fate. They'd been good people with bright futures.

His employer, Carousel Cruise Lines, wanted answers neither he nor Miami Homicide had. They didn't care for excuses; they wanted these murders solved. Now.

He was dealing with the typical "shit-rolling-down-hill" mentality from the suits upstairs: they wanted something even though he had nothing. Talk about getting old.

To top it off, he was scheduled to depart for his three-month stint on the *Ocean Duchess* in two days. Unless the killer walked into his house and confessed—a snowball's chance in Miami of that—there would be no solving these cases before he headed for the Caribbean.

There was talk, more like orders, to bring in the FBI. He hated the idea but thought maybe they should. The Feds weren't total screw-ups, at least not always. He'd even toyed with the idea of calling Detective Manny Williams from that hick town in Michigan. The guy was pretty good and might have an idea or two.

I wonder how late a workaholic like that stays awake?

The subtle knock on the front door brought him out of his trance. A quick glance at his watch showed twenty minutes after midnight.

Who in hell could that be?

There had been reports in the neighborhood of renegade teens harassing people with wild door-knocking, rocks through windows, and bright graffiti on cars, but there was nothing wild about that knock. In fact, it was a little too controlled to suit his taste. One rap and that was it, like the visitor knew what was required to get him to answer. And how did anyone know he'd be up?

He lifted his six-foot-three frame from the chair, pulled the Kimber .45 from his holster, and moved to the door. His years as a New York cop, and subsequently as security chief on the *Ocean Duchess*, had made him paranoid. That wasn't about to change tonight.

Peeking through the small window, he saw her standing close to the door, her face in plain view. He did a double take. He recognized the woman.

He unfastened the security chain and unlocked both dead bolts, swinging the inside door open.

"What are you doing here so late?"

"Don't look so damn mean. I have updates on

the murders of your people. Can I come in?"

He stared at her, and then caught himself. "Sorry. Of course. It's been a long four days."

She brushed by him.

Her touch and the faint allure of her perfume woke up more than his sense of smell.

Taking a few steps, she stopped, hands on her hips.

His eyes never left her. She was a fine-looking woman, and it had been awhile since he'd really paid attention.

"Why, Chief, were you staring at my ass?"

He looked at her sheepishly and shrugged, "Guilty as charged. I've not had anyone in my house that looks like you in a long time. Want me to apologize?"

Richardson heard the screen door creak behind him, but had no time to turn his large frame. The blow to the back of his head sent him reeling to the floor, groggy, but not out. His hand snaked for his weapon, but the furious kick to the face from his female guest ushered him to the realm of darkness.

****

Her husband closed the door and returned the dead bolts to the locked position, the smile never leaving his mouth.

"Ready?" he asked.

"In a minute." She bent close to Richardson's face and ran her tongue along his bleeding cheek. "No, Chief, I don't want an apology. I want you to die."

Chapter-3

"Dad, you're going to miss the flight. You'd better get your ass moving."

Manny Williams stopped shoving clothes into his tattered, red suitcase and stepped into the hall. "Where did you learn to talk like that, especially to your old man? From Sophie?" He was working hard to hide his virtually unstoppable smile.

Sophie Lee, his long-time partner with the Lansing Police Department, stuck her head around the corner from the kitchen. "Hey, you can't blame me for that one. Have you heard yourself? I mean, where's that damn bar of soap?"

Jen Williams hauled her overstuffed bag from her room and folded her arms across her chest. Manny felt a twinge of nostalgia. In that position, she reminded him of Louise, her mother. It had been eleven months since Louise had been shot and killed in this very house, but on most days, it seemed like just moments ago. His life had become more like that than it should be: living in the past while the future rolled away.

Oddly, at least for him, it wasn't the house, or the objects in the house, that caused him to miss his wife. It was Jen, growing into a young woman who reflected her mother in so many ways, even Louise's indelible spirit, which caused him to hurt even more for his lost love.

He supposed that's why he hadn't sold the place and moved on, and it was pretty tough to sell your sixteen-year-old daughter just because she reminded you of your dead wife . . . so they stayed.

"Sorry, Dad, but I don't want to be late. I've never been on an FBI plane before, and the cruise ship thing is, like, so cool."

"Apology accepted. Now get your bag out to the car; Alex is waiting."

"Yes, Daddy Dear."

He swatted her playfully on the shoulder as she rushed to the door.

Sophie walked in from the living room and moved within two feet of Manny's chest, welding her eyes to his. Happy Chinese-American ancestry dominated her pretty face most of the time, but not now. She was as serious as he'd seen her in months. Too damn serious.

"What?"

"Manny. Are you sure you're ready for this? I mean, you've been out of the game since Louise died."

He had taken a year off from the LPD to be with Jen. They had started to heal, together. At least they had taken some real steps in that direction. They were doing what Louise would have wanted: taking care of each other.

"I'm good. Getting to bring Jen with me is a bonus."

"Yeah. I guess it's like falling off a bike, especially for you."

"Maybe. The time with Jen has been nothing short of awesome, but God knows I've sat around here long enough. Even with the consulting work I've done for Josh Corner and his FBI team, it's been way too long for a workaholic."

"You? A workaholic?"

"Okay, smartass, make yourself useful and check the back door."

"Done. So tell me more about this Carousel thing."

"Crazy stuff. Two members of Carousel's security staff assigned to our favorite cruise ship, the *Ocean Duchess*, were shot execution-style right in their homes. Carousel security is clueless."

"You mean that almost-asshole, Chief Richardson, is clueless."

"He's not my favorite cop either, but he did us a good turn, and no, I haven't heard from him. The head of security for all of Carousel's ships, Destina Flores, contacted the FBI. Josh called . . . and I said yes."

"I'm guessing it didn't hurt that they offered you a cushy master suite to cruise the Eastern Caribbean."

"Hey, stop whining. You and Alex got suites of your own."

"True. Life's about who you know." She grinned. "And I get to show everyone my new boobs."

"I'm not sure all of us want to see them."

"Really? Men don't want to see 36 DDs on an oriental chick as hot as me? You really have been out of touch too long."

"Anyway, there wasn't a stitch of forensic evidence in either murder, except for one tiny detail that they haven't released to the public."

Sophie cocked her head. "Just don't say it's little written letters on paper shoved up the nose."

"No, thank God. Do you know what an ouroboros is?"

Sophie's eyes narrowed. "Is it kinky?"

He shook his head. "It's a symbol of a snake or a serpent eating themselves."

"You said it wasn't kinky."

"It's not. It's . . ."

"Sounds kinky."

"Stop. Each victim was branded with the Celtic version of the ouroboros, one victim on the left hand and the other victim on the right hand."

"So what the hell does that mean?"

"It has different meanings in different cultures. I have an idea, but maybe Chloe Franson will have a clue. Since she's on Josh's team—and from Galway, Ireland—she may have seen this kind of thing before."

"Cool. I like her, but the big thing I remember about her was the way she was making eyes at you."

Manny was struck with a sudden familiar pang of guilt. Sophie was only half right. He'd returned a couple extra looks himself. And they'd been more than looks, hadn't they? He had been attracted to Chloe—and in more than one way. But they'd talked and made a truce: she wouldn't jump him if he didn't touch her again, and he would stay faithful to the woman he'd married.

Four days later, Louise was dead, his heart was a massive wreck, and Chloe Franson was just a name. At least that's what he told himself. Yet, every once in a while, when he heard her name or when her green eyes arrested his memory, he became confused, then quickly ashamed. He still loved and missed his wife. However, Chloe caused his emotions to war like Democrats and Republicans.

"I hadn't noticed."

"You? Manny Williams? Didn't notice? Wow, what horseshit. But have it your way."

She looped her arm though his and they headed for the door, Manny dragging his bag. "We haven't talked about the other thing."

"You and Randy?"

Sophie's eyes flickered. "We're not talking about him. I don't care how much money he got from his parents in that trust fund deal. I'm not quitting the force."

"Because you don't want to rely on him? Or you don't want anyone telling you what time to go pee?"

She grinned. "You're so delicate, but you're

right. Never going to happen again. So he's on the way out, unless he comes back with some serious kiss-ass."

"Talk about delicate . . ." said Manny.

"Don't change the subject, Williams. The other thing, remember?"

"You mean Sampson? Louise's brother has a huge yard. Big Dog will be fine over there for a couple of weeks."

Just then, Alex Downs, Lansing's head CSI, came through the door, his jowly face wearing fresh impatience. "Good God. You two are slower than the Second Coming. Let's get it in motion."

Sophie frowned at Alex. "Just a minute, Dough Boy." She turned to Manny "You know that's not what I mean."

Manny sighed. "Argyle? He's always on my mind. He's like some damned addiction that is a split second away from sending my life flying over a cliff, especially lately."

Alex shifted his weight. "Why has that murdering bastard been on your mind lately?"

Manny ran his fingers through his hair and curled his lip. "After almost a year, he left me a message three nights ago."

Chapter-4

The new guest, the American, made her nervous. Haley Rose Franson wasn't all that sure why. He was tall, good-looking, polite, and very bright. She was forty-nine but not dead, and she could still appreciate a man. His broad shoulders invited her to steal those hidden looks that folks lie about.

Still. She didn't trust him. Nothing she could put her finger on, but there was something now, wasn't there?

She'd been around the block a few times, especially since her husband Darren had run off with that tart from Dublin, leaving her and her niece Meav to run the Bayside Bed & Breakfast. Darren hadn't fooled her with his last affair, and she had the same feeling about this American. He was hiding something. She sighed. Then again, weren't most people?

She sipped her hot tea and pulled the black, thick, wool sweater even tighter around her neck, hoping to ward off the ever-present wind whistling from the ocean. It raced through Galway Bay like some damned banshee and blew directly to her chair inside the oceanfront gazebo near the beach.

Haley Rose smiled. Even in late August, there was no expectation of warm weather on her beloved island, but that was part of the charm, the uniqueness of Ireland, and she loved it with all her heart . . . especially on nights like this. The wind was strong, to be sure, but the night sky was amazingly clear, revealing a billion stars shining like precious gems. The divine view was capped off by the twinkling lights of the villages on the Aran Islands guarding the mouth of Galway Bay, some fifty kilometers across the water.

People, her guests mostly, talked about fancy places in the world like the Caribbean or Hawaii, and she'd heard them prattle on like school children, don't you know, but one glimpse of her Heaven on Earth and they forgot all about those other places. Most of 'em just stood there with their mouths open. Even her daughter Chloe, Miss Smarty Pants Special FBI Agent, came home twice a year to shake the demons of her job and bask in the beauty of God's favorite place.

The wind abruptly stopped, at least for a moment, like it was prone to do. She leaned over the edge of the gazebo, closed her eyes, and took in a long, deep breath of fresh ocean air. The only thing better would be to have a man holding her, kissing her, touching her. Getting her ready for what was next. And she hadn't had "next" in an age or two.

"What a wonderful view."

Haley Rose jumped, tossing her tea cup into the air, and slapped her strong hand to her ample bosom, all in a nanosecond.

"Oh my. I'm so sorry. Did I frighten you?"

She turned to face the source of the voice she'd learned to welcome. "Why no. I often throw a perfectly good cup of tea far into the air in a fit of joy. You've caught me in the act, I'm afraid."

The American grinned. Even in the half-light of the night, she could see his charm.

"You Irish have such odd customs."

"Aye, we might be a bit different, but we're special, we are."

"I do apologize for the scare. Let me make it up to you. I'm going to visit Dunguaire Castle in the morning. I've been anticipating getting a good look at Kinvara Bay from that vantage point. Would you be able to tear yourself away and accompany me as a guide? I'd be so appreciative and certainly would take you to lunch in return."

Haley Rose's pulse rate climbed a notch or two as she pushed back her long, red hair. She felt something amiss with him, to be sure, but most women fantasized about the whole bad boy thing, didn't they? This American had that stamp all over him . . . and the mystery was fascinating. And what did he have in mind after lunch? She felt herself grow warmer. "Are you asking me on a date?"

He moved closer and took her hand. A sudden, totally unexpected jolt of electricity shot up her arm straight to her heart. It was brilliant.

"If I might be so bold," he said. "For the last week, I've seen your side glances, and I've prayed you haven't noticed the awkwardness of my own. You're simply too beautiful to ignore. You are a charming woman, and I never could resist green eyes such as yours. So please don't disappoint me."

She barely managed to keep her hand from shaking as she pulled it away. Haley Rose took a deep breath and released it slowly. "It is against my better judgment to go on a date with one of my guests, but it'd be rude not to show some old-fashioned Irish hospitality. And to be sure, I don't want to be leaving you disappointed. Dr. Fredrick Argyle, I'd love to accompany you on your tour."